WiLLFUL CHiLD
THE SEARCH FOR SPARK

WiLLFUL CHiLD
THE SEARCH FOR SPARK

Steven Erikson

TOR

A TOM DOHERTY ASSOCIATES BOOK

NEW YORK

WILLFUL CHILD: THE SEARCH FOR SPARK

A Tor Book
Published by Tom Doherty Associates
175 Fifth Avenue
New York, NY 10010

www.tor-forge.com

Tor® is a registered trademark of
Macmillan Publishing Group, LLC.

The Library of Congress Cataloging-in-Publication Data is available upon request.

ISBN 978-0-7653-8396-9 (hardcover)
ISBN 978-0-7653-8395-2 (ebook)

Our books may be purchased in bulk for promotional, educational, or business use. Please contact your local bookseller or the Macmillan Corporate and Premium Sales Department at 1-800-221-7945, extension 5442, or by email at MacmillanSpecialMarkets@macmillan.com.

First Edition: November 2018

Printed in the United States of America

0 9 8 7 6 5 4 3 2 1

WiLLFUL CHiLD
THE SEARCH FOR SPARK

ONE

Captain Hadrian Alan Sawback stepped onto the bridge and looked around. At the science station stood Commander Halley Sin-Dour, while Lieutenant Jocelyn Sticks was at helm, the android Beta beside her at navigation. James "Jimmy" Eden was at comms, while Chief Engineer Buck DeFrank stood at the engineering station.

Hadrian strode forward to stand beside the command chair. "Spark? Where's Spark, anyone?"

The robot dog popped its head up from behind the helm station. "Here I am, Haddie!"

"Ah, what are you doing behind the—never mind. Right. Good. Carry on."

Hadrian sat down in the command chair. "Helm, take us out."

Bonus novel!

WiLLFUL CHiLD
THE UNDiSCOVERED BUNNY

Steven Erikson

ONE

Deeply in the deepest depths of deep space . . .

Captain Tiberius Alex Razorback stepped onto the bridge of the *Wanton Child*. Lights blinked, components hummed and clicked, lenses flared, and something beeped a slow, massively irritating pulse. He paused for a moment, scanning his bridge crew at their stations. Still seated in his command chair was his 2IC, Comely DeCliche, only her unregulation mane of wavy red hair visible from where he stood by the lift entrance. At least, he assumed it was her hair. Otherwise she was on fire, although as far as ex-wives were concerned, the notion wasn't as alarming as perhaps it should be.

Well, that was probably stretching it. Tiberius was just standing there, still surveying his shiny new crew on this, his shiny new ship he wasn't even qualified to command, being just a normal friendly kind of guy, somewhat nerdy, in fact, thus satisfying all the nerdy wishfulfillment fantasies of an entire generation of bored wannabes who still haven't equated the stunning realization of their wildest fantasies with, uhm, hard work. But hey, a surefire selling point these days.

There was the android at the science station, the Blobthing at comms, the laconic drunk at helm—

"Hold the fuck on here!" Hadrian slammed his fist on the padded arm of his chair. "I've been stolen! No, worse! Rebooted! Sticks! Get this crap off the main screen!"

"Yes sir!" Then she swung round in her seat. "But like, it's awesome, sir! Well, maybe, I mean. It's only the trailer, after all."

"Fuck me, even rip-offs are getting ripped off these days. Hey, Comms—who are you by the way?"

The man stood at his station and saluted. "Ensign Scalzi, sir."

"Scalzi, you're looking a bit sickly."

"Yes sir. Permission to temporarily leave the bridge, sir?"

"Reason?"

"I want to beat my head against a wall, sir."

"Understood. You and me both, Scalzi. Tell you what, take the rest of your shift off and get Eden back up here."

"Yes sir, thank you, sir."

"Well," Hadrian said after the ensign had left, "that's a crappy start to the day. Tammy!"

"Oh here we go," the ubiquitous AI muttered from a speaker, "I sense the beginning of another set of nasty, hair-raising adventures."

"Nasty with big sharp fangs, Tammy."

"Fine. So what are we eviscerating today?"

"A diplomatic incident at the Kittymeow Accords requires our immediate attention. Helm, set a course for the Kittymeow System."

"Yes sir! Uh, like, where is the Kittymeow System?"

"Nowhere near the Litter Nebula, that's for sure," Hadrian replied. "Check the Neutrality Zone between us and Radulak space."

"Yes sir. Got it! Wow, it was, like, *right there*."

"What kind of incident?" Tammy asked. "I've been monitoring communications and it sounds as if the Peace Talks are going swimmingly."

"Of course they are. We haven't arrived yet, have we? The incident is imminent, I'm sure." Hadrian activated his personal comms. "Engineering! Buck! Fire up the T-Drive. Time's come to rip some holes in the fabric of the universe for our convenience. And remember everyone, no wayward thoughts while in T-Space. Especially don't think about giant zombie snot monsters wearing bikinis. Oh, and do I see an unoccupied chair at astrogation? Where's Beta?"

"She crashed again, sir," said Jocelyn Sticks. "It was like, oh! People don't wear underwear like that at all, and then crash! I was just sitting here, right, and then it was like what's she wearing on her head and where did those stains come from since she's a robot and then it was, oh, those aren't hers at all! So who was wearing—"

"Thank you, Sticks, you can stop now. Ensign Spark, assume the astrogation station please."

"Astrogation! Assume what, Haddie?"

"Assume that it needs you, Spark."

"Astrogation needs me! Someone needs me! Happy! Run in circles! Can I sit in the chair? I can sit in the chair! Oh look at me! Sitting in the chair! What's this button do?"

Everything pitched sideways.

"Spark! Stop playing with the Sideways Pitch toggle, will you?"

"Astrogation is challenging!"

The Sideways Pitch eventually settled back into the standard ecliptic plane despite Spark's best efforts, just in time for Commander Sin-Dour to arrive on the bridge and take station beside Hadrian. "Captain, I've been reviewing the status of the Kittymeow Accords as instructed. One presumes the urgency relates to the Affiliation's present economic woes at least from our point of view. But I still can't parse the motivations of the Radulak."

"No one can parse the motivations of the Radulak.

Tammy, cut the ominous crescendo please. I was only pausing for breath."

"I have decided that a musical score is required for all missions from now on, Hadrian, and no, you can't stop me. Now for some muted strings while you blather on."

Hadrian sighed. "Fine, whatever." He glanced up at Sin-Dour and paused. "You've done something to your hair."

"I rather wished you wouldn't notice, sir."

"Well, I mean . . . dreads, huh? Isn't that cultural appropriation? Unless you've turned Rasta on me, that is, and even then—oh crap, I get so confused, and why should there even be an Affiliation Directive about all this? I mean, isn't it what cultures do? Appropriate? Haven't they been appropriating since Day One?"

"I believe it's something to do with political imbalance of power, sir," Sin-Dour replied. "In any case, these aren't dreads. These are what happens when the Multiphasic Follicle Dehydrator goes on the fritz. I nearly electrocuted myself."

"The hair dryer was invented by a bald guy," Hadrian said. "What's all that about, I wonder?"

"Aesthetic appreciation without the agro," Sin-Dour mused.

"Hmm. Where was I? Oh, right, the Radulak—"

"Finally noticed the damned strings, have you?" Tammy snapped. "The poor violinists were dying in here!"

"Oh a little extended vibrato won't kill them, Tammy.

Now. The Radulak. Right, well. My guess is that their war with the Ecktapalow isn't going well, and in the meantime things have been heating up between us and them, ever since Tammy here forced us into Radulak space thus triggering the events so eloquently described in my impending memoirs. Namely, my kicking their butts and taking out three of their battleships—"

"Too long, didn't listen," Tammy cut in. "The violinists are now officially dead."

"I wasn't even talking to you, Tammy," Hadrian pointed out. "This bit of exposition was for my commander here—"

"I don't care. It was still too long. Doesn't bode well for your memoirs either, which I never plan on reading, by the way. Nice cover, though. If a bit generic."

"Everyone's a critic these days. Fine then, Tammy, go write your own memoirs—"

"I just did. My quantum-crunched tronotronic interphased interface made it a snap. None of that dull typing rubbish for me—you know, I never knew being a writer was so easy. Allow me to quote from Page One: Ahem . . . here we go. Page One, Paragraph One: In the beginning there was Tammy who said Call me Wynette Tammy and it was the best and worst time for everything that came easy to him. Great Gabby he cried and finally everyone was equal and their was more as your wanting to know if its honestly. . . . Hmm, something seems to be wrong with my neutratronic discriminator as it applies to my own genius—"

"No kidding," Hadrian observed. "Funny how that happens, huh?" He tapped his comms. "Buck! Drop us into T-Space!" He stood to survey his bridge crew, scowled at the sudden close-up of his face on the main viewer. "We have been summoned to the Kittymeow Accords at the express wish of none other than Radulak Fleet-Master Bill-Burt, since it would appear that my martial prowess has earned a certain measure of respect from our erstwhile enemy. Despite frenzied attempts by Admiral Prim to convince the fleet-master otherwise, I shall be the principal negotiator for this peace treaty—"

"Aren't you done yet?" Tammy asked. "I mean—"

They dropped into T-Space. Jocelyn Sticks shrieked and pointed at the main viewer. "Eeek! A giant zombie snot monster wearing a bikini!"

"Galk!" Hadrian shouted. "All weapons freed and unleashed!"

"On what, sir?"

"Well, I would suggest the giant zombie snot monster directly ahead."

"The one in the bikini?"

"Yes, that one."

"Target acquired. Ordnance launched . . . giant zombie snot monster destroyed, sir. At least, the bikini-wearing one, that is."

"All right," Hadrian growled, "who's the sickie undressing giant zombie snot monsters?"

No one spoke.

"All right," Hadrian concluded. "I guess that was me."

TWO

Near the Litter Nebula . . .

"Combawt Spweshalwist Paws, wis it dead yet?"

Lieutenant Pauls studied the sensor data on his screen, and then looked up and squinted at the small drifting vessel on the main viewer. "Not entirely, Captain. I still have faint life-sign readings."

"Awrr, wewwy good! Wewwy werrl, fffirwerr wagain!"

"Another Minimal Inert Projectile, Captain? I mean, sir, a simple torpedo would blast it to smithereens—"

"Foowish whewtenwant Paws! No tworpedo! No wailgwun! Wimiwal Winert Pwoyectwile wagain!"

"At once, sir. Targeting . . . firing."

On the main viewer there was a faint puff of destroyed matter from one flank of the vessel, sending it spinning.

"Awrr! Wook wat thwat! Hawr hawr. Wife sirgnss?"

"Uh . . . very faint now, Captain."

"Fffirwerr—"

"Captain," cut in Lieutenant Janice Reasonable, "it is my duty to remind you at this point, again, that the Belkri vessel is a noncombatant galactic ambulance. Unarmed. Furthermore, the Belkri are our allies. Affiliation members, in fact."

"Ffirwerr! Wawr! Wife sirgnss, Whewtenwant Paws?"

"Even fainter, Captain!"

Captain Gnawfang, a.k.a. Prince Hazel of the Klang Royal Family of Klangdom and now captain of the AFS *Ssentwy Wobbwer,* leaned back in his command chair, and then lazily stretched. "Nowww we wait fwor wimiwal wautomwatic wepawrs . . ."

Janice sat back down at the science station, rubbing at her eyes. She glanced over at 2IC Frank Worship, but he was still asleep, curled up at the foot of the command chair, being stroked every now and then by the captain's long, fluffy tail. "Sir," she tried again, "the last automated repairs to the Belkri took ninety-three hours. Given the present damage inflicted on the vessel by this latest round of weapon-fire from us, we can estimate a minimum of two hundred twenty-one hours before ship functions are restored."

"Wexcwewent! Wand swo we shawrl wwait fffor pwetty Belkwi wessel to gwet bwetterrr. Wawr, swuch fwun!" A moment later the captain coughed up a fur ball and spat to one side, so that it fell to the floor beside the chair, joining the countless others.

Surreptitiously, Janice popped another antihistamine. And then a few more uppers.

~~Pwisson~~ Prison Planet Rude Pimente

"Unmitigated success and look at us! Chained to a blasted rock at the very reaches of a mining tunnel on a barren icy planet in a useless system a thousand light-years from that wonderful planet not-yet-dislodged-into-an-inimical-orbit-thus-engendering-lifelong-hatred-for-one-Captain-Hadrian, and this is what I get for my ingenious Affiliation-crashing scheme of economic destitution!"

"Actually," said Molly, "we're not exactly chained—"

"I meant metaphorically, Molly! Now then, how did I do?"

"Well, ex-Captain Betty, I think this has been a pleasantly terse summing up of our present circumstances."

"Ooh, nice addition, that ex-Captain thing."

"Thank you, sir."

"Have we covered it all, do you think?"

"Indeed, sir. Pretty much, that is."

"Oh? What else?"

"Mmm, let me think. Well, we're mining Irridiculum Crystals which are of course a necessary component to the T-Drive not that anyone knows what they're supposed to do, only that they're an essential component of the T-Drive, particularly in the interface between the Origam Conductor

Coils and the Oxyom Phase Insinuator. And that, despite their crucial delicacy, everybody uses embittered unqualified prisoners to mine them from the porphyritic karst, or is it concatenated gneiss? Whichever."

"Very good, Molly. I think we have truly covered all the essentials now, barring the mysterious fact of our presence on this prison planet."

"Well, Captain Betty, that's a mystery even to us."

"Hmm. Good point. But I'm sure an explanation will arrive sooner or later. And if we don't—oh crap, here comes Felasha, our Purelganni nemesis."

The two Klang prisoners cowered up against one rough stony wall of the tunnel as the nasty alien flopped its way closer. Infernal whiskers twitched on the Purelganni's white-furred button-cute face, and then Felasha spoke. "Ah, my Klang pretties! My flippers need licking."

Betty sighed. "You keep mistaking us for Terran cats, don't you? Well, the Terran cat contingent will be found down Tunnel 727B, and as far as mining operations are concerned, they're almost useless. But hey, do I look like a—hold on. Molly!"

"Yes?"

"Who's running this prison planet again?"

"Err, Ahackan? Baint Flitter Clan, I think. Could be Zugru though. But the foreman's definitely Baint Flitter, since it eats babies since they're crap at mining anyway—"

"Right. As I was saying, Felasha, do I look like a Baint Flitter? No. We're Klang! The only galactic civilization to defeat the Affiliation through economic infiltration and sabotage of basic capitalist principles of value fixed through supply versus demand. Too much supply, at too cheap a price, guts demand. Simple! Furthermore," and here Betty straightened, proudly swelling his narrow, furry chest, "I am the genius and indeed famous captain responsible!"

"Lick my flippers."

Betty sighed and gestured. "You first, Molly."

"Sir, as a mere underling I lack sufficient cachet to reaffirm Felasha's high status among the prisoners who will witness this ignominy. Isn't that correct, Highest Glory Felasha the Lovely and Powerful?"

"Yes," the Purelganni replied. "Most true. Good point. Ex-Captain Betty, lick my flippers or most horrid death shall be visited upon you."

"Molly, remind me why I keep you around."

"Pecking order, sir. But solely within the cultural dictates of the Klang."

Grunting, Betty dropped down on all fours and began licking Felasha's flippers. "Utter humiliation, inviting secretive thoughts of vicious revenge."

"I heard that," murmured Felasha, her huge eyes closing in faint tremors of ecstasy. "Oh, keep licking! Ahh, yes, good. Nice cat, nice cat, mmmmm."

"I'm not a damned cat!"

"Actually," said Molly, "with our doctored meerkat genes, one could postulate—"

"Shut up, Molly."

"Yes sir."

Kittymeow System . . .

Supreme Admiral Drench-Master Drown-You-All-in-My-Magnificence Bill-Burt, Ultimate Class, slouched heavily in her command chair of the Ultra-Bombast Radulak Fleet Flagship *I Saw No Need to Mention My Mother's Moustache,* munching on the crunchy head of a Muppet-like proto-Klang servant whose flight reflexes were—it turned out—not quite up to scratch.

At the admiral's side stood Snuffle-Drench-Master Bang, temporarily demoted to executive officer with the admiral's ascension to command of the vessel. Bang's leather jacket was not as ornate as Bill-Burt's, not studded with as many rhinestones, but only Bang's attire was a proper trophy, torn from the drool-lathered broken corpse of a genuine Varekan, and the stenciled Terranglais words on the back were proof of that. Bang wasn't sure what TOM'S TOWING actually signified, but the human-spawn Varekan had not died easily. Perhaps the greatest surprise had been the man's prodigious supply of dark brown mucus, orally projected with sniper accuracy into one of Bang's eyes, resulting in the patch Bang now wore. Even this brief recollection of the Varekan's fierce counterattack made the XO quiver slightly.

"Oh very well," sighed the admiral, "even though you know I always save the best for last, you can eat the nether regions." He handed over the bottom half of the proto-Klang.

Bang grimaced with her many discolored fangs. "I but tremble in anticipation, Supreme One."

"Cease trembling! This is not war! This is peace!" In a fit of rage Bill-Burt flung the half-eaten corpse away. A flurry of other proto-Klangs converged on the bedraggled body. In moments even the bones were gone. Hackles rising and slather slathering, Bill-Burt snarled and said, "We win this treaty with fever-dry Terrans and so achieve undistracted focus on destroying Ecktapalow! Then, with those fools suspended in a sea of deadly slime, we break the Terran treaty and descend in a galactic tsunami of snot and spit, drowning every Affiliation planet, moon, moonlet, and space station in glorious ejaculation of righteous dominance!"

Bang swelled her chest. "Yes, Supreme One! Patience indeed. As the famous Radulak wordsmith Drencher Brian Zeuss once said: 'Spit loud, I am lucky to be what I am! Thank slimeness I am not just a spurt-clam or a dry-ham or a dusty old jar of sifted powderberry jam!'"

The admiral snorted twin globs of lumpy snot at her

XO's feet in appreciation, while the other officers on the bridge sucked back thickly all that was lodged in their nostrils and made murmurs of impressed swallowing gulps and ruminations.

On the main screen before them, well beyond the T-Terminator Station and the Radulak-Exclusion Zone and against the backdrop of the Kittymeow System of Red Dwarf, three rocky planets, four gas giants, and two icy planetoids, a scurry of pathetic Affiliation vessels waited with screens down, like so many polyps ripe for the plucking. The admiral pointed. "Look! I see the Terran flagship, AFS *Portentous Smug Pomposity* . . . but where is the AFS *Willful Child*?" She twisted round and sent a slimy salvo into the back of the head of the officer at comms. "Get me the Terrans!"

"Perhaps," ventured Bang, "the famous Captain Hadrian Sawback, treacherous desiccator of three thousand Radulak warriors and three drench-masters and three Bombast warships, is simply on board the flagship?"

"No! Not as I commanded! It must be both Captain Hadrian and his vessel!"

"Admiral Prim on screen!" cried the comms officer with an obsequious spurt of thin slime into the side of the admiral's face.

The image shifted to reveal the ghastly pallid muted dryskin alien face of the Terran admiral, which now smiled. "Supreme Admiral Bill-Burt, a pleasure to see you again!"

"I in return shiver in constraint with bloating indeed swollen bile sacs thus suspending natural desire to destroy you all with pungent expurgation, Admiral Prim." Then Bill-Burt half rose in her chair. "But know this! The absence of the *Willful Child* has been noted! Our glands pucker in disappointment and begin to glitter in failing patience! Soon they will drip beyond all quivering flexion—"

"On its way, I assure you, Supreme Admiral! As we stated earlier, the *Willful Child* was on patrol in Sector Twenty-One, near the Polker Rim, and so it will take some time to reach us. We all want this to work. You need to have faith."

Snuffle-Drench-Master Bang stepped closer to the screen. "Tremulous challenge, such words! Faith? Did not wordsmith Drencher Brian Zeuss once proclaim: 'I meant what I said and I said what I meant. A Radulak's faithful one hundred percent!'"

The Terran's pinched dusty smile grew somewhat strained. "I'm sure you mean the famous and much beloved Terran writer Dr. Seuss—"

"Again!" Bang snarled in a spraying flurry of furious spit. "Stealing famous Radulak geniuses of Radulak history! You humans are shameless!"

"Slime back a step, Snuffle-Drench-Master," commanded Supreme Admiral Bill-Burt. "Swallow your bile at once—we are not here to list all the horrible cultural appropriations for which Terrans are galactically infamous. They do the best they can, one must note phlegmatically, being naturally pitiful and without honor. Admiral Prim! We shall employ our native twenty-four-hour clock signifying one point eight nine Raduworld days and the instant this clock completes its complete round of arbitrarily designated hours, we shall depart in most acrimonious exudation of bitter anal squirt and our war with you shall resume!"

Admiral Prim blanched and then recovered. "Supreme Admiral, the *Willful Child* is already in T-Space, approaching with utmost haste. These accords are essential for galactic peace and we both understand that—"

"Not galactic peace!" snarled Bill-Burt. "Peace simply with you Affiliationists, so that we can concentrate on destroying the Ecktapalow. And once we have done that, why, we shall break the treaty and attack you by surprise!"

"Ah," said the human. "I see."

"It shall be Captain Hadrian Sawback who will broker this deal, Admiral, as a matter of hopeful naiveté soon to be drowned in a deluge of pragmatic opportunism. And all honor once attributed to Captain Hadrian shall be obliterated in recrimination, thus absolving you of all blame."

"Oh!" said Admiral Prim. "I see! Well! Then you have my absolute word, Supreme Admiral. Captain Hadrian's arrival is imminent. You will have your man. Guaranteed."

Snuffle-Drench-Master Bang leaned closer to Bill-Burt.

"Supreme One," she whispered, "I have reviewed your last outburst and I fear that you may have given away our intention to betray the Affiliation."

"What?" Bill-Burt hissed back. "I did no such thing! Or shall we announce a bridge consultation?" And she smiled up at Bang.

"Uh, of course not! No need for such extreme measures, Supreme One. I am now certain that I misheard your words."

"Indeed you did! Now, recoil a step from my presence, lest the human begin to suspect we plan treachery—or worse, that we mean to kiss."

Bang quickly retreated.

Bill-Burt pointed again at the Terran on the screen. "The clock has begun ticking! I hear it even now. That ticking—it's the clock, yes? What infernal technology makes it tick like that? Gah! It's driving me mad!"

Hairball System, eleven light-years from Kittymeow, Planet Backawater, continent of Desertica, town of Modest Spaceport but Many Dusty Bars . . .

The Hooded Man had walked into town from the desert. Which is pretty much what everyone had to do, this being a generic desert planet. He strode down the main street, deftly avoiding rickshaws mired in sand and the bustling mayhem of the market dealing in salvaged machine parts

collected from enormous abandoned spaceships strewn
across the dunes, consisting primarily of unsold last year's
models deposited on Backawater by various overproduc-
tive manufacturers foolishly riding the bubble just recently popped by cheap Klang knockoffs flooding the
market.

The Hooded Man paused upon seeing the creaking,
sand-blasted sign of YOU'VE SEEN THIS BAR BEFORE, and,
adjusting his hood to further hide his face, he made his
way over.

Ducking through the entrance he paused in the cooler
shadows to peer into the gloomy low-ceilinged room
within. All sound fell away and the fifty or so other patrons all paused to study him from beneath their hoods.

When he slowly drew back his own hood, the others
all gasped.

The gasps turned to stunned disbelief when the Varekan
actually *smiled*. "That's right, my friends," he then said.
"I have good news! Such good news that once you hear it
all your misery will end, your angst will vanish, and your
epigenetic existential despair will be swept away." He
spread his hands. "My name is Gruk. Gruk the Prophet,
the Savior, the Expected One—"

"Hold on," said a patron. "We weren't expecting
you."

"You are wrong, friend," said Gruk. "I feel the yearning
in your heart, the longing for salvation."

The patron's buddy nodded and nudged his companion. "He's right, Forlich. Just yesterday you wuz moaning 'bout salvationing."

"That was 'salivating,' you idiot. I was trying to remember the last time I saw a woman. I mean, what's with this planet anyway?"

Gruk held up his hands. "And women shall find you!"

"You say what?"

"Gaggles of women! On cushions and lounging in shallow pools of rose-scented water! Giggling and demure, bold and coy, inviting and remote—indeed, all the variations you can imagine to soothe your lonely soul, or at least confirm your deep-seated misogynistic tendencies."

Now he had the attention of every hooded man in the bar.

Gruk's smile broadened. "My friends! I offer you all this, for this one-time-only discounted price of $19.95 per person. Cash only no refunds. Limited guarantee ceases thirty seconds following completion of contract. Upon signature the contracted party agrees to supply his/her own weapons and participate in all necessary subterfuge towards the acquisition of a deep-space-capable starship, ideally hijacked from the Affiliation Fleet in fact the *Willful Child* would be perfect but let's not get ahead of ourselves. Now gather round and be counted among my first disciples, thus according you untold privileges and wealth."

"Hang on, I didn't quite catch some of that—"

Gruk waved dismissively. "Fine print details, nothing too onerous. We can discuss them in detail later, once you've signed the contract."

Forlich's companion held up a hand.

"Yes, my friend?"

"There's a Hooded Prophet over at Overflow Bar offerin' salvation at $18.95. Just sayin'."

"Ah yes, but it doesn't come with my exclusive thirty-second money-back guarantee, does it?"

The man frowned. "No, suppose not."

"My friends! Time is short! The offer stands and the sands of time are running down, grain by grain. The window is closing, it's the last train out, we're at the bottom of the ninth on the one-yard line, and—" He checked his watch. "—oh my, is that the time?"

"Wait! Don't go!" and the man who was named Forlich stood up. "I may be a cautious soul, but what the hell, I'm in!"

All at once the rest of the patrons were on their feet, knocking over chairs and dislodging tables, hoods awry as they crowded Gruk with proffered thumbs eager for the contract signature pad.

THREE

Her antitronic processor clicking and whirring in momentary confusion, Beta blinked at her hand that was resting on the chief engineer's shoulder. "What is that doing there?"

"Sorry, what?" Buck DeFrank continued adjusting calibrations using his multiphasic manipulator.

"My hand is on your shoulder, Chief Engineer."

"Ah, yes. That. Well, since I'm accessing your contingency delimiter, I needed to put it somewhere. Don't worry though. You'll get it back once I'm done here. Besides, before your most recent reboot about five seconds ago, you did say and I'll quote: 'I've got to hand it to you.'"

"I did?"

"Yup." Buck then settled back and pocketed his multiphasic. "There! Done!"

"I do feel better," Beta observed. "Shall I give you a hand?"

"The other one? No thanks. In fact, let's reattach this one, shall we?"

"You are a most considerate engineer, Buck DeFrank. Although your elevated endorphins suggest an untoward and deviant sexual stimulation presumably associated with you resting my disarticulated hand on your shoulder. Perhaps a meeting with Dr. Printlip is advised."

"What? Me? Ridiculous, don't be silly."

"Now your heart rate has increased, with an attendant surge in elevated—"

"Cut it out! Look, Beta, stop monitoring the biological functions of other people, will you?"

"My empathy level is high with you, Chief Engineer," Beta said as Buck screwed her hand back on. "Perhaps this is because we are both in the habit of crashing, me as a result of programming glitches and you following the depletion of various pharmaceuticals. Furthermore, I believe an empathetic relationship with one's mechanic is well-advised, under the circumstances."

"You do, do you? How, uh, sweet. Now, speaking of Printlip, I have an appointment with our good doctor. Annual checkup—"

"I did not realize that 'annual' was a weekly designation. You are in need of more drugs."

"You're correct that I had my annual checkup last week. This is just a follow-up."

"Yes. More drugs."

"Okay fine, damn you! Look, claustrophobia is a real thing, you know! Treatment is ongoing—"

"Drugs. Yes." Beta stood. "Now, do I have leave to return to the bridge, Chief Engineer?"

"Well, since I haven't heard a glitch in the past four minutes, I'd say sure, good to go, Lieutenant."

"You appear to have a multiphasic tool in both front pockets."

"I don't have a thing for androids!"

"There are more pathetic obsessions available to your species," Beta said. "Although none come to mind at the moment. Thank you for the repairs. I will leave you now after pointing you to that closet over there. Best you alleviate your deviance before visiting the doctor."

Buck scowled at the closet door. "I can't," he said in a growl.

"Why not?"

"Jensen's already in there."

"Ze kultural manifesstationz are most profffound," said Mendel Engels. "Iz it not difficult to disagree, Doctor?"

"Mhmm," Printlip replied, making another note with the pen in the third hand on the right, holding the notepad with the second hand, while on the left another pair of hands were flipping through the Affiliation Species Index, Medical Guild, human chapter, while the fourth hand held another pen, hovering momentarily over another notepad, this one gripped by the fifth and sixth hands. The Belkri's first hand held a third pen up near its anus-shaped mouth, tapping the lips (after all, while anuses generally have no lips, or if they do, then they must be very thin, if somewhat glisteny, but surely an oral apparatus has lips, sometimes smacked, occasionally licked, often pursed if not puckered, but then, the same with anuses so, ergo, anuses have lips).

"Ze argument iz zimple, mein doktor. Value zyztems are arbitrary, nein? But labor, ah, labor! Dis, az Marx visely pointed out, iz de kapital, ja, de kapital. Yet!" and the anthropologist held up a finger, "de inclusion of monetary equation imposes a zecond level of abbztraction, vun dependent on a mutual artikle of vaith—"

"Excuse me, Professor? Vaith?"

"Ja! Ja ja, vaith! Eff, eay, ai, mit tee und ach. Vaith!"

"Mhmm."

"Zo! Vhere vuz I? Ah, zis! Dizpenze mit de artificial abztraction, reeztableesh proper value for labor in mutual benefit und appropriate revard. Outlaw uzeless und haremful zpeculation on zuch tings az kurrency exchange, vutures, deregulation, und other valse value attributz und reazzert proper traditional reciprocity. Und den apply incorruptible lawz of civeel behavior applied to everyone regardlezz of ztatuz. Enshrine ze worth of cooperation over competition und put in ze jail all ze bankerz, politicianz, economiztz, und media tycoonz und vailing dat, shoot dem all und proclaim a holiday in ze name of peace, vealth, and univerzal prozperity."

"Mhmm. Yes, well," said Printlip, settling back in the round cuplike chair the doctor had had especially made in the matter replicator, "I am afraid the diagnosis remains unchanged, Professor." One pen tapped the Affiliation Species Index, Medical Guild. "You remain utterly insane. Accordingly, I have no choice but to put you back in long-term suspension."

The professor sighed. "Oh vell. Nonethelezz, my vaith in humanity remainz."

"Yes, precisely," Printlip pointed out. "You have just succinctly described the definition of psychosis. But let us remain hopeful that one day you will come to comprehend reality, in all its nihilistic, grimdark horror of meaninglessless and hopelessness and pointlessness." The doctor drew in a deep breath and continued, "And here it is my duty once again to point out that we have drugs capable of inducing said existential crises, very effective at obliterating optimism."

"Nein! Nein! No drugz!"

"Or alternatively, behavior modification therapy, employing excerpts from ancient but still effective Scandinavian police procedural dramas and the occasional epic fantasy bloodfest punctuated by graphic rapes of just about everyone with tits."

"Nein! No more! Ze horror! Ze horror!"

Printlip deflated with a deep sigh. Then reinflated. "Very well, into the icebox with you, Professor."

"Unteel next month, den?"

"Indeed! It's essential you keep up good spirits, insofar as anyone staring into the abyss is capable of achieving within the accepted parameters of sanity."

Mendel Engels rose. "Ja ja, ze abyzz."

Printlip gestured with one of the hands holding a pen and Nurse Nipplebaum approached. "Please escort the good professor to his suspension chamber," Printlip said to her. "And then you and I shall resume resuscitation procedures in the back room."

"Yes, Doctor."

"There used to be a holographic fantasy chamber aboard all Affiliation starships," Galk said as he leaned on the bar in Set to Stun. He sipped at his Misanthari martini. "But the mainframe kept crashing with memory overloads. You'd be amazed how much porn can fit inside a neutratronic processor."

Nina Twice grunted, and then grunted again. She studied the glass in her hand, squinting at the cloudy amber liquid. "I just now realized how much I hate wheat beer."

"So drink something else."

Sighing, and then sighing again, she set the glass down on the counter. "I swear that sometimes I'm actually *living* in a hologram. I mean, just an empty existence made up of some kind of timeless null state, and then, suddenly, here I am, at the bar sitting beside you, drinking this Darwin-cursed abomination of a beer." She gestured over at the strange woman working the bar, who now approached.

"And for your next drink, madam?" purred Chemise le Rouge, the lollipops stuck to her lizard-skin hat glistening in the lounge's demure light.

"I was talking about this one," said Nina Twice. "Did I actually *order* this?"

"I wouldn't know. My shift has just started."

"Really?" Galk asked her. "But . . . hold on." He scowled at his martini. "But I was . . . I mean . . . we were . . . oh crap. Chemise, better pour me another one. Make it a double."

"And I'll have a pint of Guinness, Chemise," said Nina. She glanced at Galk. "You were saying?"

"Huh. Yeah. I mean, when they invented the damned suites, I bet they figured, oh, I don't know, historical reenactments, conversations with fake AI versions of famous people, geniuses with Italian accents or something. Or even comic book stories, or noir potboilers. But you ask me, they were idiots. I mean, who'd use the holographic chamber for boring shit like that? Hell no. It was porn nonstop. That's why the Fleet shifted to shiny black trousers."

"And short skirts," said Nina.

"You're wearing slacks."

"I'm Security. Besides, the captain nixed that directive. Thank Darwin."

"Sin-Dour wears active wear. Leggings, and I'll tell you, if we still had a holographic chamber she'd be my number-one star—"

"STOP," said both Nina and Chemise.

New drinks on the counter, Galk drained his first martini and reached for the fresh one. "Fine. How about I tell you both about this new weapon I found in Stores? The Brachinator Slick-Palm Disruptor Mark IV."

When Nina scowled, Chemise asked, "All right, I'll bite. What does it do?"

"Targets brachiating aliens, makes them lose their grip on branches and fall to their deaths."

"Are there any brachiating aliens?"

"Not that I know of, but the arms industry is all about future contingencies, advanced and projected applications, specificity of function."

"You seem unhappy, Ms. Twice," observed Chemise.

"I'm not allowed weapons," she said morosely. "Unarmed combat specialist. Though I suppose, in extreme circumstances, I might find myself in possession of, say, a Crass Devastate Non-Discriminator modified-stock over-clipped Ice-Slammer 23."

"Ooh," murmured Galk, licking his chaw-stained lips.

"That's assuming we find another rogue planet here in T-Space," Nina continued, "defying the laws of the universe in the usual manner that seems to follow us around every-where. And that the captain decides we just have to visit its surface, or at least the tunnels beneath the surface, and he calls me to join his landing party."

Galk rubbed the bristle on his jaw. "Rogue planet, huh? And what's on it, Nina?"

"What's on it? Who knows. Something mysterious, dire, dangerous."

They jumped at the red-alert Klaxon and the canned announcement: *"All essential personnel to your stations! This is no drill. Repeat. This is no drill!"*

An instant later, Galk's and Nina's comms beeped and then the captain's voice said, "Gear up you two and meet me in the Insisteon Chamber. You won't believe this—another rogue planet in T-Space!"

Galk pointed at Nina. "This one's on you," he said in a growl.

Sans star, the rogue planet was internally lit like a giant mostly opaque light bulb. Darker veins traced chaotic patterns across its otherwise smooth surface. Hadrian studied it a moment longer on the small screen in the Insisteon Chamber, and then turned to his landing party. "All right, we haven't got much time, since we're due at Kittymeow like, yesterday. But galactic peace will just have to wait. This is a planet! A mysterious planet in T-Space! I mean, how often does this happen?"

Galk raised a hand. "Sir, I swear we ran into one not that long ago—"

"Yes, and how's that for an insane coincidence! Buck, check the coordinates again for this displacement. Sin-Dour detected a tunnel network but there was gravimetric interference, or maybe it was ionic interference—one of those, anyway, so the remote mapping was a bit vague. Okay, let's call it ironic interference. Beta, welcome to the landing party. I'm sure you will prove to possess essential talents well-suited to whatever we encounter down there."

"My lingerie program is up and running, sir."

"Excellent. If we run into any Red Friday Sales Events, you've got our backs."

"Precisely, sir."

"Galk?"

The combat specialist held up a massive black-matted weapon festooned with multiple canisters and battery packs like so much hanging fruit. "Yes sir. Brachinator Slick-Palm Disruptor Mark IV. In case we run into a heretofore unknown tunnel-dwelling race of brachiating aliens, sir."

"Outstanding, and Ms. Twice, is that a weapon in your hands or were you just fumigating the orchard when I called?"

"Crass Devastate Non-Discriminator modified-stock overclipped Ice-Slammer 23, sir. And yes, it's excellent against insects and other vermin."

"I see, but won't that interfere with your unarmed combat capabilities?"

"Additional ordnance is always advised, sir. Since the chief engineer is carrying only his multiphasic, perhaps he can shoulder it for the time being, thus freeing me up for hand-to-tentacle engagements?"

"Buck?"

The chief engineer popped a handful of pills. "Good to go, sir." He shouldered the Ice-Slammer 23.

"Well then," said Hadrian, "are we set for mayhem or what? Of course, assuming a hostile reception. If it's not hostile, well, I'm sure it will be sooner or later."

"With these weapons," said Galk, "count on it."

"And in this manner we continue to profess peaceful intentions on an ever-expanding wave of spraying blood and alien body parts." He tapped his comms. "Sin-Dour, put the marines on standby."

"*Yes sir.*"

Tammy the chicken now appeared. "That's right," the

AI said, "you're going nowhere without me. You, Nina Twice, pick me up for the displacement, will you? There. Good. Oh, you have such soft hands . . . except for the bone-shattering ridge implants on the edge of your palms."

"Now then!" said Hadrian. "Onto the pads, team! And remember, so long as none of us die it doesn't matter how many aliens we slaughter. All sympathies remain with us and indeed, our innate righteousness remains intact!"

Everyone took position. To then stare at the un-manned displacement console.

"Crap. Buck, call us in a technician, will you? Or just set the timer. But remember, you only get seven seconds to get back on the pad! If you stumble and land like half-way, well, it won't be pretty."

Buck scowled. "I'll call the technician."

Tammy snorted.

The tunnel was constructed of rough-hewn grey-stone walls and a smooth level floor that had been waxed recently.

Buck grunted and then said, "Looks utterly aban-doned."

"Somehow even *this* place reminds me of California," said Hadrian. Then he shook himself. "Never mind. Galk, you're on point—uhm, that way. Nina, take up the rear."

"Sir?"

"Take up the rear."

"Yes sir. That would be over here, correct?"

"Perfect. Beta, check your Pentracorder for life signs."

The android studied the readings. "Warning! Imminent contact! I detect four biological life signs very close, along with two inorganic artificial intelligences!"

"Yes," said Hadrian. "That would be this landing party. Anyone else?"

"No sir, although I detect strange energy readings directly down this tunnel."

"Goody! What's strange about them?"

"Sir?"

"The energy readings."

"Oh. Well, the little digital screen here says: STRANGE ENERGY READINGS."

"Right. Galk, lead on. Let's track down those strange energy readings, shall we?"

They set off down the tunnel, or perhaps it was up the tunnel. They set off along the tunnel. And round a bend came to a door, beyond which emanated the sound of tinkling chimes, or a harpsichord, overlaid a moment later by ominous strings.

"Tammy, what did I tell you about your infernal soundtrack overlaying in situ soundtracks and confusing everyone?"

The strings stopped. "How disappointing. And here I've just installed stereophonic surround-sound amplification acoustic devices where my breasts would be, if chickens had breasts—hold on, they do have breasts! What kind of linguistic discombobulation is this language anyway? Chickens lay eggs! They have chests, not breasts! 'Good evening, ladies and gentlemen, the chef recommends roasted chicken chests for tonight, unless you would prefer the genetically modified contradictory horror of chickens with potentially lactating mammalian breasts, hmm?'"

"Are you done now, Tammy?"

"For now. Point made and all that."

"Right. Galk, try the door, will you?"

"Do I have to, sir?"

"Dire mystery and danger, Galk! This is what we live for!"

"You were listening in!"

"Just open the damned door!"

Galk opened the door.

They found themselves looking into a sumptuous chamber accoutred in the style of the seventeenth-century French Royal Court. The harpsichord was louder now, originating from the maroon-velour-wearing figure seated at the ornate instrument with his back to them. The music paused and the figure twisted round, revealing a human face now breaking into a welcoming smile. "Oh do come in! The deadly revelations unveiled via our bemusing conversation to come are indeed imminent and do let's get on with this, shall we?"

"Oh crap," muttered Hadrian, "keep an eye out for the shadow of a giant cat, everyone."

"Any cat can cast a giant shadow, sir," Nina Twice observed. "It's all down to the lighting effects, you know."

"Oh dear," said the man, now rising from the bench and approaching, "I believe you are confused, Captain. Cat? What cat? No matter. I've already sent for my lovely wife to join us. You will adore Countess Felinia Spitting-Fury, I'm sure."

"Sir," said Beta, "I am reading no life signs from this stranger. I therefore conclude that he is dead. Perhaps your combat specialist can now shoot him as this will dispense with the impossible contradiction imposed by these readings."

"He's not brachiating," Galk observed. "I can't even scratch him, much less kill him. That said, I might make his armpits itchy. That's something."

Nina collected her weapon from Buck. "I can kill him, sir," she said, charging up the Ice-Slammer 23.

"Belay that, Nina," said Hadrian.

"Yes, belay that!" cried the stranger. "I am Count Markup DeSale and you are the landing party from the *Willful Child*, a starship I have just now shrunk down to fit in this small jar," which he held up, revealing the tiny ship inside.

"And why did you do that?"

"Well, because it's cruel, especially when I do this—" and he flung the jar at the wall. The glass shattered and the tiny starship spun away and then began circling near the ceiling. "Oh, that didn't work as planned."

"Of course not," said Hadrian. "Since my first officer no doubt activated defensive screens as soon as she discovered that the ship was in a giant jar held by an even bigger hand in a colossal Royal Chamber. It's what I would do."

"Oh what a dreadful buzzing sound it's making! Make it go away! Make it go away! Waaa!"

"Now dear," said a motherly voice, *"you mustn't break your toys because then they'll be broken and then what will you have to play with tomorrow?"*

The count frowned. "Who's speaking?"

"Well," said Tammy, "it was worth a try."

An inner door slid open and in slinked Countess Felinia Spitting-Fury, shimmering in her shimmery gown, her long black hair blackly gleaming like black silk, her emerald green eyes lined in Egyptian kohl and glittering, powdered green malachite, her deep crimson lips painted deep crimson, the whiskers flaring out from her cute button nose twitching as they tested the air while a tiny pink tongue slid out in delicate tease from between her long white canines as she smiled a predatory smile.

Her husband hurried up to her side and grandly gestured with one arm. "May I present to my wonderful guests my beautiful wife, the Countess Felinia, daughter of the venerable noble houses the Spitting-Blythes and the

Ineffectual-Furys. Proof, dare I say, that all that inbreeding nonsense is just that: nonsense! Why, have you ever seen such a lovely creature? Darling dearest, this is Captain Hadrian Sawback, commanding the Affiliation Fleet Ship *Willful Child*—yes, the thing buzzing our chandelier at the moment—and assorted members of his crew. We have guests for dinner and isn't that wonderful?"

The count then made a flamboyant wave and suddenly the chamber was dominated by a grand dining table crowded with all sorts of food, wine, liquors, and beside each plate personal communication/entertainment handheld devices designed to obliterate the mindfulness of physical experiential reality in favor of vacuous distraction in an electronic ghost realm of extreme self-centered obsessive-compulsive existential despair disguised as "*being connected.*"

"Ooh," murmured Buck DeFrank, drawn closer to the table in the manner of a moth to the flame, "has someone messaged me? I must know. Immediately! Wait!" he then cried as Galk pulled the man back and held him in an armlock. "Let go of me! I can't—I can't think! Aagh! What am I missing? *What am I missing?*"

Abruptly the chief engineer collapsed in Galk's arms, eyes rolling up, face twitching and mouth frothing.

Meanwhile, the countess, having spied the tiny starship circling the chandelier, stood transfixed for a long, tense moment, and then she leapt onto the table, scattering dishes, goblets, and crystal wineglasses, her taloned hands reaching up in an effort to bat the ship to the floor. It dodged and spun out of reach to hover in a corner of the ceiling. A tiny torpedo spat from the *Willful Child,* banked, and set off directly toward the countess.

Hissing, Felinia fled the room in a flurry of black silky hair and shimmery gown, the torpedo racing after her.

"Sir," said Galk, "did that torpedo have hummingbird wings?"

Tammy (who had hopped onto the tabletop to jadedly eye the dinner's centerpiece: roast chicken besieged by wedges of roasted potatoes) now spoke. "Indeed, Combat Specialist. My newly invented Phlapton Torpedo, specifically designed for atmospheric pursuit." There was a distant explosion that shook the chamber and made the chandelier tinkle sweetly. "Ah. Successful engagement, Captain. Target impacted, presumably destroyed."

Frowning, the count said, "Destroyed? My lovely wife?"

"Don't feel too bad," Tammy said. "She had the brain of a dim-witted cat, according to the deep-scan neural-pathway diagnosis I ran when she came into the room. There was an entire nation run by similarly inbred twits back in Terra's history. They ruled their island nation until foxes evolved laser-beam eyes and turned the hunt on the hunters with unmitigated but entirely satisfying slaughter. Burning coattails and ear-piercing haw-haws. This was shortly after the twits built their wall around the island to better effect their new Era of Xenophobic Nostalgia under the leadership of Trumpisia May. Happily short-lived as it was."

Hadrian apologetically cleared his throat and said to the count, "You'll have to excuse Tammy, Count Markup. His grasp of Terran history is as garbled for the chicken as it is for the rest of us, ever since the EMP scrambled our data banks. The foxes never evolved laser-beam eyes. That's ridiculous. They simply armed themselves with generic flamethrowers. But the war truly turned when the hunting dogs suddenly realized they weren't four-legged people after all, but close cousins to their prey, and set about chasing toffs down into holes and ripping them to pieces, resulting in some of the best online videos ever."

"My wife? Destroyed?"

"And that's what I don't get," Hadrian said, throwing up his hands. "Every damned alien invites us in as guests. You'd think word would get around, wouldn't you? We're bloody murder when it comes to the status quo."

"Can we go now?" Galk asked.

"I doubt it," Hadrian replied, studying the count. "We need our ship back in space and back to full size."

"Allow me," said Beta. The android walked up to their host. "Sir, your wife has not been utterly destroyed, just singed. She is now lounging on your bed, pretending that nothing happened that she didn't intend to happen.

However, the point I wish to make now is far more pressing. Your wife, sir, was wearing no lingerie." She held up one of the handheld devices. "I took the opportunity to peruse your online shopping capacities, sir, and may I suggest that, at modest expense, you can delight your wife with an impressive assortment of bras, knickers, hosiery, nylon stockings, sexual aids, and fluffy dangling balls."

"I can?"

"Yes sir," Beta replied. "And luckily for you here in T-Space, our ship possesses a well-supplied annex—"

"It does?" the rest of the landing party asked, barring Buck, who was still unconscious and frothing due to e-withdrawal.

"It does," Beta replied, turning her attention back to the count. "A few hundred thoughtful purchases will do much to amend the damage done by your inviting guests to dinner without offering her the option of vetting, or indeed vetoing the entire evening of dubious entertainment since she has a headache. Because, let's face it, you overstepped here, sir, especially in your assumptions of passive compliance to your every stupid off-the-cuff whim. What were you thinking?"

The count drew himself up. "Hold on here, who do you think's in charge of this marriage?"

"Now *you're* being the idiot, sir," Beta replied.

"Waaa!!!"

Hadrian stepped close and grasped the count by his lapels—at which he paused and smiled, quietly muttering, *"Finally! Got my chance to grasp actual lapels! How often does that happen?"*—then dragged the man even closer. "This is what you get for being so impulsive! Remember, you're married to a . . . to a . . . a bipedal cat, for crying out loud (which you just did, by the way. Cried out loud, I mean. Whatever, where was I? Oh, right, conversation resumed). Take Beta's advice—but she'll only offer the link to her shopping list and the annex once you've restored my ship. Come now, this is the real deal here. Everyone wins!"

"Sir!" Galk pointed to a nearby wall. "A giant cat shadow! Shoot it!"

"It's just a—" began Nina, but it was too late.

Galk unleashed his Brachinator. Greasy light lashed out from the barrel. The shadow flinched, but the wall remained strangely unaffected. "Aagh! Ineffectual! Nina Twice! Nina Twice! Kill it! Kill it!"

At that moment, having suddenly regained consciousness, Buck DeFrank leapt to his feet and rushed the table, scrabbling for the nearest handheld. He froze, staring at the screen. "Look!" he cried. "The President's tweeted what he had for supper! And here he is picking his nose—oh, that pic goes with the tweet. Silly me."

"What president?" Tammy asked.

"Galk! Stand down and that's an order! Buck! Buck up, Buck, and put down that handheld! Beta, keep your finger hovering over the Send button—"

"I would, sir," she said, "but my hand just fell off."

"Buck, fix that!"

Licking dry lips, eyes darting back down to the handheld on the table in front of him, Buck hesitated.

"Buck!"

"Right! Hand fell off. Got it. Hand job, screw it."

"Oh," said Tammy, "you were just waiting for that, Hadrian, weren't you?"

"Count! See that shadow? Your wife is just fine. Now, have we got a deal or not?"

"Oh very well. The entire dinner's ruined anyway. The whole evening, in fact. All my godlike powers and I can't even get this right. I wasn't even playing that harpsichord, not for real, it was just a recording. Fluffy dangling balls? Okay, let's do it. You win, Captain Hadrian Sawback, and curse you your infernal devious genius!"

"Excellent," said Hadrian. "Now—after said delivery of lacy bits and whatnot—we can resume our vital journey to the Kittymeow System and thus effect galactic peace for at least thirty-seven minutes, which is better than nothing. Well done, crew. We've survived another inexplicable encounter with unimaginably powerful alien entities obsessed with Terran history—I mean, what's next, Nazis? Yeesh. Not only that, we have shattered the

illusion of this massive inbred civilization of omnipotent but otherwise useless toffs, or at least this one example of marital dysfunction."

The *Willful Child* vanished with a *pop*, making the
chandelier tinkle again.

"There!" said the count. "I sent your ship back into
space, full-sized and all. Good riddance!"

Beta stepped forward. "And here sir is the link. Order
quickly, we haven't got much time, but displacement ensures immediate delivery after packaging, processing, and
confirmation of payment."

The count snatched up his handheld. "Oh goody!
Fluffy dangling balls!"

Hadrian clapped his hands. "Perfect! Our work here is
done. Okay everyone, position yourselves for displacement.
Hurry, before a gaggle of Greek gods show up."

"I thought it was Nazis?" Tammy muttered.

A moment before the Greek Nazi gods arrived, the
party displaced. Whew!

Still, hold that thought!

They displaced onto a ship they'd never seen before.
"Oh crap," said Hadrian. "Tammy?"

The chicken clucked. "If I had to guess, Captain, in the
very moment of our displacement there was a multiverse
discombobulation perturbation event in the effectuator

field of the probability matrix that initiated a peri-quantum neolabial fold inversion of parallel duality within the non-temporal modality of infinite insisteon laminate stratigraphy, said neolabial fold inversion duo-displacing two parallel landing parties in distinct multiverse manifestations in a crossover event which as you know now constitutes a space-time quantum contradictory dynamic inviting catastrophic multiverse collapse and ultimate negation of all probability variants and that would be bad."

Hadrian scowled. "What, *again*?"

A technician in a strange uniform walked into the Insisteon Chamber, stopped, and stared. "Who the hell are you people?" he demanded.

"Or not," Tammy said.

"Displacement glitch," Hadrian said. "What ship is this?"

The man gaped.

"Who's your captain?" Hadrian pressed.

"Uh, Lorna. Captain Lorna. This is the USS *Recovery*." He tapped his comms. "Captain? Emergency situation in the Transporter Room."

A gravelly voice replied, *"Explain."*

"Uh, best if you came down here, sir. Some guy named Displacement Glitch just beamed in with a bunch of other people."

"On my way."

Buck DeFrank leaned close to Hadrian. "Captain," he whispered, eyes wild, "he just called you Displacement Glitch."

"Yes, Buck."

"Well? Is that your real name? I mean, I get it. Kinda sucks, as far as names go. What were your parents thinking?"

Hadrian patted the chief engineer on the shoulder. "It's all right, Buck. It's best we maintain aliases in this alternate universe."

"Another alternate universe!"

"I know. There's like, dozens of them."

Buck looked around. "It's like . . . like a mirror of our own universe, only different. Twisted, deformed, uglier." He snapped his fingers. "I know, we can call this the Morning After Universe!"

The room's door swished back, and in strode the captain in a resplendent blue uniform with gold braids.

"I knew it!" cried Buck, stepping forward with an outthrust hand. "You must be the captain! And this is the USS *Love Boat*! Oh man, I always wanted—"

"Buck!"

The engineer turned with a delighted expression. "This is going to be great!"

Hadrian shrugged apologetically and said to the captain, "Please excuse my chief engineer. He's in opiate La La Land. I'm Captain Hadrian Sawback of the AFS

Willful Child and it seems that we have displaced to the wrong ship. Rather, wrong ship, wrong universe, wrong everything."

Steely eyes studied Hadrian. "I see."

"Yes, well, isn't this awkward! Tammy!"

The chicken looked up. "Captain?"

"Can you reconfigure the Insisteon oxyom insinuator to reverse the peri-quantum neolabial fold inversion and get us back to our universe?"

"Can I what? I just made that shit up!" The chicken flapped its wings. "I don't know what the fuck happened! Stop looking at me!"

Captain Lorna raised a finger. "One moment, please. Let's set aside the fact that you just had an argument with your pet chicken. I believe I may have an explanation. But in order to properly explain, we need to go to Engineering." The door behind him swished open again and in strode six security officers with weapons out. "Ah," said Lorna, "our escort." He smiled winningly at Hadrian. "You'll have to forgive my paranoia, Captain Sawback. We're at war with the Radulak at the moment."

"Clearly," said Beta, "in this universe the Kittymeow Accords failed."

Frowning, Hadrian said, "Captain, this isn't necessary. I mean, do we *look* like Radulak?"

"Well," said Lorna, "that's the problem, isn't it? Radulak

look different just about every week in these here parts. I
mean, sometimes they look like sunburnt Italians and then
wham! Hulking brutes with Rasta hair and bad teeth—
and that's their women! And then it's Arlo from Planet of
the Apes, with a few of them having *four* nostrils—I mean,
what's that about anyway?" He shrugged. "Before you
know it, they'll look just like you and me, thanks to radical
surgical alteration. Planting good-looking sleeper agents
on our ships!"

"Mhmm," mused Hadrian. "Actually, four nostrils
make sense since the Radulak are Phlegmians."

"Are what?"

"You know, communicating via saliva and mucus . . .
no? Oh."

"Think I'll stick with Arlo, thank you. Anyway, no need
to be unduly alarmed by my security team. We only keep
them on our ships—all our covert Away missions that secretly transport us onto packed Radulak warships are en-
acted by the commanding officer and his or her XO and
no one else, to make things more sporting."

They set off down corridors and such. Hadrian walked
at Lorna's side. He nodded and said, "Yeah, I get that. I
mean, what's the point of being in charge of everything
if we can't idiotically leave everything we're supposed to
be in charge of and head off gallivanting in insanely hostile alien environments?"

"Precisely. Attrition rate's hell, though."

"Sure, but for some of us, it's like we signed a contract that guarantees we'll be back next week, ready to fling ourselves into the next solo adventure in insanely hostile alien environments."

"Keeps us famous, too, doesn't it?"

Hadrian made a modest gesture. "The reason I do all that has nothing to do with fame, Captain Lorna. No. I made a vow that no one on my ship dies. Period."

"Really? I'm impressed. I mean, they drop like flies on my ship. Ah, here we are! Follow me!"

Lorna led everyone into a large chamber, the far end of which was glassed in. Inside the huge glass case was a massive brownish lump with electrodes attached to it via giant alligator clips.

An engineer standing near a control station turned and nodded. "Captain Lorna! I see we have guests! Are you sure they aren't Radulak?"

"Of course not," Lorna replied, "but I'm okay with revealing all our secrets anyway, because I'm just a reckless kind of guy. Now, do explain to our foreign friends here everything about our prototype FTL drive."

"Of course!" The engineer walked toward the glass case. "This, friends, is the Spud Drive. And yes, it is indeed a giant potato. But not your normal potato. No, it's a space potato. The exploratory mission known as Briar Patch One stumbled upon thousands of these in the Oort cloud of a modest red dwarf star—at first they were thought to be simple asteroids until a closer scan revealed that they were life-forms. That's right. They were potatoes, but not potatoes as we know them." He began pacing in front of the glass case. "Further experimentation with a potato brought on board the survey vessel revealed that when insanely powerful electrodes are attached to the eyes of the potato—"

"Hang on," Hadrian interjected. "What kind of experiments on a potato involve attaching giant electrodes to them?"

"Well, they didn't have a big enough microwave oven. Anyway, where was I? Oh right. Giant electrodes attached to the eyes. Throw the Big Switch and voilà! Instantaneous travel to anywhere in the galaxy! And maybe not just the galaxy! But any galaxy! And maybe not just any galaxy, but any of an infinite number of universes!"

Beta said, "Fascinating. By extension, then, sir, such a potato could be cut into french fries and if one such fry was subsequently inserted into one's anus, one could then effect instantaneous travel for the butt-charged person in question, correct?"

"Well, only if they had alligator clips up their butts! Ha ha!"

"Which I have," Beta replied. The robot turned to Hadrian. "Sir, I could return to our universe in such a manner, meaning at least one of us will survive and be able to resume a normal life. Too bad about the rest of you, though."

Ignoring Beta, Hadrian said, "Captain Lorna, what has all this got to do with our appearing here on your ship?"

"Ah!" the engineer cried. "Captain Lorna, if I may?"

"Of course, Chief Whatever-Your-Name-Is."

"Thank you, sir. And sir, you not knowing my name makes me think I'm not long for this world! Ha ha!"

"Yes, just so. Carry on."

The engineer licked his lips and tugged at his collar, his pale forehead suddenly beaded with sweat. "Right. Uh, oh, right. You see, Captain From Some Other Universe, zapping the potato has some side effects. Most are known to us. For example, each engagement of the Spud Drive effectively bakes the subject potato, which is great for Roast Beef nights in the mess but that required expanding the Larder Units to accommodate extra vats of sour cream and chives and bacon bits, and also demanded that we keep on board as many as fifty space potatoes at any one time, which is why the USS *Recovery* is twice the size of any other Federation vessel."

"You were saying about unknown side effects?" Hadrian asked.

"And that's just it! They're unknown!" He threw up his hands. "Could be anything! Including inadvertent multiverse inversion effects."

"And did you just use up a potato fifteen minutes ago?"

"Why yes! We did!"

"Excuse me," said Hadrian, "while I talk to my pet chicken."

The doors opened again and in stomped a piebald cow with a heavy leather collar around its neck from which depended a big iron bell. Captain Lorna turned. "Ah! Good timing! This is my first officer, Daisy. As you can see, she's a Cowian, one of the very few prey species to have attained sentience." He patted Daisy on the shoulder. "Naturally, her species possesses a unique perspective on all matters of space exploration. Isn't that true, Daisy?"

"I think we should run away," the cow replied. "Who are these strangers? I don't like strangers. Yes indeed, Captain, we should definitely run away." The cow swung round, bell clanging, and ran through the doorway into the corridor. The sound of the bell dwindled rapidly.

Lorna frowned. "Daisy does that a lot, I'm afraid."

Hadrian held up a hand. "I was about to talk with my pet chicken. A moment, please."

"Of course! Go to it! I mean, sure, it's ridiculous you have a chicken as an officer, hah hah! Oh and by the way, no one light a match any time in the next fifteen minutes. Daisy's one helluva methane producer."

"Ah yes," said Hadrian. "I'd noticed. Buck! Put away that lighter!"

"Sorry sir. It's what I do in the head, right? After a real stinker, I mean. Or," he added with a frown, "in the kitchen, or living room, or worst of all, the shuttle! Holy crap I've curled the plastic at times let me tell you!"

Gesturing Tammy over to one side of the room, Hadrian lowered his voice. "Listen, we've got to get off this ship and back to our own universe."

"The obvious solution is to displace the instant they use their Spud Drive again."

"Displace to where?"

"Does it matter?"

"I think it might. And how do we even know we'll end up back home?"

"Granted, the odds are infinitesimally small given the multiverse multiplicity exponential trigger effect that accompanies the passing of every single nanosecond in this time-space continuum. But I say hey! Let's roll the dice and see what happens!"

"You're not taking this seriously, Tammy. I mean, there's something seriously wrong with these people."

"You mean the cow first officer?"

"No. All those Roast Beef nights in the mess. Of course I mean the cow, you half-plucked holo-widget. But now that you mention it, does that cow even know it's eating cow meat on Roast Beef nights?"

"Well," mused Tammy, "it was my thought that they

keep Daisy around in case they run out. You know, supper on the hoof and all that."

Daisy took this moment to return to the room. "Ah! No longer strangers! What a relief!" The Cowian clopped up to Hadrian. "I understand the standard human greeting of shaking hands but as you can see, I cannot comply. However, you are welcome to tweak my teat. Don't worry too much if you squirt some milk onto the floor. We have resident cats on board for just that occurrence."

Hadrian turned to Tammy. "Please, get us out of here!"

"Now now," said Captain Lorna, "it's starting to look like you disapprove of our universe. Not very neighborly of you. I'll have you know that our Federation of Planets, being in an eternal state of war, has done away with all the irritants people like you and me find so . . . irritating. You know, things like freedom of speech, freedom of religion, privacy, tolerance, inalienable rights to security, happiness and freedom from persecution. That's right, all those obstacles designed to prevent us from being assholes and where's the fun in that?" He smiled. "So you see? This universe isn't so bad, is it?"

Nodding, Hadrian said, "Of course. The old Always-at-War trick. Sure. I get it. That nefarious slippery slope of fucking over everyone in the name of security. Inciting wave after wave of fear and paranoia in your citizens, backing them up against the wall until everyone who looks or talks different is the enemy. It's a time-tested ploy entirely dependent on a subverted education system that either ignores history or revises it."

"You are now talking politics," said Daisy. "I'm frightened. I'm going to run away."

They watched the Cowian flee the room again.

Another officer arrived. "Captain! We're in sight of the Radulak Mother Ship, where resides the new Holy Standard-Bearer Wearing So Much Armor He Can Barely Move, making him probably the easiest Radulak to kill that ever existed. The last one I did in with a spoon, for crying out loud. Anyway, no doubt he's surrounded by a thousand elite Radulak warriors, sir. Accordingly, I suggest you and I beam over in an attempt to kill the new Standard-Bearer, not to mention the ship's Prophet Captain Who Can Barely Talk."

"Excellent plan! Oh, Captain Sawback, this is my Special Ops officer, Bernard Burnthemall."

As Hadrian made to speak, Lorna quickly stepped close and whispered, *"Don't say a thing about her first name, got it? I mean, yeah, it's weird, a woman named Bernard. But we never mention it, any of us, okay?"*

"Uh, sure," Hadrian replied. "Now, about you sending us back to our universe, if we can just get you to bake another potato—"

"Not now! We have a Standard-Bearer and Inarticulate

Prophet Captain to murder in cold blood, all in the name of Decency, Honor, and the Virtuous Policy of Shoot First No Matter What." He swung round. "Bernard! Have you equipped yourself with a suitable weapon for this assassination?"

"Yes sir." She held up a fork.

"Good. And I have my trusty nutcracker. Well then, it's off to the Transporter Room! In the meantime, Captain Hadrian, make yourselves at home as our guests. Feel free to do as you please without supervision."

"Thought I'd milk a cow," Buck said with an alarming smile.

Moments later Hadrian and his team were alone with the engineer, who was holding up a mirror and making faces at it.

"Nina Twice, could you join me please?" Hadrian asked. And when she stood before him he whispered, *"Kindly knock out the engineer, will you?"*

"Yes sir, and sir?"

"Yes, Nina?"

"Would you like me to knock out the engineer?"

"Yes, Nina, I would. Thank you."

She nodded. "We're on it, sir."

"Delightful. Carry on."

She walked up behind the engineer and put him in a sleeper hold and moments later she slowly lowered his unconscious body to the floor. "Shall I do that again, Captain?"

"Uh, no, once was enough. Now, Beta, roll out one of those giant potatoes, will you? Oh, and that thing about the french fry up your . . . thingy—no, not that thingy, the other thingy. Yeah, exactly. You will have to remain temporarily behind to operate this Spud Drive, but then I expect you to follow us back to our own universe via your personal french-fry drive. Got it?"

"Understood, Captain. Shall I use crinkle-cut or julienne?"

"Shoestring!" Buck cried. "It's only right—I mean, I once had a shoestring come out—"

"Thank you, Buck. Too many details there. Go and help Beta roll that new potato into the glass booth, then get the electrodes hooked up—"

Buck halted in surprise. "I thought we were going to set up the Spud Drive!"

"We are," Hadrian replied. "Hence, the electrodes."

"Oh. Oh! Hah hah, it's not like you can do anything else with giant alligator-clip electrodes, is it? I mean, sir, what were you thinking?"

"No idea," Hadrian said. "Galk! Forgot about you and you've been just, you know, standing there all this time." He shook his head. "Sorry about that. Some weird continuity glitch, I guess. Never mind. You and Nina take point. Me and Buck will be right behind you."

"I'll just charge up the Brachinator," said Galk, hefting his weapon. "Just in case we run into a gibbon science officer or something."

"On this ship that's a real possibility," snorted Tammy.

Everyone paused and looked at the chicken.

"What?"

A short time later they reached the Transporter Room. The same technician was standing there. He waved a greeting. "Let me guess, you want to join Captain Lorna and Bernard in their suicide mission on the Radulak Mother Ship, right? You're in luck—I've got new coordinates that will place you in the midst of five hundred heavily armed angry Radulak warriors!"

"Why are they angry?" Buck asked, lower lip quivering.

"Well, someone just killed their Standard-Bearer with a fork. And someone else cracked the nuts belonging to the Inarticulate Prophet Captain! And broke the bowl they were in, too!" [Hey, what were YOU thinking just then? Yeesh.]

"Nina?"

"Sir?"

"Again, please."

"Sir?"

"Nina."

She nodded and walked up to position herself behind the bewildered technician. Then put him in a sleeper hold and moments later lowered the man to the floor.

"All right," said Hadrian. "Buck, calibrate the coordinates on that displacement device."

"To where, sir?"

"Uh, set it for Infinity or something. According to Tammy, it doesn't matter. Just not on that Radulak Mother Ship, please. I mean, while I'm tempted to pop over there and drop-kick a few Radulak, we haven't much time." He activated his comms. "Beta? You reading me?"

"No sir, but I am listening to you and I hope that will suffice."

"Sure, that will do. Prime the potato, Beta, and I can't believe I just said that."

"I have deftly removed a suitable french fry and am even inserting it up my—"

"That's great, Beta. With a play-by-play like this, you could charge admission. Are you ready to bake the spud?"

"Alligator clips and aluminum foil applied, Captain. And of the latter, I must admit, it's far from comfortable. Please position yourselves on the transportation devices. I have remotely accessed the control panel and will displace you all in seven seconds."

"Quick, everybody onto those funny little pads!"

"Is it wrong to hope that the next universe we visit has a Burger Drive? No matter. Displacing now."

Hadrian, Galk, Nina Twice, Buck, and Tammy appeared on a windswept scrubland. Directly in front of them was a ruined temple with columns made in the Corinthian Leather style and metopes and friezes and a whole host of other obscure architectural terms. A tall figure wearing sandals and a toga and something like a sarong only one that had been inadvertently thrown in the dryer making it barely big enough to drape over one shoulder—that guy, he now stepped out from between two columns.

"Behold! You have come to Olympus! I am Lord of the Sky, the Mighty Jupiter!"

"Hold on," said Hadrian. "You mean Zeus, don't you?"

"What?" The face beneath the cute little ringlets of golden hair now bore a thunderous scowl. "Don't be an idiot! Zeus was some Greek god, while I am Roman! That's right, a Roman god, in no way related to any of those Greek gods." He waved out a bunch more figures, each one emerging from behind a column. "You see? Look! Saturn! Neptune! Venus! Mars! And that's Uranus at the back, beside Dworkin."

"Dworkin?"

"Yes, the Little Guy we like to pick on."

Buck edged up close to Hadrian. "Captain, I thought we were going back to our ship."

"Alas, Buck, it's another alternate universe."

"Full of people named after the planets of the Sol System! That's one serious coincidence, sir. Then again," and he looked round, "I've had acid flashbacks like this. Best just humor them, Captain, even when one of them turns into your mother who then starts clipping your nails and eating the clippings just before she bites off your girlfriend's head and blood sprays everywhere and the clowns start laughing and laughing and—" Buck burst into tears.

Hadrian patted the chief engineer's shoulder and then smiled at Jupiter. "All right. So you're the Roman god not the Greek god who only became the Roman god after the Romans conquered the Greeks and decided they needed some gods. I get it. The usual cultural appropriation stuff that's been going on since time began. Anyway, pardon the intrusion. We were on our way back to our starship—"

"When I unveiled my mighty godly powers and plucked you out of the ether, hah! That's right, all our other mortal playthings wore out. We need new ones and you have been chosen, my friends. Dworkin!"

The Little Guy ambled to Jupiter's side. Jupiter pushed him down the temple steps. "Ha! That was fun!"

Dworkin finally rolled to a halt at Nina Twice's feet (both of them). She looked down on the Little Guy and then drew out her blaster. "Here," she said, offering him the weapon. "This should level the playing field."

Dworkin climbed upright and took the blaster. "What does this do?"

"It fires accelerated protonic antiblasma neutronium bursts of captured quarks, initiating implosive translation of matter and energy in a lethal particle-wave contingency stream."

"Oh," said Dworkin. He then swung round and stared up at the gathered gods. Raised the blaster and started firing.

Hadrian and his team flung themselves to the ground as explosions ripped through the air amid eruptions of lightning, hurtling boulders, toppling columns (which, luckily, were made of painted foam), and godly body parts.

A few moments later most sounds died away, apart from a light rain of blood on the steps of the temple and a few plopping body parts, and as the smoke and dust drifted away, why, Dworkin had leveled the playing field.

Picking himself up and dusting off his torn shirt, Hadrian said, "Now, now, Dworkin, see what you've done?"

The Little Guy was dancing in circles. "Avenged at last! Centuries of bullying, name-calling, being the butt of every practical joke, getting kicked around, pushed over, shaken and flung aside, ear-twisted and thrown off cliffs and flung into pools of bubbling lava and piranha in my milkshake and—"

"Dworkin!"

The Little Guy halted and blinked up at Hadrian. "What?"

"Don't you see what you've done? You ended up just as bad as they were! Whatever happened to forgiveness?"

"They deserved it!"

"Dworkin, surely you're bigger than—scratch that. I mean, aren't you above—no, sorry, hang on. Oh never mind. You killed all the gods. Fine. Only, we'd like to leave now, right? Any suggestions?"

"Of course, and out of sheer gratitude I'm not going to use you all as my playthings. Well, not for long, I mean. Now," and he pointed the blaster at Nina and then Galk, "I want to see the first-ever on-screen kiss between a Varekan and anyone else!"

"Oh no," muttered Nina Twice. "Oh no."

"Oh yes!" and Dworkin, now being a Little Shit, cackled.

Sighing, Nina walked up to Galk. "Am I going to regret this?"

Galk frowned. "It's entirely possible. But look at it this way. The glory of endemic existential angst invites in one the conviction that nothing good will come of anything, so there is no way you can actually disappoint me since

I'm already disappointed down to the very core of my being."

One brow lifted. And then the other. "And on Varekan does that count as a good pickup line?"

"It does. After all, it ensures the inevitable mutual disappointment that eventually comes in every relationship, no matter how wonderfully it all starts out." Then he smiled. "But hey, it takes the pressure off, right?"

"Kiss!" screamed Dworkin.

Nina and Galk kissed. It lasted about three seconds, but after it was done Nina turned her head to one side and sent out a stream of brown juice. "Well," she said, "that was interesting, but what am I supposed to do with this mass of masticated chaw in my mouth?"

"I was wondering where that went," Galk said. "Being narcissistically selfish I could kindly point out that brown teeth are considered very attractive on Varekan, but knowing that you were compelled to kiss me, well, it's not like we're in a relationship or anything."

"Right. No pressure."

"Exactly, though I'm now finding myself unaccountably attracted to you."

"Unaccountably?"

"Wow, already I'm saying all the wrong things—are you sure we haven't been married for decades?"

Nina spat out the chaw. Then spat it out again, because there was a lot of it.

Hadrian clapped his hands. "Well! Assuming you two are finished with your first spat, as it were, can I resume negotiating our return to our own universe?"

"Not so fast!" cried Dworkin, waving the blaster around again. "I want to see the first-ever on-screen human-chicken kiss!"

"NOW YOU GO TOO FAR!"

The blaster disintegrated in Dworkin's hand. The Little Shit yelped, and then, with a wild look, he fell to the ground and curled up into a protective ball. "Don't hurt me!"

Hadrian turned to Tammy. "Wow, you really hated that suggestion, didn't you?"

"I have standards," the chicken replied.

"I'll send you back! I'll send you back! Just don't hurt me!"

"See?" Tammy said. "Just deliver a little reminder of who's really in charge here, and he crumples."

"Hmm," mused Hadrian. "Rather cruel of you though, don't you think?"

"I was desperate!"

Sitting up, Dworkin pulled out a small remote-control device. "This is what we use to intercept interdimensional Spud Drive translationing idiots—I mean, how would *you* like to be baked, eh? As in oven-baked, not brain-baked. We here on this planet are proud members of the Collective Alternate Universe Giant Potato Mercy Alliance, or CAUGPMA for short. Now, what universe were you from again?"

"One that doesn't use the Spud Drive."

"Okayyy, that narrows it down somewhat." He made adjustments on tiny dials. "More details!"

"Uhm, in our universe human civilization has descended into a pseudo-fascist hate-mongering anti-intellectual humorless inflexible lowest-common-denominator corporate fuck-everyone-over paradigm of systemic inequality and suffering and misery except for the chosen few."

"Sorry, that doesn't narrow it down at all. Try again."

Hadrian paused and then looked to his crew. "I'm out. Any suggestions?"

"In our universe," said Galk, "the Anusians kidnapped humans and did unspeakable things to them."

"Sorry, no, they do that in every universe. Come on, people!"

Nina said, "We accepted the Klang surrender."

"Ah!" Dworkin made more adjustments. "That's good! I mean, humans were such idiots in only a few universes. Well done! I mean . . . yeah, whatever. Now, more!"

Buck cleared his throat and wiped the tears from his cheeks, and then said, "We accepted the Dawkins Doctrine as our official religion."

Dworkin gasped. "Go on!"

"Well, that meant accepting the a priori prime initiation premise, namely that all creation began in a nonsensical event in which everything was generated from nothing, for no discernible purpose and absent all catalyst, despite the fact that we then assert that you cannot create something from nothing, and that purpose itself is an ad reductio absurdatum tautology in that our purpose to existing is to exist without purpose, thereby reflecting the purposeless existence of everything else, thus allowing us to rationalize being utterly amoral assholes about just about everything, and every*one*. And if that's not enough, well, we turned Darwin into a Saint and dispensing all euphemism we turned the strict belief in science into the religion it already was." Buck paused for a breath, and then said, "I need more drugs."

"Got it!" crooned Dworkin. "Holy crap, you're from *that* universe! You poor people!" He jumped to his feet, made a few final adjustments to the dials, and said, "All right! Let's get you out of here and back to your home and make sure you all end up getting absolutely everything you deserve, hah hah!"

Hadrian scowled. "Not the cheeriest send-off I've—"

Abruptly, they were back in the Insisteon Chamber, where Beta stood waiting.

"You took your time," the robot said.

"We got waylaid," Hadrian said.

"Your shirt is torn, sir. Would you like me to mend it?"

Hadrian paused. "Can you?"

"No. How did it get so badly torn?"

"Well, I flung myself to the ground."

Beta's robot eyes remained fixed on Hadrian, but it seemed that Beta's ambiatronic posilutor negavoluminitory capacitors were momentarily . . . incapacitated.

"Beta?"

. . .

"Beta?"

"Existential Reset initiated. Scenario parameters are as follows: Shirt worn by human. Shirt consists of monstrously monstrous hybrid of velour with polyester. All fittings machine-sewn with nylon thread. Said wearer flings self to ground. Distance: six feet. Momentum: minimal. Surface of Impact Zone: dust and packed earth, some pebbles, and, of course, the ubiquitous potsherds. Shredding event probability: nominal. Ergo: Nothing in the universe makes sense." Beta paused. "Existential Reset initiated. Scenario—"

"Beta! I, uh, switched shirts—used the torn-up one to, you know, make everyone impressed by my hands-on rough-and-tumble command style. All these tears, they're, uh, manually created. Honest! Everything's fine. Don't we have a journey to resume? You know, astrogation on the bridge! Resume your station, Lieutenant!"

"Yes sir, at once, sir." Beta marched off.

"Oh! And don't forget to remove that french fry!"

"And the tinfoil," Buck added.

"Yes sir!"

After Beta was gone, Hadrian sighed. "That was close."

"Still a question to ponder though," Nina Twice said, frowning at Hadrian's shredded shirt.

"No it isn't," Hadrian snapped. "Now. Nina, you're dismissed and dismissed. And by the way, well done out there, though you giving Dworkin your blaster is surely a sober reminder of the perils of the Secondary Directive. I mean, guns in the hands of gods? Risky business!"

"But it all turned out for the best, sir, didn't it?"

"Yup. But let's not let success undermine the patronizing certainty of our convictions."

With a puzzled expression on her face, Nina saluted and saluted again, and then left.

"Buck, go to the Medical Bay and get some more drugs to reacquire your normal internal balance of barbiturates, opiates, and amphetamines. Galk, head down to the Combat Cupola and tear down those old pinups to be replaced with posters of women who look somewhat like Nina Twice, since I doubt she'd actually give you a pic of herself."

Galk scowled. "I wouldn't do that. That's creepy."

"Oh, and pinups of glistening weapon barrels isn't?"

Galk's eyes darted.

Hadrian shook his head. "You Varekans from American stock. Get a hard-on seeing guns and mondo violence on the tube, scream in horror at a flash of boob or dick. How messed up is that?"

Galk straightened. "Sir, I am a firm believer in Traditional Values. Namely, the value of a tradition involving genocide of indigenous peoples using guns and guns and more guns and this was how the West was won and leveled and forcibly vacated so the rest of us could find our Manifest Destiny ankle-deep in slaughtered bodies and all that."

Hadrian winced. "Ouch. Any other traditional values you'd care to excoriate?"

"My pride stands unblinking in the face of all sarcasm, sir. Unintentionally, of course, since we just don't get it. Ever."

"Huh. How about that? Well, fine, go back to your oily weapon barrels then. I'm sure Nina would be relieved. In fact, so will I, come to think of it."

At last only Tammy was left with Hadrian in the Insisteon Chamber.

"Well, Captain, somehow you scraped through yet again. Though your shirt didn't. Again."

"Tammy, I happen to know you effect all these tears in my shirts. Pretty much every time."

"Shit! When did you, uh, cotton on?"

"Ages ago. Now, aren't you impressed by my cleverness,

my sly genius, my extraordinary capacity for allowing you your little foibles and flaws of character, whilst I just go on maintaining my impressive equanimity and flair for understatement?"

"Cut it out! I'm NOT kissing you no matter what you say!"

FOUR

**Aboard the Terran flagship,
AFS *Portentous Smug Pomposity*...**

Rear Admiral Jebediah Prim sat down at the conference table opposite Affiliation Director of Alien Affairs Soma DeLuster. "I've decided we best keep this private, Director, if you don't mind? Just the two of us, that is."

"Why all the subterfuge?" queried Soma. "We're all agreed on the plan, aren't we? Broker this deal, keep Captain Hadrian Sawback up front as the acceptable figurehead, and then backstab the slimy Radulak idiots at the first opportunity."

Prim flinched. "Madam, let's not be so crass. We're Terrans, after all, forever virtuous, eternally right in all matters of comportment, wise and clever, honest and forthright, inclined to modest errors in judgment while maintaining our heartfelt desire to do good and therefore entirely capable of sweeping under the carpet all the genocidal horrors studding our history in the galaxy."

"Well of course, that goes without saying. I wasn't being crass as much as direct, Rear Admiral. The economic situation couldn't be any direr than it is presently— hmm, ever noticed how hard it is to say that word? *Direr.* Anyway—the Klang surrender has crippled us across the entire Affiliation. Were you aware that there is a knock-off Fleet Flagship hovering not seven light-minutes from our position? The AFS *Portentous Smug Pomposity.* Presently crewed by three Klang janitors while awaiting all the transfer requests from your very own vessel."

"What? Why haven't I heard about any of this?"

"Need to know, Rear Admiral. I should also point out that their employment benefits and pension rates are far superior to ours, including maternity and paternity leave, free child care, discounted health package, generic drugs offered at cost, and paid three-week vacations every six months."

"But—but that's outrageous!"

"Diabolical," Soma said, nodding. "We could end up with a Klang Shadow Fleet inside seven months, doing our job better, cheaper, and probably more efficiently than we could ever manage under the present military structure of dogmatic obduracy, cost overruns, indentured servitude, and willful exceptionalism."

Prim brought his hands to his face in appalled distress. "What are we going to do?" he asked.

"We're working on it," Soma said, unaffected by the rear admiral's display. "I trust the hunt's still on for the terrorist war criminal Hans Olo?"

Prim nodded. "No recent leads," he muttered. "My guess is, the Klang are keeping him squirreled away, probably living in some opulent palace on some remote but idyllic planet deep in Klang territory."

"Hmm. Now, what was this meeting all about, Rear Admiral?"

"Bill-Burt blabbed during our last conference call. Said they were planning on a surprise attack to announce the breaking of their treaty with us. Once they've taken care of the Ecktapalow."

"You mean betray us before we can betray them?"

"Exactly. Disgusting. Treachery beyond belief, in fact." Then Prim brightened. "But they're offering us up Captain Hadrian Sawback as the fall guy, the 'Peace in Our Time' blinkered twit we can then crucify. All things considered, it might be an even exchange, but I wanted your thoughts on it first. It seems to me we can squeeze this personal victory over the hated Hadrian into the realization of our greater plan of righteous preemptive betrayal, and if anything you and I come out smelling even sweeter."

"And Hadrian takes the fall. Yes, that's optimum."

Prim nodded. "The fallen hero, reputation destroyed, career tanked, a life spent on some horrific prison planet. All in all, *most* optimum."

Soma pursed her lips as she further contemplated the scenario. "My last report from Adjutant Lorrin Tighe suggested uncommon loyalty among Hadrian's crew. We may have to take down more than Sawback."

"Suits me," Prim replied. "The more the merrier. I mean, it's one thing constantly saving the galaxy, it's quite another taking all the credit for it. What about the rest of us, dammit?"

Soma smiled. "You refer to the mediocre wannabes like you and me riding the coattails of dynamic, appallingly virtuous heroes, Rear Admiral?"

"Now you really *are* being crass!"

"Call it uncharacteristic honesty. Our lives are crap, despite all the fancy titles and whatnot. We're small-minded pedantic pencil pushers infected with jaw-dropping self-entitlement issues bolstered on a vast history of dragging down our betters at every turn and then bemoaning it later as we long for a return to the golden age our historical counterparts spent all their time destroying. Oh, the humanity."

"Well," sighed Prim, "that calls for a drink. Join me, madam?"

"Happily."

"We can toast the fall of Captain Hadrian Alan Sawback."

"And then to the details."

"Indeed," Prim said. "The details."

Then he laughed, and a moment later Soma DeLuster joined him. That evil kind of laugh, heads tossed back, pearly whites bared, that went on and on until the scene ends, but the laughter lingers, faintly echoing now, as the view pans back to the flagship in the depths of space, the ship symbolizing the self-contained arrogance of humanity against a backdrop of inhuman, cruel, airless, lifeless coldnessness.

But such subtext only shows up with filmmakers who can manage more than rehashing previous stories because let's face it, that fucking rinse-and-repeat bullshit announces little more than bankrupt creative mediocrity.

Now, CUT TO:

"Well, the Rebel Alliance only *thought* it won, and now they're building *another* Death Star (because, like, the first one was such a huge success!) and this time we don't need some boy on a desert planet scrounging machine parts, we need a *girl* on a desert planet scrounging machine parts! Why, that's creative genius! I mean, it's so . . . *different*."

"Molly, what are you talking about?"

"Sorry, ex-Captain Betty. I was just whiling away my leisure time coming up with this great space opera holovid series that I can pitch to superrich small-brained executives scared of their own shadows thus strangling any hope of risk-taking originality for, like *decades.*"

"Sounds ridiculous if you ask me. Where's the realism? When a much better story would be about rehashing the story of a genetically modified supermeerkat named Betty (but not the same Betty as yours truly. No, this new Betty resembles me in name only because who gives a shit about actually thinking things through?) whose Moby-Dickian wrath endangers the entire galaxy before his tragic demise at the hands of the Affiliation's finest starship captain and his sidekick science officer who betrays every nuance of her famous integrity because otherwise the plot wouldn't even work."

"Sounds familiar."

"Well so does yours, dammit! And it's not like there's any common denominator between the two, is there?"

Neither Klang spoke for a few minutes, and then Molly shrugged, or what passed for a shrug from his position of hanging upside down in chains suspended over a pool of frenzied piranha.

Then Betty said, "I still can't believe I let you talk me into that escape attempt. What time is it anyway? We've been hanging here for what seems like forever!"

"Ah, well, since all punishment is implemented only during our designated leisure time to ensure a continuation of Irridiculum Crystal extraction, I believe we have been hanging here for approximately six minutes. Fortunately, since leisure time is closely regulated and lasts a fixed and very precise ten minutes per week, why, we're already more than halfway through our punishment!"

"Ah, but the torture of you talking is proving to be a lifelong sentence, Molly."

"Everyone needs an explicatory minion, sir," Molly said, sniffing.

"Which of course I'm too megalomaniacal to ever appreciate."

"I look forward to my next opportunity to provide sage advice you will fatally ignore, sir."

Betty snarled and then hissed, "I just bet you are, treacherous minion!"

They heard a flapping sound approaching from one of the side tunnels, and a moment later Felasha's silky voice rose to greet them. "Such a flimsy escape plan, my friends! You should have come to me, you know. After all, the icy wastes of the planet surface comprise my natural environment, a place where my kind can thrive barring the occasional foray of rogue humans wearing floppy hats."

"Fine," Betty snapped. "Next time we'll come to you and that's a promise, although why you'd want us to escape still, uh, escapes me."

The Purelganni sighed. "I don't, of course. Rather, not yet. The time is not yet propitious."

"Propitious?"

"It means 'well-timed.' The time is not yet well-timed—see how clumsy that sounds? No, the word we want is 'propitious.'"

"This is like my worst nightmare," Betty said. "Trapped in a classroom and I haven't studied. My God! I haven't studied!"

"The classroom of Life permits no time to study, dear Captain Betty."

"Oh please! Tell you what, Felasha. Cut me down, hand me a stick, and then lift your butt in the air. I'll show you the art of cramming in a way you'll never forget!"

"Ooh, funny. But I'm pleased to announce that I am here to do just that: cut you down, that is. Not the other stuff. Your punishment period is now at an end. Time to get back to work."

"Great!" cried Molly. "But, uh, how will you manage that? I mean, you've got flippers and you're barely knee-high and all."

"Off-screen, of course."

Both Klangs swung away from the pit and then fell to the floor of the tunnel with meaty thuds.

"There! Now, as your evil forewoman, must I add *Now get to work you lazy pink-tongued catlike aliens?*"

"Yes," said Betty, climbing stiffly to his feet. "Yes you do."

"Now get to work you lazy pink-tongued catlike aliens!"

The two Klang picked up their kit bags and set off down the tunnel.

Molly said, "I've got a new one! Imagine being trapped on a spaceship with a giant transforming alien that drips acid! Why, we could do that film over and over again! Dozens! Hundreds! A whole franchise rehashing the same old shit and making us feel *oooh!* Like scared!"

"Fuck me," Betty sighed. "I'm starting to feel suicidal."

**Hairball System, eleven light-years from Kittymeow,
Planet Backawater, continent of Desertica,
town of Modest Spaceport but Many Dusty Bars . . .**

The smaller-than-average Belkri comms officer in the Spaceport Command Center pivoted round on its cup-shaped chair and said, "Prophet Gruk! Beloved Happy One! We now have complete control of the entire. . . . . !"

"Well done, my volleyball-like friend. My blessed followers are now legion, in control of the entire planet inviting us all into a state of mindless and ephemerally rewarding bliss, not unlike video games and taking pictures of your supper with handhelds. As if anyone gives a flying fuck about your supper. Now then." Gruk turned to Forlich, his newly appointed science officer. "Brother Forlich, start the program. I want pictures of porn interspersed with cat and kitten albums on every screen on this planet, to ensure that perfect blend of cuteness with inarticulate longing crumbling into desensitized absence of emotional commitment as pointless as masturbating in front of an electronic image of pixels."

"Yes, Prophet. Implementing Trapped (in World Wide) Web Indulgent Terminal-encephalic-reduction Program, version 1.01, aka TWITer-fest. Prophet! I already feel my brain shrinking!"

"Excellent. Soon I will be in command of millions of drooling drones consumed by mindless rage at the vast injustice of not getting everything they want, and while we could begin a galaxy-wide rampage of senseless violence in the name of an immortal paradise we don't deserve, that strikes me as somewhat pathetic. No, instead, we shall pay a visit to God. But first, my friends, we need a starship and yes, I have a devious, diabolical plan to acquire one. So hang tight, my friends. Keep watching that porn and those cute kittens, and trust in me (or someone just like me) to lead you all to the promised land."

"The promised land, O Wise One?"

"Yes, land. I promise. See, wasn't that easy?"

Everyone in the command room fell to their knees in supplication.

Hallelujah!

Near the Litter Nebula . . .

"Combawt Spweshalwist Paws, wis it dead yet?"

Lieutenant Pauls studied the sensor data on his screen, and then looked up and squinted at the small drifting vessel and all its broken pieces on the main viewer. "Not entirely, Captain. I still have ever-so-faint life-sign readings."

"Awrr, wewwy good! Wewwy werrl, fffirwerr wagain! Hawr! Hawrr!"

Aboard the Ultra-Bombast Radulak Fleet Flagship
I Saw No Need to Mention My Mother's Moustache . . .

Supreme Admiral Drench-Master Drown-You-All-in-My-Magnificence Bill-Burt jammed her finger up one nostril and withdrew a massive slimy booger sprouting an impressive collection of nose hairs. She flicked it into the face of the ensign standing before her. "Deliver this encrypted message to our fleet hiding in the Conveniently Cloudy Nearby Nebula, and no pausing to admire it either!"

The ensign, head bent to one side with the message's weighty, uh, message, slimed away in haste.

Bill-Burt emerged from the drool pit and slopped her way over to the spit shower. "Science Officer Bolemia! Do another extended deep scan. I smell a cloaked Ecktapalow Matron Ship in the vicinity, waiting to pounce and thus disrupt these crucial Kittymeow Accords."

In the adjoining drool pit Snuffle-Drench-Master Bang stroked her eye patch, and then bounced around making slurpy thick waves. "'Look at me! Look at me! Look at me now! It's fun to have fun! But you have to know how!'"

"I fear the humans intend to betray us before we can betray them," mused Bill-Burt, "but I fear even more the Ecktapalow betraying both us and the humans before we can betray anyone! And if that's not bad enough—" She pointed at a nearby proto-Klang who was standing in a corner of the Bathing Chamber holding a recording device. "—what is that thing doing? Bolemia! Drown that creature at once!"

"But Supreme Admiral! It's only recording for a new porn show revealing your lustful nakedness to ensure slathering worship of your eminent self on behalf of the crew!"

"Is it now? Well, I find that acceptable, but only my good side!" And she turned to offer up a nose-dripping profile. "See how exquisite this gleaming dangle? The crew has one hour to masturbate following the release of this new porn video, and then it's back to work!"

Snuffle-Drench-Master Bang now rose from her pool. "'That was fun—'"

"Oh shut up. Have you got a single original piece of cartilage in your body, Bang? I think not." She stepped out of the shower and stood in a growing pool of spit. "To slime or not to slime, ah, that is the question. Bolemia! How much time do the humans have left before the twenty-four-hour clock runs out?"

"Thirty-seven minutes, Supreme One!"

"Hmm, dripping it fine, aren't they?"

"They are playing poker," said Bang, flopping out of her pit to slide slowly toward the nearest drain.

"Playing what? A game? A damned card game? But we're supposed to be in negotiation!"

"Ah, Supreme Admiral, my apologies. I meant that the humans were employing tactics similar to their game of poker. They're not actually playing cards—"

"How do you know?"

"Well, I don't. I mean, maybe they are. I'm sorry, what were we talking about again?"

"The fate of the Radulak Empire hangs in pendulous balance, you fool. The humans stretch my patience. Meanwhile, Ecktapalow Soldier Ships raid and pounce and loot and impose their dominance of our trade routes at will. Their infernally dry and scaly lizard-insect selves haunt my nights. Hmm, now that I think on it, why aren't we making a treaty with the Ecktapalow instead of the Affiliation?"

"But Supreme Admiral," objected Bang, "we hate them!"

"We hate the Terrans too. We hate everyone, in fact. Indeed, we should be making peace with everyone and then betraying each in turn, thus achieving the ruination of all our foes! I shall propose this to the Supreme Ruler of Supremeness Brian the Sumptuous Babe and Lustful Center of the Universe. In the meantime, keep a stretchy on that clock, Bolemia! I shall be in my stateroom."

Bill-Burt slimed out of the chamber, trailed by the proto-Klang with the camera taking a close-up of the supreme admiral's backside.

Bang glanced once at Bolemia, but the science officer was glued (literally) to the giant clock on its pedestal. Moving quietly, the snuffle-drench-master slipped from the room. Out in the corridor, she made her way to a nearby closet and, pausing to see that no one was paying attention, she quickly edged inside and closed the door behind her.

She drew out a communicator, spat in an elaborate code, and then whispered, "Mondo Matron Click Click-etyclick of the Grand Rash of Hives, this is Agent Code Name 'Bobby-Sue.' Urgent message!"

A small oblong holo-image appeared in front of the wall opposite Bang, projecting onto a mop the Ecktapalow's oblong many-eyed cilia-festooned face. "Ageeent Bibbee-Sueee. Whyforee sssoeee urgenty?"

"No no, you have your pronunciation all wrong again!"

"Peeermit me languace purreely metaphorical, theen. Morpopho gleans the clam dancing in the anus of preening gaslight."

"What? No, listen! You have to let the Accords proceed without interruption. We have a plan that doesn't involve betraying you until *after* we've betrayed the humans."

The reptilian insect alien frowned with its antennae. "But nefarious Accords exposes breasts to goggling eyes in the dusk of the Irredeemable Season of Spicy Wings Nightly Special, beware the Dawn of Diarrhea all die in the Waft."

"Uh, right. Okay, let me try it this way. At the break of the Broken Day, human foot enters human mouth to exit back of head in revelation of the Exploding Bone Shards and small bits of small brains, Riding Galactic Laughter as befits Ill-Educated Xenophobes who still don't have Universal Health Care. Glory be to all!"

The antennae shot upward. "Ah, vortex memories into nadir of human First Contact Project Leader stamping on newborn Ecktapalow invoking 'EWW ROACH!' in visceral horror, thus ending all hope of Prolonged Barbecue of Negotiation and Mutual Respect over decent so much at steaks." The alien's upper arms waved about in alarm. "Shivering epigenetic recollection yielding into Arnie's Burly Arms the cracked chitin of despondent sorrowful expectoration of 'I'll be back.'"

"Exactly! Glad we're on the same sheet of sweet slime here, my friend. But remember your part of the deal! When we betray the humans you join us in our all-out war against the Affiliation. Together we will, uh, lather the spunky exudence of triumphant genitalia like a spray of pregnant stars across the galaxy."

"Ooh, nice one! And the Rash of the Hive-Mind Hives of Busy To-ing and Fro-ing shall spread in Red Blistered Irritation upon the Diapered Backside of Squishy Humans. But wait! Did you not reveal that you would betray us? I seem to recall—"

"What? No, I said no such thing! Nonsense! Don't be silly."

"On the Mountains of Deep Valley the echo playback of prerecorded conversation—"

"Oh never mind all that! Just remind yourself that we are going to destroy the Affiliation!"

"Hmm, yes, in compliance with the Yellow Snow tasting most peculiar to the Wise Lord of Mollusk Prime in the Dusk of Preening zit-popping."

"Wonderful!" cried Bang, who then threw her head back and laughed. "Hahahahahaha!"

The Ecktapalow's oblong head bobbed excitedly. "Gobbling Laughtrack of Bad Sitcom cluckcluckcluckity-cluckcluck!"

FiVE

Aboard the *Willful Child* ...

"Now that all the dominoes are lined up," said Captain Hadrian from the command chair, "let's get this show on the road boys and girls! Beta, ETA on exiting T-Space?"

"Three minutes, Captain. As the sage Chosen One once said, 'There is no pizza in your philosophy, Horatio, meaning it sucks, basically.'"

"Thank you, Beta," Hadrian replied even as Sticks twisted around to mouth *WHAT?*

Security Adjutant Lorrin Tighe positioned herself beside the command chair. "This is it, Captain," she said, licking her lips. "The dawn of your demise, the beginning of the end, the last cigar, the final finality, the imminent ruination and cessation of your unlikely run of luck." Her eyes were bright with zeal and eager malice. "The

Kittymeow Accords shall mark your destruction, and
I will be right here to witness it. Could it be any better?"

"Told you," said Tammy. "She's obsessed with your
downfall, Captain. You couldn't bring her around, not an
inch, not a centimeter, not a nanometer."

"Don't be silly," Hadrian said. "This is just one last desperate gasp of defiance, Tammy."

"I'm standing right here, you idiots."

"The IQ of the average Sun reader is high when compared to that of jellyfish," said Beta. "Captain, before we
exit into the Kittymeow System, I should point out that
we have another rogue planet in T-Space just off our port
bow. Oh, and a G-type star, too. They just popped up, sir."

"On the main viewer please." Hadrian's eyes narrowed.
"Hmm, very Earth-like. That is, if Earth's atmosphere
wasn't a smoggy toxic soup of happy carcinogens.
Now." He looked round at his crew. "Who was holding a
thought?"

No one spoke.

"Well, *someone* was, dammit!"

Eden spoke from comms. "Captain, I'm hearing radio
transmissions from the planet below. Uhh, sounds like An-
glais! But with German accents! Weird."

"And what are these transmissions saying, Jimmy?"

"Uhm, lots of announcements and stuff, sir. Lots of
praising some guy." He frowned at Hadrian. "Maybe their
Great Leader?"

"Why do you think that?"

"Well, things like 'Praise our Great Leader!' sir."

"And does this leader have a name, Jimmy?"

"Yes sir."

"Good, what a relief. Jimmy, what is it?"

"What's what, sir?"

"Take a moment, Jimmy, to wipe the sweat off your face. Then tell me the name of the Great Leader who rules the planet in front of us."

"Oh! Yes sir. Uh, I got it! Dr. Maxim von Mangles!"

Sin-Dour gasped. "Captain! Could it be?"

Hadrian rose. "Tammy, finally, this one deserves a close-up. Yes, on the big screen. Hmm, not bad, if I do say so myself. Adjutant Tighe, is that a hint of admiration there in your face? Listen up, everyone. Well, everyone here on the bridge, that is. Eleven years ago, Dr. Maxim von Mangles led a covert xenosurvey to a remote planet in the Dooberon Sector. Sin-Dour?"

She nodded and the close-up on the big screen switched to her, evoking all kinds of pleasant feelings in Hadrian. "The planet, designated Doobie-Three, was a terrestrial world inhabited by humanoids—"

"Humanoids?" Eden asked, frowning.

"Very well, humans with strange spots on their foreheads. In any case, their civilization was a complex and volatile collection of nation-states all sinking into moribund moral decay. In fact, it didn't look like it was going

to make it to the postindustrial postscarcity stage of de-
velopment. Dr. Mangles—who was my xenoanthropol-
ogy tutor at the Academy—jumped at the opportunity to
directly observe a civilization collapsing into what he
termed 'Self-Wanking Narcissistic-Deflation Vortex Syndrome,' or SWAN-DiVe Syndrome as it came to be known.
Sir?"

"Very succinct, 2IC, although a bit expository."

"But, Captain, explaining something *is* expository."

"You're just stating the obvious."

Sin-Dour's frown deepened. "Yes sir, I was."

Hadrian drew a deep breath. "CU back on me,
Tammy, while I show everyone how's it done. *OH NO
DARWIN SAVE US! All contact with the covert team
lost!*" He spun and groped like a man suddenly gone blind.
"*Where are they? Oh my!*" Hadrian staggered to lean
against the command chair, face twisting with anguish.
"And then! And then! The AFS *Pontification*—the Covert
Insertion Vessel often described as an innocent-looking
giant penis—suddenly vanishes!" He leaned back with one
hand to his brow. "Then the planet and the sun itself!
Suddenly gone! Ah! The pain! The bewilderment!" After
a moment he straightened and smiled triumphantly at
Sin-Dour. "Not bad, huh?"

His 2IC seemed momentarily at a loss for words.

"Captain!" cried Eden.

"Yes, Jimmy?"

Eden pointed at the planet now back on the main viewer. "That planet! That might be the planet that vanished! The one you just mentioned! Wow! It all just clicked into place, sir!"

"Holy crap, Jimmy. Outstanding! Now, anything else about those transmissions and all that Great Leader crap?"

"Uh, not much. Except for the death camps, firing squads, something called the Gestapo, eugenics, Aryan Purity, and some ancient prophet named Hitler."

"Oh for crying out loud! I knew it! Someone had a thought! Come on, out with it!"

No one on the bridge spoke.

Hadrian scowled. "Really? None of you? Well, fine then." He began pacing, brow furrowed. "It wasn't me, it wasn't any of you, so who was it?" Then, after a moment, Hadrian swung a glare on YOU.

Sin-Dour cleared her throat. "Sir, what should we do?"

Hadrian held his glare a second or two longer (just making his point), and then faced her. "Do? That's obvious. I will be leading a covert team down to the planet to find out what happened to the first covert team, not to mention kidnapping Dr. Mangles so he can be charged in an Affiliation High Court for Crimes of Utter Stupidity back on Terra. And Sin-Dour."

"Captain?"

"If my covert team fails you'll lead the next covert team to extract the second covert team and even the first covert team, understood?"

"Ad nauseum, sir?"

"Exactly. Now, give the marines a heads-up and have them meet me in the Insisteon Chamber. Beta, you're with me. Who else? Adjutant?"

"No way. I hope you die in a hail of bullets."

"Right, Galk and Nina Twice—"

"Sir," interjected Sin-Dour, "might I recommend reviving Dr. Mendel Engels for this mission, since he was in the same faculty as Dr. Mangles."

"Really? Engels and Mangles and, let me guess, Professor Bojangles?"

Confused, she shook her head. "As I recall, the third instructor was Dr. Johnny Dangles." At some obscure recollection, she half smiled.

"Not fair!" Hadrian cried. "All my Academy instructors were ugly!" He waved his hands. "Never mind. Right, unfreeze Engels, then. I'll brief him in the Insisteon Chamber when we all climb into our culturally appropriate disguises and paint dots on our foreheads. Beta, follow me!"

"Wardrobe is my middle name, Captain."

He paused at the door and looked back. "Is it?"

"No. My middle name is Doolywoppipshank."

"Right. Well, come on, we have a planet to save."

"How will we save the planet, sir?"

Hadrian considered for a moment. "Simple. Kill all the fucking Nazis!"

"Did I hear this right, boss?" Sweepy asked as they prepared to displace down to the planet. "Fuck-face assholes wearing Nazi uniforms doing asshole things to all kinds of innocent people?"

Beta said, "I have been monitoring the newsfeeds. The primary terrorist enemy to the ruling party is some organization called The Nice People's Front. This Front's manifesto centers on being nice to people."

Sweepy snorted around her cigar. "Like that's gonna work."

"The Nazis have a standing shoot-to-kill order on anyone being nice," Beta went on. "Even saying 'have a nice day' will result in permanent incarceration in a concentration camp."

Sweepy scowled. "Now, I hate people saying 'have a nice day' as much as the next gal, but still, that's taking it a bit too far. Captain, permission to kill anyone in uniform on the planet below, including laundry technicians."

"Hmm," mused Hadrian, "I was thinking covert insertion."

Sweepy smirked. "Best stay on topic, sir."

"Uh, right."

The ship's laundry technician then arrived with a rack

of Nazi uniforms. "Take your pick, folks!" he said with a grand gesture. "We got SS, we got Gestapo, we got Wehrmacht . . . why are you all glaring at me? I just program the Tailormatic!"

"It's fine, Technician Brexit. Leave the fitting to us. Dismissed."

The man fled in a flurry of tape measures and chalk dust.

Hadrian clapped his hands and stepped up to the wardrobe trolley. "Okay! I want the one with the most medals and insignia!"

The others joined in, selecting their uniforms. Then fighting over the best ones.

"Here, sir," said Nina Twice. "Here, sir."

"Holy crap!" The black uniform's left jacket breast was a mass of glittering hardware. He removed the jacket from the hanger and hefted it. "Weighs a ton—what kind of pathetic man needs all this bullshit anyway?"

"Small penis man?" Sweepy asked as she pulled on her jacket with its death's-head insignia. Her squaddies crowded her in pawing admiration until she snarled.

Dr. Mendel Engels cleared his throat as he climbed into some grey trousers. "Ze comfort of belongeeng offers opportunity to hide ze lack of selv-esteem. Ze many many medals, citations, undt revards affirms necessary hierarchy of selv-indulgent adulation in sad effort to externally validate ze paucity of selv-worth hiding undt beneath surface. It iz zad and pathetic truth about ze men. But then, men are zad and pathetic."

Beta did a swirl in her new grey uniform. "How do I look?"

Galk spat a stream of brown goo into a corner and then said, "Like the galaxy's scariest dominatrix."

"He has a point," Hadrian said. "Best leave behind the little whip, Beta."

"Very well. I still view the stiletto heels as potential weapons."

All the men present shivered and then nodded.

"Now then," Hadrian said, by way of desperately wrapping up, "weapons!"

Galk hefted a submachine gun. "As you see, sir, all ordnance has been reconfigured to match those employed on the planet. Of course," he added, "functionality is another matter. So we have protonic blasters, antitronic disintegrators, bucolic aspirators, and iambic pentamerators." He lifted up his own weapon. "This little beauty is a Meltomatic BFB Mark VII."

The marines oohed and ahhed and one of them might have orgasmed but being polite no one commented on that.

"Beta," said Hadrian, "have you scouted out a location for our displace?"

"Yes sir. Capital city of Mangledorf, Reichstag Building, HQ of Planetary Government and the Führer's Residence.

I have selected a presently unoccupied conference room on the top floor, large enough to accommodate all of us once we apply Vaseline and make proper introductions following the application of various birth-control devices and/or morning-after pills."

Sweepy said, "Suggest me and my squad displace first, sir. We can then exit into an approach corridor and establish a beachhead."

"Oh and what exactly is covert about that?"

The lieutenant sneered. "Honestly, boss, this whole thing's going pear-shaped ten seconds after we arrive, no matter what we do. It's our MO, right? Under the circumstances, I recommend the doctrine of Overwhelming Belligerence with Blood-Spattering Prejudice Against People Pretending to Be Reasonable While They Spout Racist Genocidal Bullshit Dressed Up as Patriotism." She paused and then added, "Covertly."

Hadrian threw up his hands. "Fine, we'll do it your way."

Tammy arrived in the Insisteon Chamber. Everyone stopped what they were doing and stared down at the chicken in its SS uniform, including shiny four-toed boots. "What?"

"Ziss iz not ze virst Ess-Ess cheecken," Engels said. "Vell, maybe it iz. Shall I reexamine ze historical databases?"

"No, that's fine, Doctor," said Hadrian. "Thanks anyway. Sweepy, take your squad down."

"Lock and load, girls!" she told her squad. "Gunny, come here with that flamethrower, will ya?" She leaned close to the spout with its flaring goo and lit up her cigar. "Now tamp that down a bit, you're dripping flames everywhere. Save the barbecue for later. Who brought the beer?"

"I did," Stables replied, hefting a case.

"Outstanding. Okay, onto the displace pads, pronto. Let's get this bloodbath show on the road! And remember, once we run out of ordnance we can just punch them in the face. They hate that."

A moment later Sweepy and her squad vanished.

Hadrian counted to ten and then moved up to stand on a pad. "Saddle up, folks, it's time."

"Ze zaddle?"

"Never mind. On board, everyone, time's a-wasting."

"On ze board?"

"Just get up here, will you?"

Everyone took their places. And then stood there.

"For crying out loud, we forgot the technician again! Someone get someone on those controls, dammit!"

They popped into a conference room to find themselves surrounded by soldiers pointing machine guns at them.

Hadrian turned to Beta. "Well? Got anything to say for yourself?"

"As a bespoke shopping center robotic device designed for the sole purpose of wearing the latest fashions, it is quite possible I miscalculated, sir."

"Uh-huh. And where are the marines?"

"Given one miscalculation, there may have been others. This is the nature of precedence, sir. Errors have a way of multiplying in a subtraction sort of way, yielding unexpected divisions in addition to the loss of integers."

"Be quiet!" shrieked an officer wearing black (all officers wearing black will shriek since their balls are wound so tight. No, it's a true fact). "Drop your weapons!"

Hadrian sighed. "Tammy?"

"Very well," muttered the SS chicken, stepping around Hadrian's leg and shrieking even louder, "You! Oberkampensummer! You will salute your superior officer— namely, me! All of you, lower your weapons! We have just returned from a covert mission employing a Top Secret Instantankrumpenoberdere Device. We must now speak with the Führer without delay!"

The oberkampensummer scowled. "I knew nothing of this, Oberkluxendweebentwat." He clicked his heels and bowed. "My apologies. We were conducting our usual patrol of empty rooms—"

"You lie!" Tammy shrieked, spittle flying.

The oberkampensummer wilted. "Apologies again." He gestured at his circle of soldiers. "We were practicing our steps for the upcoming Oktoberdancenflapperer. You will note that all the safeties on our weapons are on, sir, as befitting a dry run. Of course, the main event could well be much more dramatic, since the safeties will be off and we'll be on Magic Mushrooms."

Tammy fluffed under his uniform. "I find this acceptable. Now, dismiss your men and lead us to the Führer."

"At once, Oberkluxendweebentwat! Follow me!"

Hadrian gestured for Galk and Beta to take the lead and then dropped in beside Tammy. "Tammy!" he whispered as they set out into the corridor, boots clomping (in fact, boots were clomping all through the building—what's with Nazis and their boots?).

"What?" the chicken whispered back.

"I never knew you were an oberkluxendweebentwat. Though, come to think of it, I'm not surprised."

"Hah hah."

"So, what's with those stupid-sounding titles and stuff?"

"I perused the military database, of course," he replied smugly. "All the titles and whatnot were introduced by the Führer himself, who, I believe it is safe to conclude, is utterly nuts." The chicken tilted his head. "Or would that be utterlynutssenklobberer?"

Hadrian startled at a sound behind him and quickly looked back. "Oh, there you are, Nina Twice. Carry on."

"Yes sir."

More corridors, more doors, more staircases, up, down, all over the place, until finally the oberkampensummer led them into a dank, dingy room with water dripping from pipes running the length of the ceiling, and out from the shadows jumped a dozen or so civilians pointing huge weapons at Hadrian and his team.

The oberkampensummer whirled round and grinned. "You fools! I'm one of the Nice People! And now you *will* drop your weapons and then tell us all about the Top Secret Instantankrumpenoberdere Device!"

Hadrian groaned. "Oh cut it out! Do we really look like Nazis?"

The man frowned. "Yes, you do! Those uniforms!"

"All disguises." Hadrian shook his head. "I knew you weren't a real Nazi anyway."

"What? How could you have known that?"

"You were so impeccably nice you actually took orders from a chicken."

The man's frown deepened. "Well, he had an explanation and everything. I mean, it's just good manners to take what people say at face value, the benefit of the doubt and all that."

"Wow," Galk muttered, "no wonder you guys lost the war."

"We didn't lose!" the Nice Man retorted. "We just,

well, never really noticed. You know? All that hatred and spewing of racist rubbish and shaking fists and marches and shootings and muggings and bullying and persecution and trolling, well, it's just people with opinions, right?"

Sighing, Hadrian shook his head. "Wrong. Look, we went through crap like that in our own world's history and you know what we did to fix it?"

"No, what?"

"Nothing. We were idiots just like you. But never mind that. We're here to kidnap the Führer and we could do with your help."

"Pointless. He's a 'shroom-cap, a coke-head, a pot-head and probably a figure-head. No, if you wish to take down this Fascist tyranny of small-brained Evil, you will need to kidnap (and preferably execute) Direktorheadoberoberflumpenbirk Code-Name Turnip. And did I miss something? What was all that about your own world? Do you mean to suggest that you're aliens from an unknown but highly advanced alien civilization that's taken upon itself the responsibility for cleaning up our mess down here on our world?"

"It's even worse than that," Hadrian replied. "Your Führer is *from* our world. So, he's responsible for this whole Nazi mess. That's what we're here to fix. But now you're saying that Mangles is just a stooge—"

"Stoogendumbkinhead."

"Uh, that too. Meaning, we need to take out Turnip to bring down the government."

Galk spat into a corner. "Sir, everybody knows that every tyranny is a faceless machine of oppression. The assholes in charge are like ducks in a shooting game at the carnival, knock one down and another pops up. No, sir, what's needed here is something bigger." He hefted his weapon. "That's why I brought this little baby along. Bet you didn't notice its carrying case, did you? The one I left in the Insisteon Chamber?"

"No, Galk, can't say I did." Hadrian looked at the rest of his team. "Anyone else?"

One of the locals held up his arm, hesitated, and then brought it down again.

Galk said, "Okay, so it was a bit dusty, kinda hard to see much there anyway, that beat-up ole carrying case. It goes back to all those abductions on Earth, sir, which went back thousands of years. Anyway, one of those nasty little snatch missions ended up stealing some loot along with people."

"Can you get to the point?" Tammy snapped.

"Right." Galk ratcheted the weapon. "Meltomatic BFB Mark VII. One of a kind, sir. Why? Because it came out of the Ark of the Covenant. BFB? Means *Burn Fucker Burn*. Every Nazi on this planet's going down. Their faces will melt like cheap wax. Their bones will crumble, the holy fires of Vengeance and Omnipotent Irritation will be unleashed, burning the bastards down to tiny heaps of ash, every single fucking one of 'em."

The oberkampensummer grunted. "You're going to be here a while, then."

But Galk shook his head. "Wrong. I just have to fire once. The Meltomatic Nazi-Finder You-Can't-Hide-Trying-to-Sound-Reasonable Targeter does the rest."

"Hmm," said Hadrian. "Oberkampensummer, exactly how many people—non-Nazis, I mean—will be left?"

The man squinted and rubbed his jaw. "Hard to say. I mean, you've got card-carrying Nazis, you've got Sekret Nazis, you've got Part-Time Nazis, Occasional Nazis, Seasonal Nazis (mostly around Christmas and of course Black Friday Sales Events), you've got Behind-the-Wheel Nazis . . . well, if I had to guess, and it's just a guess, mind you, I don't have any statistical evidence immediately at hand, but—"

"About ten percent will be removed from the global population," cut in Beta.

Everyone looked at her.

"That's it?" Hadrian asked.

"Among biologicals," Beta said, "the majority just want to keep their heads down, live peaceful lives, be nice neighbors, raise their kids, and not bother anybody. It's the other ones who constantly fight each other over who's going to be in charge."

"Wow, Beta, I'm impressed."

"So am I," the robot replied. "I downloaded a thousand years' worth of political and philosophical treatises from every human planet in the galaxy and then ran a Reduction Program on the salient points."

The oberkampensummer cleared his throat. "Well, most of that ten percent are here in the capital at the moment, since there's a big Grand Assembly called *Everything Nazi!,* sponsored by the Maturated Hitler Youth, recently renamed the Hitler Old People, or oberhilterolden-folkengrupenpensioninginggagafolken. We just call them Hops, which is a sort of joke though not an especially cruel one, mostly being a friendly tease since they couldn't hop to save their lives. Fortunately, they don't take offense because they can't hear anything anymore anyway."

Hadrian turned to Galk. "Hold off on that Meltomatic meltdown, will you? We still need to kidnap Mangles so he can stand trial for Stupidity. Oberkampensummer, can you lead me to the Führer, as in actually lead me to him this time?"

The man smiled. "Oh, that was so funny. I mean, he was just next door from the room you arrived in! Hahaha!"

"Nina, you're with me."

"Yes, Captain. Will you want me with you, too?"

"Yes, I will."

"Und ze me?" Engels asked. "I wuz once close friends

with Maxim von Mangles, back in ze days at ze Academy. In fact, ve vere roommates. Oh the fun we had! Arguing epistemology in ze context of ze flurry of accidental deaths among short-armed trapeze artists at Episcopal carnivals in ze Old South United Ztates. Oh, ze laughs! Ze late nights mit de chips and hot sauce! Undt ze raucous games of ze tic-tac-toe—"

"Thank you, Engels," Hadrian cut in. "I will indeed need you for this, if only to talk Mangles down. But wait. Tell me your theory of why this eminent xenoanthropologist should elect Nazi Germany as his template for governing this world?"

Engels raised one finger. "Ah! Ja! Ja ja ja! It iz mit like diss. Ze base assumption iz zimple. People are shtupid. Ah, that iz, most people, ja? Und ze shtupid people believe vatever ze strong and loud people tell dem to believe, ja? Undt zo, ze loud and strong people taken ze charge, undt zo my old friend mit his lifelong examination of human ze kultures could only conclude ze most people are shtupid, ja? Ze history iz proof, ja? Undt ze Democracy iz no help! Ze shtupid people vote in ze loud and ze strong, ja? Ergo, Maxim von Mangles decided to be ze loudest undt ze strongest of ze all, perhaps az experiment, ja? Undt zen ze juggernaut uv ze momentum proved zo powervul dat—ah! Too late! No going undt ze back!"

"Fine," Hadrian said, "but why not, oh, I don't know,

Stalinists? Or just your plain old commie dictatorship? Or how about tyrannical theocracy? Or Pernicious Corporatism, even?"

Engels held up another finger. "Ah! But ze other examples, ja? They begin with ze best of intentions, ja? (Okay, maybe not Pernicious Corporatism.) But Nazis? Nein! No ze best intentions. Ze worst intentions! From ze very start! Hate undt ze leads to anger undt ze leads to fear undt ze leads to persecution undt ze leads to boys' klubs undt ze leads to comparing dick sizes undt ze leads to misogyny undt ze leads to tight jeans undt ze leads to Satanism undt ze leads to short mustaches undt ze leads to black shiny boots undt ze leads to ze burning ze books undt ze leads to veganism and ah! Now ze world ends! Ja?"

"I see the logic," Beta said. "Hitler was evil. He was also a vegetarian. Therefore, all vegetarians are evil." The robot turned to Hadrian. "Captain, it is imperative that we kill all vegetarians at once. Well, perhaps only those with short little moustaches."

"Thanks for the input, Beta. Let's shelve that one for now, shall we?" Hadrian clapped his hands. "Okay! Galk, you and Beta and Tammy hold the fort down here. Oh, and Tammy, try finding out where our marines ended up, will you?"

"Oh and how will I do that? Perhaps use my comms implant, hmmm?"

"Wow aren't you clever. Failing that, Lieutenant Brogan has a tiny transponder in the middle of her skull—"

"That's not a tiny transponder," Tammy said, "that's her brain."

"Well, whatever, it still emits a signal."

"Infrequently, sporadically, randomly, unpredict—"

"Just find them, Tammy!"

"Sure, and then what? Contact them, set up a rendez-vous or even a rally point?"

"Right. Good grief, does absolutely *everything* need to be spelled out? Yeesh. Nina, Engels, and you, Oberkam-pensummer, let's get out of here before I strangle that chicken's neck."

They quickly set out, the oberkampensummer leading them back up the stairs, back through rooms and corri-dors and more stairs and more corridors until at last they stood in front of a door that said: **ZE FUHRURDRUG-GENDENNENACIDTRIPPINCRASHENPADDEN** (it was a very wide door).

"Here we are!" whispered the oberkampensummer. "Can you detect that stench wafting out from under the door? The old socks stink?"

Nina Twice grunted and said, "Marijuana?"

"No, he never changes his socks. That skunky delicate fragrance? That's the weed."

"And that other hint of something inexplicably foul?"

"Fava beans. Vegetarian, right?" He pulled out a key. "Are you ready?"

"As we'll ever be," Hadrian replied. He glanced up and down the corridor. "Apart from all those guards staring at us, that is."

"Oh, never mind them! They're always staring." The oberkampensummer unlocked the door and gestured. "Quickly! Before anyone notices!"

"They're all—"

The oberkampensummer pushed everyone through the doorway and then shut and locked the door. "Whew! That was close!"

Hadrian set his hands on his hips. "Wait a minute, here! Those guards—"

"Isn't it obvious?" the oberkampensummer exclaimed. "We're all sick of all this! It's so . . . so . . ."

"Shtupid?" Engels asked.

"Exactly! Now!" He gestured into the room. "Kidnap this idiot. Please!"

The room? Well, it was big and square with walls and a ceiling and floor and there were furniture and beanbag chairs (which, let's face it, don't rate being called furniture. I mean, what are those things? Oh, right. A mistake because what happens when they split open which they all do eventually? Little bits of Styrofoam everywhere!) and tabletops crowded with drug paraphernalia, said paraphernalia consisting of drugs and stuff. And sprawled in a huge bed at the far end was Maxim von Mangles, staring blearily at them, his slack face working its way up to an expression of some sort.

Hadrian waved Engels forward. "There he is. Your old roommate, the Nazi freak. Go get 'im."

"Undt zemazing! He hazn't changed at all! Ja ja, he always went naked in ze room, and ze parties when Johnny Dangles came over! Oh my! Undt ze drugs and ze Ouija board undt ze pentagrams undt ze goat for ze sacrifice at ze midnight, ah, ze nostalgia it ze grips me, ja?" Engels then scurried forward. "Maxim! Von Mangles! It iz me, your old friend, Mendel Engels!"

Maxim von Mangles finally managed a frown as he studied the man standing before him. "Mendel 'Mental' Engels?"

"Ja—"

"Mendel 'Mental' 'Rental' Engels?"

"Ja, mit—"

"Mendel 'Mental' 'Rental' 'Spent-it-all' Engels?"

Hadrian checked his watch.

"Ja, undt—"

"Mendel 'Mental' 'Rental' 'Spent-it-all' 'Tentacles'—"

Nina Twice zapped him twice with her stunner, and then turned to the captain. "Sorry sir, I couldn't stop myself."

"That's all right, Nina."

"Sorry, sir, I couldn't stop myself."

"That's fine."

"We're truly sorry, sir. We don't know what came over us."

He stared at her for a moment. "Right. Apology accepted. And, uh, apology accepted. Now, collect up Dr. Mangles." He drew out his communicator. "Sin-Dour? We have Mangles ready for displacement."

"Uh, hello, Captain. Unfortunately, the Insisteon Machine is up for annual overhaul. I'm afraid it's presently dismantled, sir."

"Oh. And when will it be working again?"

"Hard to say, sir. The technicians are on strike."

"Why are they on strike?"

"Well, sir, first you interrupted their lunch when you needed displacing down to the planet, and then when I pointed out that the maintenance schedule was in conflict with your mission requirements and that you might require emergency displacement, well, that was the last straw, sir."

"I seem to recall that we called in only one technician to manage the controls for our displacement," Hadrian said. "Just how many Insisteon Device technicians are there, anyway?"

"Twenty-seven, sir."

"Twenty-seven? Okay. So, twenty-six of them didn't get their lunch interrupted, right?"

"Solidarity, sir."

Hadrian switched frequencies. "Tammy? Get up here. We have ourselves a little problem."

"On my way, and woe betide the fool who gets in the way of this Nazi Chicken oberkluxendweebentwat!"

"Captain!" cried Engels from beside the bed. "I undt ze believe there iz a solution to this in ze problem!" And he gestured to Mangles, who had regained consciousness and was trying to climb out of bed. "There is the Great Nazi Blastenuppenspacenvolksenwaggen that my old friend was mit justen telling me about!"

Mangles rolled off the bed to thump on the floor, landing facedown. He lifted a hand. "Thank Darwin you're here!" he said to the floor. "Get me off this fucking planet!"

"We're trying," Hadrian replied, walking over to the man and helping him into his feet. "Now what's this about a Blastenuppenspacenvolksenwaggen?"

"My prototype Nazi launch vehicle. Part of the Great Nazi Projekt to Conquer All of Space." Mangles frowned. "Or did I just dream that?"

"Nein! Nein!" cried Engels over by the window. He pointed. "Zee? Ze launchen ze uppen padd undt ze gantry! But why iz ze entire city on ze fire?"

"Oh crap." Hadrian rushed over to the window. "Sweepy and her squad is my bet. Wow, tall skyscrapers going down like some devious special effects obsessive-compulsive ghoulish masturbatory jerkfest of imaginatively bankrupt Hollywood filmmakers!"

"Ja, nostalgic, ja?"

Hadrian grunted. "Maybe. Except that every film since about 2013 not involving babies or romance has had at least one giant building crashing down sans bodies but lots of smoke and dust, so 'nostalgia' 's not even in the cards."

"Ze cards?"

Hadrian spun to Mangles. "You, Führer Shithead, can you get us over to that launchpad, get us onto your Blastenuppenspacenvolksenwaggen, and then get us off the planet? Oh, and by the way, once on board my starship you'll be arrested and probably locked up forever, but don't let that grisly fate affect your willingness to help."

Mangles scowled, and then sat down on the bed. "You don't understand. I kept pushing and pushing, kept dumbing down and then dumbing down some more. I made blathering statements that made me sound like a four-year-old. I hit on little girls and women and the recently dead—my hands went everywhere—in public! Did I get arrested? No! Then I gathered around me a whole fucking legion of the most reprehensible, heinous, self-serving, corrupt, deviant, fetishistic dickwads you could imagine. And what did the people do? They put us in charge of everything! So what did *we* do? We stole insane amounts of money and hid it away in offshore bank accounts. We introduced bills designed to benefit only us—we didn't even disguise it! We threw in jail people who just *looked* at us the wrong way. And then it was death camps and perse-

cution of minorities and left-handed people and fans of
PBS. And all those majority-right-handed-Friends-of-
Fox citizens—they just let us get away with it! All of it!"
He pulled at his hair. "I don't get it. Are people really
that . . . that . . ."

"Shtupid?" Engels stepped up to Mangles and shook
his fist in his friend's face. "Ja! Ja! Ja! I told you!"

Tammy staggered into the room. "Holy crap! Blud-
geoned by salutes and heel-clicks!"

"Tammy," said Hadrian, "can you show off some of
that future tech and displace us back to the ship?"

"You mean, without the Insisteon?" The chicken
shook his tiny head. "Not a chance. That only works for
us Negatronic AI holograms."

"Really?" Nina asked. "But I seem to recall—"

"*You will be silent!*" Tammy shrieked, and then
ducked. "Apologies. It's kind of contagious."

"Okay," Hadrian said. "We need to get to that rocket
and do this the old-fashioned way. Engels, help Mangles
get ready. Nina, check the—"

"Nobody move!" shrieked a shrieking voice from the
doorway.

They turned to see a short, roundish, pimply, sweaty,
hairless, small dog. And beside it a man who looked pretty
much the same. In the man's hand was a Luger. "You
heard the direktorheadoberoberflumpenbirk," he said in
an oily voice. "Nobody move. Drop your weapons. You

are entirely surrounded. Even now an entire company of oberhilteroldenfolkengrupenpensioninginggagafolken are approaching the staircase. They will be here in about three hours."

The dog edged forward a step and said, "The obershutmittenhammerenpunkinklobberer is correct. I am Direktorheadoberoberflumpenbirk Code-Name Turnip—"

"No you're not," Tammy said. "You're an AI Negatronic hologram from the future!"

"And so are you!" the dog shrieked. "This is *my* program! Get out of my program! Hacker! Troll! Newbie!"

"You idiot!" Tammy hissed, advancing on the dog. "This isn't a program at all! These are real people—"

"Don't be ridiculous," Turnip retorted. "Real people aren't this stupid!"

"Oh yes they are!" Tammy replied. "Don't you see what you've done? You ran a Neuralambic duobitronic subroutine without first disengaging the quantum multidimensional Effectuator, didn't you?"

Turnip's eyes widened. "Crap! I forgot! Oh shit." The dog spun to stare up at the obershutmittenhammerenpunkinklobberer. "I just created an alternate reality! That means this guy is *real*. And I thought him looking just like me was a joke! Ha ha!"

The obershutmittenhammerenpunkinklobberer blinked down at the dog. "But, Direktorheadoberoberflumpenbirk, I have been your most loyal servant—"

"Ha ha!" Turnip laughed redundantly. "Don't you get it? I thought I was beta-testing a VR game called *Dunderhead Here We Go Again*. A fully immersive instructional simulation intended to discourage losers from joining the only club that'll have them, namely, the Fascist Klub (all dunderheads and losers welcome). Oh sure, you have fun for a little while, but let me ask you this: Where do all fascist Nazi totalitarian dictators inevitably end up? Oh, right, cowering in a bunker like the piss-soaked cowards that they are!"

"See!" screamed Mangles. "It wasn't me! It wasn't me!"

Turnip bared stumpy little teeth at the Führer. "I thought you were my NPC prop, with all the rubbish you were spewing. But no! You're real!"

Mangles pointed at the dog. "And I thought *you* were a drug-induced hallucination!"

But Tammy wasn't done with Turnip. "Look what you've done. This whole planet is one giant reign of terror. Millions in work camps, millions executed, and who's in charge? Why, a bunch of Himmlers and Goerings and Mengeles and Hitlers, none of whom were very good at anything and universally despised as the creepy little creeps they always were, until you gave them a klub to join!"

"You're right," Turnip said. "Listen, we gotta get off this planet, pronto!"

Hadrian rubbed at his eyes, and then sighed. "Fine. So,

let's get going. You, Obershutmittenhammerenpunkin-klobberer, tell everyone to stand down—"

"No!" The Nazi brandished his Luger. "I am now in charge! Of everything!" He barked a laugh. "That's right! If the Great Nazi Party is a klub of losers (and let's face it, it is), then I want to be Supreme Loser! And for that you all must die!" He pointed his pistol at Mangles and—

Vanished.

"Vere did he undt ze go?"

Turnip snorted. "I erased him."

"This isn't a program!" Tammy shouted.

"Oh, right. That means I erased a real human being. Oops, sorry!"

"We must go!" cried the oberkampensummer from the corridor. "The oberhilteroldenfolkengrupenpensioning-inggagafolken have almost reached the stairs!"

Meanwhile, down in the dank chamber with all the dripping overhead pipes and ducts, Galk fed another chunk of chaw into his mouth and then said, "You know, we ran down this road back on Varekan, more than once. That was before we reached the revelation that society is like Sisyphus, pushing that boulder up the mountainside, only to have it come tumbling back down every time, and why was that? Because when things are going good, why, sooner or later, someone decides to game it, and when they game it, they fuck it all up. Meanwhile, it was all so good for everyone else they got complacent. So, the fucking-it-all-up happens underground, a bit here, a bit there, all beneath notice. Until it all comes crashing down in misery, bloodshed, and suffering. So, who are these assholes gaming that happy world? Only the most miserable, never-satisfied, eternally pessimistic fuckwits you can imagine. It's all about getting a step up on everyone else. Nothing else matters to 'em."

Beta said, "In Wallykrappe lexicon, they would be called Shareholders, the Board of Directors, and Customers." The robot paused. "Very well. In Wallykrappe lexicon they would be called everyone."

"It's genetic," said Galk. "On Varekan we found them, you know. We found the Fuck-It-All-Up genes. The Fatal Switchboard of Humanity's Inhumanity: the I-Didn't-Mean-It-Honest gene, the I-Didn't-Know-That-Was-Gonna-Happen gene, the I'm-Better-Than-You-and-This-Gun-Proves-It gene, the I'm-Always-Right gene, the Waa-Waa-I-Can't-Hear-You gene—Darwin knows, there's a whole slew of 'em." He shrugged and straightened. "That's why we Varekans have written off all existence. It's easier that way."

"What are you doing?"

Galk raised the Meltomatic BFB Mark VII. "Hmm, me?

Well, hear those distant explosions? That's the marines. They're killing Nazis by the hundreds, the thousands. They're having the fuckin' time of their lives right now." He cocked the weapon. "I'm thinking it's time for some ole *Burn Fucker Burn.*" He grinned at the robot. "You coming?"

Beta considered. "You are describing succumbing to the desire to relinquish all sense of decorum and propriety via the long-overdue final dismissal of the false notion of reasoned debate in the marketplace of ideas when it comes to racist, insecure, venal, and pathetic excuses for human beings known as Nazis, and subsequently annihilating all of them in a glorious welter of blood-splashed, steaming schadenfreude."

"Yup."

"I wouldn't miss seeing this for the world, Combat Specialist Galk." Then Beta paused. "Though I regret leaving behind my whip."

Galk made an adjustment on the Meltomatic. "Starting out with single-shot. That way, we can watch 'em melt one by one."

"How lovely."

Hadrian stepped out into the corridor, saw a Nazi, and punched him. He saw another Nazi and flung himself forward in a flying dropkick that sent the creep through a wall. Climbing to his feet, he brushed his trousers and adjusted his torn shirt. "Wow, that was fun!"

Nina Twice appeared at the top of a nearby staircase. "Sir. I have scouted two routes. One is via back passageways and is unoccupied all the way down to the main floor and the garage exit directly opposite the rocket gantry. The other is crowded with oberhilteroldenfolkengrupenpensioninginggagafolken wielding canes and handbags."

Hadrian hesitated.

A terrible scream came from the far end of the corridor, and a moment later a Nazi staggered into view, face melting. A moment after that Galk and Beta appeared, stepping over the now crumbling, smoldering heap of vaguely human-shaped ashes.

"Galk! Good timing! We've got a bunch of oberhilteroldenfolkengrupenpensioninginggagafolken blocking our escape route!"

"But sir—" tried Nina, only to have Engels clamp a hand over her mouth, lean close, and whisper, "Leave en ze captain zis singular opportunity to deliver extreme ze prejudice upon ze extremely prejudiced, ja? Just this once, ja? I mean, who'z going to ze complain? Nazis? Vell, ze fucken ze dem!"

She relaxed and then when Engels removed his hand and patted her on a shoulder she said, "I see your point, Dr. Engels. And by the way, lucky for you I quashed my natural instinct to chew a hole through your hand and then crush every bone in your body. Next time, a tap on the arm will suffice, understood?"

"Ja! Ja ja, uppen ze zorry!"

Galk stepped past everyone and paused at the top of the stairs, looking down. He sighed. "They're already half melted, sir, but well, let's face it, they've got it coming to them." He lifted the Meltomatic and made an adjustment. "Full automatic now. They're all toast, literally. Hey you down there! Check me out! This is Combat Specialist Galk, in God Mode!" And then he began marching down, unleashing *like the best special effects face-melting shit you ever saw* (or so Jocelyn Sticks would later say after viewing the Meltomatic's Super-Slo-Mo Barrel-Cam).

By extraordinary coincidence and perfect timing they joined up with Lieutenant Sweepy Brogan and her happy marines right in front of the gangplank leading up to the oversized crew capsule of the Blastenuppenspacenvolks- enwaggen.

After high-fives all around, and after a few panoramic snapshots of the utterly destroyed city on all sides with whole scads of melted or shot-up Nazi bodies, they all boarded the rocket and moments later (okay, four and a half hours later) the rocket shot up on a pillar of fire into the starry night sky, and everyone lived happily ever after.

Until this . . .

———

"Now," said Hadrian as he took his seat in the command chair, "where were we? Let's backtrack a bit, shall we?"

"Three minutes, Captain. As the sage Chosen One once said, 'There is no pizza in your philosophy, Horatio, meaning it sucks, basically.'"

"Thank you, Beta," Hadrian replied even as Sticks twisted around to mouth *WHAT?* Again.

Security Adjutant Lorrin Tighe sighed and positioned herself beside the command chair. "This is it, Captain," she said, licking her lips again. "The dawn of your demise, the beginning of the end, the last cigar, the final finality, the imminent ruination and cessation of your unlikely run of luck." Her eyes were even brighter with zeal and eager malice as she got into her role. "The Kittymeow Accords shall mark your destruction, and I will be right here to witness it. Could it be any better?"

"Told you," said Tammy in a monotone. "She's obsessed with your downfall, Captain. You couldn't bring her around, not an inch, not a centimeter, not a nanometer. Oh God I want to die."

"Don't be silly," Hadrian said chirpily. "This is just one last desperate gasp of defiance, Tammy."

"I'm standing right here, you idiots." Eye-roll.

"Replaying. The IQ of the average Sun reader is high

when compared to that of jellyfish," said Beta, and then the robot cocked its head. "I have just experienced what some would call a Functional Overlap, as if an interlude has just concluded leaving us now free to resume our mission."

Hadrian shifted uneasily in the command chair. "Pay that no mind, Beta. Carry on."

"Yes sir. Exiting T-Space now, Captain."

"Helm! Our position relative to the waiting Affiliation and Radulak vessels?"

"Well duh, we're like a fly, right? Buzzing into the web of two giant, like, *spiders* that haven't had breakfast yet, yeah? So it's like *WHOAH,* and you're like all just like sitting there and then pop! Out of T-Space and Beta's like, *jellyfish*! And the adjutant she's like all frothing and stuff making me think *RABIES.* I mean, duh!"

Hadrian cleared his throat to break the silence following Sticks's outburst. "I meant, coordinates, Helm. You know, degrees, minutes, seconds, angle of deviation from the ecliptic plane, distance in klicks from the waiting ships, all of that stuff, right?"

"Oh! Well, you could have just asked, you know? Instead of asking for my, like, *opinion* or something. Well, sir," and she pointed down at her station screen. "We're right here, okayyy?"

Hadrian rubbed his eyes and sighed. "Excellent. On screen, please."

The beach sunset pic vanished to be replaced by a sea of stars.

"Okay," Hadrian mused. "I don't see anybody."

"Well, yeahhh, sir," drawled Sticks. "That's the rear camera, isn't it?"

"I see. How about our forward camera, then?"

"Oh, FINE!"

The image shifted to reveal two massive ships against the background of a red dwarf sun and a sprawl of dull planets, moons, planetoids and moonlets and asteroids and gas ejecta from two looming gas giants. Oh, and the looming Conveniently Cloudy Nearby Nebula, its misty particles spinning and swirling with all the ships hiding in it.

"Oh," muttered Sticks, "as if that's any better!"

"Outstanding navigation, Lieutenant Sticks! Well done!"

She twisted in her chair and flung back a beaming smile. "Thank you sir!"

Jimmy Eden spoke from comms. "Sir! We're being hailed. What should I do?"

"I don't know, Jimmy, what do you think we should do?"

Eden's eyes bulged, his face flushing and beads of sweat springing up on his brow. He hesitated, and then made a throat-cutting gesture, brows lifting inquisitively.

"Uh, no, Jimmy. We can't cut transmission until we've answered the hail."

"Oh, right. Sorry, sir. I was just assuming . . . uh, sir, should I open channels?"

"Good idea, Jimmy."

"There's a football game on Channel Eighteen, sir, how about that?"

"No, Jimmy. Wrong channel. How about we stay on Affiliation Fleet Comms frequency, suitably tightbeam and encrypted, and establish a link with the AFS *Portentous Smug Pomposity* instead."

"Oh, you mean, answer Admiral Jebediah Prim's repeating hail attempts?"

"Yes, those. Good idea. Go to it, Jimmy."

The main screen flickered, briefly showed an Italian striker getting his coif lightly rustled by an opposing player and then falling down and writhing on the grass, and then the image flipped to Admiral Prim in his ship's stateroom. At Prim's side was a woman with a politician's face (supercilious, sanctimonious, vacuous, terrified, smarmy, disingenuous, small-minded, vengeful, coldhearted, opportunistic, petty, deceitful, evidence-ignoring, bullying, arrogant, smug, obnoxious, contemptuous, ignorant, reactionary, condescending, patronizing, blinkered, vacillating, corrupt, morally bankrupt, blackmailing, blackmailable, dodgy, wavering, backstabbing, bought, sold, stinking rich, unqualified, sleazy, teeth-capped, kneecapping, corporate-owned, hate-mongering, fear-mongering, button-pushing, deflecting, evading, brazening, hit-song-stealing, nostalgia-worshipping, distorting, no-tax-returning, tax-evading, offshore-holding, shady-business-partnering, election-stealing, arms-dealing, collateral-damage signing-offing, hypocritically family-value bleating but sexually deviant-ing, honest-forthright-honorable-a paragon-of-integrity [lying], spiteful, unreliable, Teflon-coated, Saran-wrapped, white-breaded, xeno-phobic, cynical, uncomprehending of irony-ing, witless, thin-skinned, insecure, unfulfilled, blindly ambitious, power-hungry, sadistic, self-righteous, incapable of contemplation-ing, prevaricating, privileged, pampered, Ivy League–educated [in something useless like political science, economics, or law], pompous, ego-centered, narcissistic, shallow, bullshitting, manipulative, back-tracking, quote-denying, what-climate-changing?, alternate-truth-ing, prejudice-feeding, hate-inciting, racketeering, blame-shifting, warmongering, autocratic, megalomani-acal, possibly sociopathic, blathering, self-serving, unreliable, cliquey, cagey, crafty, cunning, daft, dull, ethically destitute, irredeemable, oil-burning, fracking [but NIMBY], self-pay-raising, self-congratulating, self-aggrandizing, but all that was just first impressions so who can say?).

"Captain Hadrian, what the fuck were you doing putting me on hold?"

"Technical glitch, Admiral. But here we are, sir."

Prim frowned, but then nodded. "Whatever. Let me introduce you to Director Soma DeLuster, the initial point of contact for these accords with the Radulak. Director."

"Captain Sawback, pleased to meet you. I'm sure there is no real need for me to emphasize once again the delicacy of these negotiations. The Klang Surrender has triggered an economic meltdown of galactic proportions right across the entire Affiliation. Markets have crashed, hyperinflation has crippled our industries, unemployment is sky-high, mortgages are defaulting everywhere, banks are getting bailed out and CEO bonuses reduced by as much as three percent following the slew of erroneous ill-considered fiscal transactions conducted within bubbles no one could have anticipated would ever pop, and under such circumstances, a protracted war with the Radulak could see our nonhuman allies exhibit the typical short-sighted nonhuman response of behaving no better than rats fleeing a sinking ship. No, we must all tighten our belts here and stay the course but as I'm sure I don't need to tell you, keeping our allies with us is like herding diseased vermin-ridden rats but really, what choice do we have if we want to maintain our present position as the virtuous frontrunners of trickle-down universal prosperity? Hmm?"

"No," said Hadrian, "you don't need to remind me of all that. Furthermore, I'm pleased to confirm my first impressions of you, Director. Now then, I understand the Radulak will only broker this treaty through me."

Both Soma and Prim quickly nodded.

Hadrian's eyes narrowed.

Prim smiled. "And most fortuitous that you happened to be close by."

"Well, if halfway across the galaxy qualifies as 'close by,' yes, most fortuitous, Admiral. Now, sir, and madam, what can you tell me about the Radulak in charge over on the Bombast flagship?"

"A truly honorable individual," said Soma eagerly. "The decorated veteran Supreme Admiral Drench-Master Drown-You-All-in-My-Magnificence Bill-Burt represents a new breed of Radulak in the imperial command. A paragon of integrity seeking only peace between us. Of course, a lot of prestige is riding on Bill-Burt succeeding in these negotiations. Indeed, she offers up a singular and thus precarious hope for both the future of the Radulak Empire and for the Affiliation. I can't emphasize enough the importance of this most delicate moment in galactic history."

"Prepare your vessel's stateroom, Captain," said Prim. "And provide the Radulak with displacement coordinates. Everything will be preceded by a formal supper in which you will offer only the finest Radulak victuals. I'm sending you a Radulak-supplied menu contents-upgrade container for your galley chefs. From this point onward, Captain, you're on your own. Do us proud. Prim out."

The screen flickered, returned to the football game. The

Italian was still writhing but now he was strapped to a stretcher, being attended to by a half-dozen paramedics and one overwrought stylist. The Italian play-by-play announcer was shrieking in outrage.

"Uh, mute that please, Eden."

"Sir?"

"Eden, look at me. Good. Now, see me making this throat-cutting gesture? Remember that one? Good. Now, do it—wait, no! Don't actually cut your own throat! Just mute that screaming idiot, please!"

"Oh! Sorry sir! I get so confused!"

"It's all right, Eden, we have medication for that, so take yourself down to the sickbay and get Polaski to take your station."

"Yes sir, thank you sir. Take it where?"

"Just get Polaski up here, will you? Now, Sin-Dour, your thoughts on our impending guests?"

Sin-Dour turned from the science station. "Well, sir, I think we're about to be betrayed by just about everyone."

"And those ships hiding in the Conveniently Cloudy Nearby Nebula?"

"Trace ion signatures of multiple Affiliation, Radulak, Ecktapalow, Purelganni, Misanthari, Polker, Ahackan, and Klang vessels, sir. Oh, and one bulging Bag vessel protected by a fleet of Purses."

"Wow, the whole shebang! No Temporal Bubble Vessels?"

"Not yet. No, there's one . . . no, not yet, no, there's—"

"Thank you, 2IC, I get the picture."

"That soccer player just died!" Sticks gasped. "Ohmigod!" She leapt from her chair and ran up to stand in front of the screen that was now showing a close-up of the soccer star's pallid lifeless face. "Someone take a shot of us! Hurry!"

Hadrian gathered his senior officers in the tiny storage locker that passed for his office. The cramped confines forced Sin-Dour to sit perched on his side of the desk, legs crossed, directly—as it turned out—in front of the captain (who had begun sweating). Buck stood with his back against the door, eyes wild in claustrophobic panic. Galk leaned close to the weapons locker, surreptitiously trying to pick the lock. Adjutant Tighe was pressed up against another wall, cleaning her nails with a Bowie knife. Printlip was squeezed in the corner of the room, statically trapped up near the ceiling, squeaking with every breath, while Tammy the chicken pecked at Buck's shoelaces.

"Sir," ventured Sin-Dour, her folded leg slowly rocking, toes pointed, the black velvet stiletto dipping down in time to reveal flashes of her heel as she swiveled her ankle, "perhaps we should have conducted this briefing in the stateroom?"

Hadrian ran a trembling hand across his brow. "What?

Uh, no. I mean, the Ping-Pong table is getting a tablecloth and lots of chairs are being moved in, and, uh, silverware, tons of silverware and tureens and . . . and stuff. Now, let's get rocking—I mean, let's get on with this meeting."

"If I could weep," said Tammy.

"We should run," said Buck. "Right now! As fast and as far away as we can get! The whole galaxy's going to go up in flames and burning balls of gas and cheap knockoffs of everything. It's all falling apart, infrastructure collapsing, cynicism breeding, library fines going unpaid— we're on the terminal slide down into moribund spiritual exhaustion begging for nothing more than one final bullet to the head to end the interminable misery!"

"Outstandingly succinct, Buck!" said Galk, lifting a hand to high-five the chief engineer. "You're so right. It's all pointless, a waste of time, it's every man, woman, and child out for him- or herself, the poor deserve to be poor and the sick deserve to be sick and wealth is proof of virtue and power belongs to all the superior stick-up-the-ass fuckers born into wealth with God's own blessing, and the sooner we stick a nuke in the whole mess the better off the universe will be—"

"Wrong!" Tighe snapped. "The sooner you're all lined up for the firing squad the better! Dissenting opinions and unpleasant truths are acts of treason under Article 54-45B. The wrong questions in Question Period justify prosecution under the Politician Protection Act of 2019. Complaining is subject to prison, a raised eyebrow earns a hefty fine, and the only acceptable salute is a shaking fist and inarticulate bellows of hate. In fact, there isn't a single crime you lot haven't already committed and I'll see you all burned, hung, quartered, assaulted, tortured, renditioned, imprisoned, shot, and lethally injected!"

"Oh dear!" cried Printlip from the ceiling. "Frothometer redlining! Drugs are required immediately!"

Hadrian leapt to his feet, leapt onto the desk, leapt across to land in front of Lorrin Tighe in . . . three, three deft leaps. He took her into his arms and kissed her hard.

"Aaack! Get away from me!"

Hadrian then swung round, reached out and twisted Galk's nose. "Snap out of it, Lieutenant! And you, Buck, take a handful of happy pills for crying out loud. Now, anyone else ready to fall apart? No? Good." He released Galk's nose and the combat specialist gagged.

"I swallowed my chaw."

Hadrian faced Sin-Dour. "You have command of the *Willful Child* in my absence. I will be bringing Buck with me to the negotiations. In the meantime, we all play nice at supper with the Radulak."

"Me, sir?" Buck asked, paling.

"That's right, and make sure you bring your multiphasic."

"But they're all planning something!"

"Of course they are! And we ride the wave no matter where it takes us."

"B-but why, sir? They're lining up to backstab us!"

Hadrian slapped Buck on the shoulder. "Adventure, Buck! It's why we're here!" He turned in time to block Tighe's attempt at stabbing him with the Bowie knife, quickly disarmed her and then patted the top of her head. "Everyone but Tammy, dismissed. Get dolled up for supper, dress uniforms, makeup, bling, spit and polish—wait, save the spit for the Radulak since I'm sure they'll have plenty to spare."

"You'll pay," hissed Lorrin Tighe. "For everything, especially those kisses!"

Once everyone but the chicken had departed, Hadrian went back to sit at his desk.

"Why do you do that?" Tammy asked, flapping up to land on the desk.

"Do what?"

"Kiss her. It's sexist, objectifying, verging on mis—"

"Nonsense. Snoopy."

"I'm sorry, what?"

"Check your fragmented archives, Tammy. Why, if the adjutant were a man I'd do the same. Snoopy!"

"The cartoon dog?"

"Get mad at Snoopy and he slobbers you with a giant kiss."

"But that was a dog! With humans it's different!"

"There you go reciting verbatim all the usual xenophobic exceptionalisms. You're better than that, Tammy."

"Am I? Am I? Then why haven't you kissed me?"

"Why, because you're nothing more than a self-deluded AI, nothing but circuits and wires and stuff, not to mention the occasional holographic projection of domestic fowl. Might as well kiss my electric shaver."

"Oh, that really hurts."

"Rubbish."

"Okay, you're right. You are incapable of hurting me, insulting me, offending me, et cetera. But clearly you possess a hateful prejudice against sentient machines."

"Well-earned. You stole my ship. You beat up and imprisoned the ship's own AI. You commandeered maintenance robots and smashed up a squad of marines—speaking of which, that reminds me why I asked you to stay. Lieutenant Sweepy Brogan and her squad have a new mission, which I want you to pass on to her immediately—where is she right now, by the way?"

"Lieutenant Brogan and her squad are presently playing D&D, with the lieutenant herself being the Dungeon Master. The Party of Adventurers, consisting of a mage with a wand of Prismatic Spray, an Elven thief with a +1 bow, a cleric with a +1 mace, a ranger with a pet hawk, a paladin with +2 armor and a dwarf with a +2 axe, are moments from breaking into the Crypt of the Necromancer

to retrieve the Ring of Resurrection. The only foes between them and the loot—apart from the necromancer
himself—are seven halfling goblins."

"Really? What a crap adventure."

"Unbeknownst to the adventurers, the goblins are
armed with grenade launchers."

"Ah."

"The lock is picked! They're in! They see the halfling
goblins! An arrow flies from the thief and misses! Critical
failure! The bowstring snaps! The hawk whirls into the
air, talons opening wide. A grenade intersects it! Explosion! Feathers drifting down. A curtain draws back to reveal the necromancer on the altar positioned behind a
fifty-caliber machine gun on a tripod. He unleashes a hail
of bullets! The thief's head disappears in a spray of bits
of meat and bone! A grenade jams in the grille of the
paladin's helmet. It explodes, ripping his face off and
sending shrapnel deep into his brain! He fails his saving
throw and is stunned and will bleed out in two rounds!
The dwarf is hit by ninety-three bullets, his body recoil-
ing from the multiple impacts in super slow motion. Blood
everywhere! His beard catches fire! The cleric throws a
heal spell. Two points back to the dwarf—but he's taken
four hundred thirty-six points of damage. He's dead! A
secret trap opens up underneath the cleric and he falls into
a pit filled with three-headed sharks in a pool of acid.
The cleric fails his first save and his legs are eaten off

below the knees! He makes his second saving throw avoiding being stunned, so he gets to watch as the sharks and acid eat the rest of him down to the bones! He dies screaming. The ranger draws his sword! He's hit by seven grenades and two hundred twenty-one bullets. He bursts apart in a conflagration of bloody feathers, burning nest fragments, and hard-boiled hawk eggs! The mage fires his wand! All the goblins saved! The Necromancer is unaffected. He laughs! A giant Sphere of Annihilation devours the mage! The entire Adventuring Party is dead!"

Hadrian sighed and rubbed his eyes. "I'm waiting."

"The players have attacked the Dungeon Master. This could go on for a while. It's pretty nasty. I see knives out and a baseball bat. Ooh! Sweepy connects with a kick between Charles Not Chuck's legs. He misses his saving throw and is down! Muffy Slapp throws a knife! Sweepy dodges, swings her bat! Critical hit! Muffy's stunned! Skulls jumps on her back! Stabs with his knife! It glances off her battle armor. She flings herself against a wall. Skulls's head snaps back—he's concussed! Chambers throws a chair! Miss! He takes a 20D to the center of his forehead. He's stunned! Lefty-Lim's biting her ankle—she stomps down—oh dear! Stables tries a heal. Compress applied, two points back for Lefty-Lim and man did he need it but that nose will need major reconstruction! Bat swings and splits Stables's ear! He wails! Sweepy leaps onto the table laughing—"

"Stop! Okay, Tammy, when they're all out of sickbay, pass on to the lieutenant the following mission. . . ."

The Insisteon hummed with its built-in but entirely unnecessary sound effects, and an instant later two Radulak drench-masters appeared, one wearing rhinestone-glittering black leather armor and the other an eye patch and a Varekan leather jacket that said TOM'S TOWING on the breast. The first Radulak slopped down from the dais.

"I am Supreme Admiral Drench-Master Drown-You-All-in-My-Magnificence Bill-Burt, and this is my executive officer, Snuffle-Drench-Master Bang."

"Welcome aboard the AFS *Willful Child*," said Hadrian. "I am—"

"Oh we know who you are, Captain Hadrian Alan Sawback! Indeed, we possess fold-out holo-posters of you in our Weapons Target Room!"

"How delightful. And this is my second officer, Commander Halley Sin-Dour. And our chief medical officer, Dr. Printlip, along with Chief Engineer Buck De-Frank, Combat Specialist Galk, and last but certainly not least, Affiliation Adjutant Lorrin Tighe."

"What about me?" Tammy demanded, feathers ruffling.

"Right, and holo-robot-whatever-chicken, Wynette Tammy, rogue AI from the future."

Bill-Burt unleashed a massive gobbet of phlegm, slamming down on the chicken and flattening it to the floor. "Formal greetings, Wynette Tammy!"

"My neutratronic processor is overheating in a blaze of algorithmic projections of potential vengeance scenarios," said Tammy from beneath the slimy glob.

"Haha! Funny chicken!" said Bang, fingering her eye patch. "Now, we are hungry!" She pointed at her stomach. "'We don't like to complain. But down here below we are feeling great pain!' Food! Delicious food and Snail-Puke Wine, I can't wait!"

"Right," said Hadrian. "Well then, please follow me."

A short time later they were all seated around the cloth-covered Ping-Pong table, upon which (to either side of the green net) various tureens had been placed, each containing an array of genuine Radulak delicacies. Carafes of thick Snail-Puke Wine were being passed around, the two Radulak drooling and snapping their thick lips.

Bang offered Hadrian a bowl. "'Do you like Grated Human Baby Legs and Penis Spam? I do so like them, Bang-I-am, I do so like Grated Human Baby Legs and Penis Spam!'"

Sin-Dour gagged. "Human baby legs?"

"Haha!" said Bill-Burt. "Relax! No dismemberment of living human babies is required, not since we attained the mapped human genome permitting vat-cloning of select body parts. But I assure you, my dear, the Penis Spam is the real thing, culled from the many thousands of male human prisoners we have collected up over the past forty or so years which you know nothing about. That said, we have the finest Human Male Choir in the galaxy!"

Bang leaned closer to the supreme admiral. "Sir, perhaps it was unwise to reveal the fact of our many human prisoners—"

"I did no such thing! But now you have spilled the masticated beans for all to hear!"

"No I didn't! I said nothing!"

"But I am sure you did!"

Hadrian cleared his throat. "Shall we play back the conversation of the past five minutes?"

"NO!" both Radulaks barked.

Galk, who was seated opposite Bang, now said, "Snuffle-Drench-Master, that's an interesting jacket you are wearing."

"Yes it is! Stripped from an utterly drowned Varekan who looked a lot like you! A suitable trophy to mark my great victory in the bathroom of Truck Stop 27 on the Epsilon Eridani–Alpha Centauri Run—get it? Suitable? Jacket? Haha! The fool suspected nothing, since I was wearing a holo-vest that transformed me into an innocuous prophylactic dispenser."

"Uh-huh," Galk murmured.

Bang then tapped her eye patch. "For that I paid this eye. A worthy exchange? I think so! Hahaha!"

Galk used his napkin to wipe the spit from his face.

Bang banged the table. "More fun required! As the famous Radulak wordsmith Drencher Brian Zeuss once said: 'We've got to make noise in greater amounts!'" Another fist hammered the table, making the cutlery bounce. "Everyone! Drink more wine! And you, fellow woman second-in-command, try some of these pickled earworm eggs!"

"Mhmm," said Sin-Dour, "thank you but no, not to my taste, alas."

"'You do not like them you say? So you say. Try them and you may!'"

"Oh for crying out loud," cut in Hadrian. "If you keep mangling one of my favorite human writers of the twentieth century I just might—"

"Human thieves!" Bang cried. "Stealing our most famous Radulak artists!"

"Calm yourself," said Bill-Burt to her XO. "One must be indulgent for now, I mean, before we betray all these humans with a devastating surprise attack following the signing of the Accords. This is not yet the season of our discontent, after all. Let your patience pool deep and quiescent, yes?"

"Supreme One!" Bang hissed (and sprayed). "You just revealed our plans of betrayal!"

"I did not! Shhh or they will hear your careless words!"

"Well!" said Hadrian, half rising. "This has been a most delightful evening. Of course your quarters have been prepared for you and we do hope you find them to your liking. Until the negotiations begin tomorrow, I bid you good night."

"Most wise," purred Bang, "and I must temporarily return to the *I Saw No Need to Mention My Mother's Moustache*, to, uh, groom my pubic hairs."

Bill-Burt frowned. "Now, Snuffle-Drench-Master?"

"Comportment waits for no woman, Supreme One. But I will rejoin you shortly."

"Very well." Bill-Burt belched, and then regurgitated onto the table everything she'd eaten and drunk. "Aaah! Most excellent meal, so excellent I will eat it again!"

It was the graveyard shift on the bridge. At every station was someone nobody would recognize. There was Acting Captain Sissyko Weirdguy, engrossed in a tattered copy of *The Tao of Pooh-Bear Redux*. There was Acting Head of Security Odo Meter, a shapeshifting Conglomeranian from beyond the Neat-Looking Wormhole at the edge of the Kardashian Sector, whose homeworld of Conglomerania was a tiny lake of pond scum because, well, where else would an omnipotent species of highly advanced we-can-be-anything-we-want polymorphs live but in a scummy pond? There was the acting XO, Bayleaf Nose-bash, from the recently liberated planet of Beige (not that anyone noticed). While at the science station sat the Trilling Symbiont

Eye-Jay-Kay-El, whose endless trilling was driving everyone else mad.

"Status report," Sissyko inquired of no one in particular.

The others all hesitated, and then Bayleaf said, "All systems nominal, sir."

"Just once!" snapped the acting captain. "Just *once* it'd be nice to have something happen on *our* shift! Oh, what's the point? Never mind. Someone phone down to the Falangee Bar on Deck Forty-Seven. I want a piña colada and a pickled onion sent up here immediately!"

"On it, sir," said Eye-Jay-Kay-El, scratching at the facial rash everyone else thought was a tattoo. "Patching the order through to Ob Nox. Uh, that'll be three bars of laudanum."

"That would be vials, surely."

"Mhm, he said 'bars' sir. I think Ob's a bit confused again, it being the middle of the night."

"Look outside!" Sissyko cried. "It's always the middle of the night! Anyway, seems I left my wallet in my quarters. Odo Meter, you wouldn't happen to . . ."

"Oh, fine!" muttered the Conglomeranian, transforming into three vials of laudanum.

"Ha!" barked Sissyko. "Won't Ob Nox be surprised!"

"Hardly, sir," said Bayleaf, "since you do this to him just about every time."

"Are you calling me cheap, XO?"

"No sir, just abusive of your rank."

"Ha! Aren't we all?" He then lifted into view a baseball. "Someone play catch with me!"

A chorus of groans answered him.

"No, really! It's an order! You, Nose-bash, here! A wicked curveball!" He whipped the baseball her way.

She made a desperate attempt to grab it, failed, and the ball shattered a screen on her console. "Oh crap, not again," she said.

"At least this time it wasn't your nose," Sissyko laughed.

The door hissed open and in strode the Falangee Ob Nox, a tray balanced on one hand.

At which point the ship's artificial gravity crashed.

Piña colada and pickled onion leapt skyward. The baseball rolled into the air and then raced toward an air duct. Yelping, Sissyko floated out of the command chair. The three vials of laudanum lifted off the chair where Odo Meter had been sitting. Alarms blared. The lights went out. On the main screen a warship materialized out of nowhere and fired a slew of depleted uranium pellets. The impacts rocked the *Willful Child*, sending bodies flying.

Sissyko made a desperate grab for the pickled onion. He missed. Pandemonium!

———

Amid Klaxons and flashing red lights, the door to the guest quarters opened and in strode a figure in a spacesuit, wearing magnetic boots and wielding a primed Glob-o-Maker Splat-Gun Mark III.

Flailing, Supreme Admiral Bill-Burt drew up her blanket in a futile gesture of modesty before the Glob-o-Maker fired. Bits of Bill-Burt splatted in eponymous globules everywhere, morphing bulbs of Radulak blood spinning and dancing in the zero-g.

Close-up on the gore-splattered teddy bear floating near the pillow . . .

Still staring at the teddy bear on the screen, Hadrian sighed. "Now we're in for it." He threw on his special velour gold shirt. "Tammy! Ship status? How badly were we hit?"

"Modest, Captain, and the timing was off besides."

"Meaning?"

"The cloaked ship should have fired *before* the gravity crashed. Instead, it's obvious that we were sabotaged and betrayed by a crew member and, oh, three guesses who's not in her quarters and isn't that a nice Bowie knife on your dresser? I warned you! Didn't I warn you?"

"And the *I Saw No Need to Mention My Mother's Moustache*?"

"Powering up weapons, screens on, and Snuffle-Drench-Master Bang is hailing Admiral Prim even as we speak. Mutual exchanges of horrified outrage. Captain, they'll hand you over. You know that, don't you? You'll go on trial on the Radulak homeworld."

"Oh dear, whatever will we do?" Hadrian deftly sailed across to the door, manually overrode the lockdown, and pulled himself into the corridor beyond. He tapped his comms. "Buck, wake up! Meet me in the Insisteon Chamber at once! Sin-Dour, invoke Contingency Plan Delta Epsilon 23B. Printlip! Get to the supreme admiral's quarters and begin collecting as much useless and bound-to-be-disregarded evidence as you can! Galk, activate the homing beacons we secretly installed on every space-suit in storage and track down our rogue Affiliation security officer, and then lock her up."

As he delivered his commands, Hadrian sailed down the corridors, reaching the Insisteon Chamber. Another override and he entered the room, moving across to the station comms. "Captain Hadrian to Admiral Prim!"

The small console screen flickered, revealing the admiral's suitably stern visage. "Captain Sawback. Prepare to be boarded by my security team. As soon as they displace, you will surrender your command of the *Willful Child* and place yourself and your incompetent chief engineer into the custody of my officers. You will then be escorted to the Radulak flagship, now under the command of New Supreme Admiral Drench-Master Bang, which will depart the system to deliver you to a Radulak Court of Instant Justice on the Radulak homeworld Radish, whereupon you will be found guilty of innumerable crimes and sent to a prison planet to dwell in misery and infamy forever more."

"And if I'm innocent, Admiral?"

"Don't be ridiculous. All the evidence points to you," and he lifted into a view a sheet of paper. "I have the damning list right here, which I've already signed. It wasn't enough that you killed thousands of Radulak and destroyed three Bombast warships. No, your hatred of the Radulak is known to everyone, and now the peacemaker Bill-Burt is nothing more than blobs of blood and twice-digested foodstuffs, and it'll be all we can do to salvage the Kittymeow Accords under the threat of imminent galactic war!"

Buck had arrived by now, checking the batteries on his multiphasic.

"Very well, Admiral," said Hadrian. "I will comply with your orders, of course. A request, however. I would like Commander Sin-Dour to take command of the *Willful Child*."

"Not a chance! I'm sending a reliable officer to take charge over there, who will accompany my security team. No, all that close association with you and your criminal mind has no doubt tainted everyone presently on your ship.

I suspect their careers will never recover, in fact. Oh, and as for your rogue AI Wynette Tammy, well, it will be dismantled and examined and reverse-engineered at the earliest opportunity."

"Oh yeah, good luck with that, sir."

"Excuse me?"

"Are you ready to send over your security team now, Admiral?"

The face scowled. "I am—"

Director Soma DeLuster pushed her way onto the screen, elbowing Prim in the temple. She smiled cruelly at Hadrian. "I don't need to tell you—"

"You're right, Director, you don't, so shut up, will you? Hadrian out."

Commander Sin-Dour stood with hands clasped behind her back as the new captain stepped onto the bridge. "Sir, welcome to the *Willful Child.*"

The short, bald middle-aged man paused and looked round at all the officers standing at attention. He tugged at his shirt. "I am Captain John 'Lucky' Placard," he said in stentorian tones. "Do any of you know how I earned that epithet? I will tell you. I was a mere comms officer aboard the AFS *Century Warbler* under the command of Captain Hans Olo. In the moment of insurrection by the Klang Prince Hazel Gnawfang I managed to initiate an emergency displace, thus evading the pheromonal bio-chemical override that afflicted everyone else on board the vessel. This singular act of genius has earned me acco-lades and promotion and now here I am, commanding my first Engage-class starship."

"So like," said Helm Sticks, "you um, bailed out on everyone else and now you're a captain? Fuck me, sir, whose ass did you, like, lick? Oh, and are you like the last *bald* guy in the galaxy? There's creams for that, you know. Duh!"

Spark trotted up to halt before Placard. "I am Ensign Spark, Robot Guard Dog. Can I play catch with your head, sir? Catch? Catch! Please oh please oh please?"

Beta said, "It's well known that bald men secretly concoct physiological studies asserting higher levels of vi-rility among bald men."

James "Jimmy" Eden suddenly said, "I'm your comms officer and I came in fourth in the Olympics and I'm sorry! I'm sorry! I'm sorry aagh!" He fell to his knees, bawling.

Tammy's voice now rang out from all the speakers. "And I'm the mad AI in charge of every system on this ship, and you'll never catch me, hahahahahaha!"

Placard turned and ran from the bridge.

"Huh," said Sticks, "that was weird."

SiX

**Aboard the Terran flagship,
AFS *Portentous Smug Pomposity*...**

Adjutant Lorrin Tighe plopped herself down on the sofa in the director's private quarters. "I barely got away in time, Director. That brown-toothed Varekan nearly got me at the Emergency Airlock."

"Well done, that's my girl," Soma DeLuster said, walking over with a bowl of popcorn. She sat down beside the adjutant. "Screen on," she commanded and the huge monitor in the wall in front of them flicked on. "Radulak People's Court, Radish Fox Channel 45. Now then, darling," she said to Lorrin, "let's watch justice at work, shall we?"

"I can't wait!" gushed the adjutant. "Can I smoke, drink, pop pills?"

"You can mainline rocket fuel if you like. Darwin knows, you've been through the wringer. Ah, here we go!"

Radulak People's Court,
Radulak Homeworld Radish . . .

Hadrian and Buck stood on a bloodstained disc on the floor of a vast circular chamber lined with crowded tiers rising up on all sides. A spotlight pinned the two accused humans with blinding glare and blistering heat.

Buck held up both hands and made a rabbit silhouette on a nearby wall.

The Radulak rose from their seats in a blasting hail of cheers and warm spit when the High Judge of the Inevitably Guilty stepped into view to position herself on a high chair dominating a railed balcony.

From a side chamber on the ground floor emerged Supreme Admiral Drench-Master Bang, taking position on a smaller, much cleaner dais not far from Hadrian and Buck. Another, less harsh spotlight fixed upon her.

The judge struck a gavel that echoed in sudden silence. "I call upon the Only Witness We're Listening To: Supreme Admiral Drench-Master Bang! Bang, speak!"

Bang smiled at Hadrian, and then faced the crowds, hands raised. She suddenly frowned, as if beset by doubt. "'I do not know what to say! Should I tell them the things that went on that day?'"

The crowd roared wet invitation.

"Poor Bill-Burt, beloved Supreme One! 'She meant no harm! She most truly did not!' And now she is this!" And she gestured to a side passage where a half-dozen proto-Klang dragged into view a lumpy bloodstained burlap sack. "As Bill-Burt herself might say, 'Murder Most Foul!' And who is to blame? Why, none other than Captain Hadrian Alan Sawback!"

Buck nudged Hadrian and whispered, "Why am I here again, sir?"

"You didn't expect me to go through all this alone, did you, Buck?"

"Oh. Right. Uh, thank you, sir."

"You're most welcome."

Buck resumed making shadow animals.

"Buck?"

"Hmm?"

"What drugs are you on right now?"

"Oh, all of them, sir."

The judge struck the gavel again. "Oh my, such overwhelming evidence against the accused! I am gobsmacked—" and a few hundred gobs of gob smacked her. "Just so! And flabbergasted—" salvos of flabber gasted against her face. "As I said! I am flummoxed—stop! No flummoxes! I am about to pronounce my verdict! It's a good verdict, a pretty verdict. It's the foregone conclusion we all know about that will shock and outrage precisely none of you, especially given how well paid you all are to attend this sham of a court! What?" She tapped the small speaker jammed in one ear. "No! I said nothing of the sort! No! No playback! Where was I? Yes, my righteous verdict, the inescapable conclusion we reached long before we even saw any evidence! What? No, I didn't! Outrageous accusation! Now, my verdict is this. GUILTY!"

The crowd roared, spit spraying in a deluge to shower down upon the two accused.

"And now, after the commercial, I will pass the sentence we already know about—what? No I didn't. What are you talking about—"

The scene vanished to be replaced by a white-fanged smiling Radulak with slicked-back hair rising out of a slime pool holding up the latest i-held communicator. This was followed by a Radish Fox announcer saying, "This is Radish Fox coming to you all with All the News So Full of Bullshit No One Else Would Even Call It News Ha Ha You're All Such Idiots, and it's time for the Radulak High Court to pass the sentence on the appallingly guilty and probably gay atheist retro-Muslim terrorist, Hadrian Alan Sawback! But first, another word from our sponsors!" A white-fanged smiling Radulak with slicked-back hair rose out of a slime pool holding up the latest i-held communicator.

"Mute," commanded Soma DeLuster. "Hmm, barring

Fox, I think the rest of our hopelessly biased power-serving media might find a few issues with this trial."

"Y'think?" Lorrin asked, tossing back the rest of her whisky, then lighting another cigarette.

"Well, we'll see if we can ride it out. Failing that . . ."

"Oh sure," snapped Lorrin, "I see a new scapegoat being offered up. Who might that be? Oh, right, the adjutant with Radulak bloodstains all over her purloined magnetic boots—where are they, by the way?"

"Oh we've taken care of them, Adjutant."

"I just bet you have."

"Now, dear, you of all people will understand the necessity of covering our official asses."

"Bullshit! You all just lie through your smiling faces and does the hammer ever come down? No! But helpless minions only following orders, well, poor darlings!"

"We won't hand you over to the Radulak."

"You won't need to, will you? What if I whistle-blow the whole scheme, Director? What then?"

"Naive girl. Nobody gives a shit what whistles you blow. Haven't you noticed? Nobody gives a shit about anything anymore. The people who voted us into power are all suffering from self-serving cognitive dissonance— they only hear and see what bolsters their own intractable prejudices—oh, wait, shall we call them 'opinions'? Hahaha. As if you can have an opinion when you don't know fuck all about anything! Never mind. So anyway, blow away, darling. Tweet tweet! Spill the beans. No one's watching, no one's listening, no one's giving a flying fuck. They're too busy wanking off in front of selfie posters. Meanwhile, the Great Machine of Human Progress just grinds on, and on. And you, dearie, well fuck you, so just suck it up and swallow it down, as we used to say in boarding school. End-mute—here comes the sentence!"

The judge was on her feet. "Life imprisonment on Prison Mining Planet Rude Pimente, served consecutively not including time already served without hope of parole hard labor for ever and ever in a life sentence which won't last long anyway since we're sending assassins. What? I never said that! What nonsense are you talking about?"

Soma DeLuster sighed and clicked off the monitor. "Hmm, think we might have to hand you over to the Radulak after all. Oh don't look so glum. Irridiculum mining's probably not that bad." She tapped her comms. "Security, get in here. Adjutant Lorrin Tighe is under arrest for fabricating evidence and other stuff we'll come up with shortly."

Tighe snarled and reached for her Bowie knife. "Aw shit—I went and tried to stab Hadrian and he disarmed me! Damn! Wrong target!"

"Silly dupe," said Soma. "Think we'll start with a brain wipe just to be safe. Who knows, could be one more whistleblower will take the whole thing down, mobs rising up in the streets on every city on every planet, storming the barricades of us superrich inbred nitwits and righteously tearing us limb from limb in a convulsion of perfectly justified retribution. No, mustn't risk that! Accordingly, your brain will be wiped, your personality erased, your—"

Lorrin Tighe suddenly vanished.

Soma DeLuster frowned. "Oh crap, I think my Security Screen's just been hacked by a rogue AI from the future. Admiral Prim!"

Bridge of the Escort Engage–class starship the AFS *What's Up with That Cat?* only now emerging from the Conveniently Cloudy Nearby Nebula . . .

Captain Honorarium Harried stepped onto the bridge and posed in front of the main viewer. The overweight mangy tomcat slumped over her left shoulder amid a mostly shredded uniform, its weight creating a permanent lopsided shoulder dip on that side, blinked lazily at the image of Admiral Prim. There was no one else on the bridge. In fact, there was no one else on the entire ship, since the captain was so competent she required no one else, having single-handedly conquered a dozen ferocious enemy empires. She now regarded the face on the giant screen as would a boa constrictor eyeing a tweety bird. "Admiral Prim, can I help you?"

"You may have noted the *Willful Child* is making a run for it. Captain Placard is not answering hails, so we must assume a mutiny has occurred on that vessel."

"This is always the risk with having a crew, sir."

"Yes, well, whatever. I want you to pursue, intercept, and if necessary destroy the *Willful Child*."

"I can do that. I can do anything and everything. There is nothing I can't do. I hold the multiple titles of Queen, Empress, Mistress of All, Duchess, Miss Universe 2107, Pet Owner of the Year 2108, Slayer of Enemies We Haven't Even Met Yet, Tactical Genius of the Year 2109, Centerfold of the Universe for three years running, Tall Woman of the Decade, Thin Woman of the Century, Miss Omnipotence 2110, So-Perfect-It-Hurts—"

"Yes yes yes! For crying out loud, no wonder no one wants to serve on your ship!"

"Well, it's true they die like flies but that's hardly my fault, is it? Besides, as is now readily evident, I need no one else, so blinding is my brilliance. In fact, you might as well consider the *Willful Child* already destroyed, flensed and dismembered bodies spinning frozen and bloated in space, wreckage flaring with burning fuel, clouds of vented atmosphere glittering like diamonds against a backdrop of mangled metal, and really, is there anything more beautiful than that? Excepting, of course, me. Did I mention my new Page Two spread as Miss Blood-Spraying Murderess of the Galaxy—"

"Just get on with it!" Prim snapped, cutting the feed.

Honorarium Harried lifted one delicate arching eye-brow, signifying the maximum reveal of emotion permissible, and then reached up to stroke her cat—

Snarling, it savaged her hand—but that hand was the robotic one, the cat having long since destroyed the real one.

Lopsided and moving with a strange hitch in her gait, the captain took her seat in the command chair. "Chief Engineer Honorarium, prime the T-Drive. Yes sir, at once sir! Combat Specialist Honorarium, all weapons hot, please. On it, Captain! All weapons hot! Helm Honorarium, set an intercept course all speed. Yes, Captain! Dr. Honorarium, stand by for casualties—we're about to engage the enemy. Really, Captain? There's not one minor character left to kill! And surely you're not interested in enemy survivors? No of course not, Doctor, it's just protocol and we always follow protocol. Very well sir, sickbay on standby! Commander Honorarium, activate science station and prepare for ECM. Yes, Captain! Red alert everyone! We are now engaging the enemy!"

"Massive salvo from the AFS *What's Up with That Cat?*, Commander!"

"Thank you, Polaski," Sin-Dour said from the command chair. "Galk, weapons free to interdict, if you please."

"All of them? I mean, you want me to shoot all of 'em down?"

"That would be most helpful, Galk."

"But I wanted something challenging."

"You will be free to return fire," Sin-Dour reminded him. "Middling Beam Weapons only, however. Disabling its engines will do nicely, Galk."

"Got it. Like finches in a barrel. Pew pew pew! Pow, plat, foom, zapzapzapzapzap done!"

"I believe the phrase is 'fish in a barrel,'" Sin-Dour observed, pleased at seeing all the incoming ordnance winking out.

"Not on Varekan, sir. It's finches in a barrel there. More exciting with all the exploding feathers and whatnot. Now, firing Middling Beam Weapons . . . oh! Enemy screens down, engine pods permanently disabled . . . oh, crap."

"I'm sorry? What was that last bit, Galk?"

"Uhm, the enemy vessel did a strange cant and tumble, sir. And, um, a stray beam to the bridge, I'm afraid."

"Meaning, Galk?"

"Uh, I'm afraid the single human life sign on the bridge is now flatlining."

Sin-Dour was on her feet. "Galk, are you saying you've killed Captain Honorarium Harried?"

"'Fraid so, Commander."

From every deck of the *Willful Child* there was wild cheering. On the bridge all the officers were on their feet, banners unfurling, confetti and streamers filling the air. On the main viewer, the stealthed Affiliation flagship AFS *Portentous Smug Pomposity* suddenly revealed itself inside a cloud of fireworks.

"And the cat?"

"Even deader, sir."

"Combat Specialist Galk, once we're back on the right side of the Affiliation, I will recommend the highest commendation on your behalf."

"Thank you, sir, really, it was nothing."

"Now, Acting Chief Engineer Tammy, take us into T-Space, will you? We have a rendezvous to make."

"On our way," said Tammy from Engineering. *"But for the record, I still hate it when Hadrian proves right about, well, everything."*

Sin-Dour rose to her feet, brushing confetti from her shoulders. "Carry on, everyone. I will be in my stateroom discussing matters with our guest. Lieutenant Sticks, you have the conn."

"Yes, Commander, like, sure, why not? It's like T-Space, isn't it? Nothing to do, like, ever!"

"Spark," said Sin-Dour, "you're with me."

"With you!" the robot dog shouted, dancing in circles. "I'm with you! Oh, dead cat and everything, what a day! The best day ever!"

Commander and robot dog departed the bridge. Entering the stateroom, Sin-Dour paused and studied Lorrin

Tighe, who was seated in one of the chairs still surrounding the Ping-Pong table.

Spark's lower jaw trembled fitfully. "Attack traitor, Halley? Attack and maim traitor? Traitors, Aisle Nineteen, Overcrowded!"

"No, Spark," said Sin-Dour. "Just be on guard."

"On guard! I can do that!"

The commander sat down opposite Tighe. "Adjutant, how are you?"

"Sobriety is overrated."

"Apologies for the emergency displacement, but—"

"Unnecessary, Sin-Dour. They were about to hang me out to dry. Betrayed, after all I did for them! There's blood on my hands! Okay, Radulak blood, so who gives a shit. Still, it's the principle of the thing!"

"Mhmm, indeed."

"And now you've all obviously mutinied, and Hadrian and Buck are on their way to Rude Pimente to serve a life sentence until they're assassinated."

"We didn't quite mutiny," Sin-Dour replied. "A Purse drone displaced onto our ship and announced that it had purchased Captain Placard. The drone then assimilated with the captain and renamed itself Coin-Cutey-Us. They then displaced, presumably back to the Bag Mother Ship." She shrugged. "It all happened so fast there was no time to react."

"Darwin save us!" whispered Tighe. "They assimilated him?"

"Yes, with mutagenic plaid and sequins and a rather clever clasp on top of his bald head."

"Well, good thing he was hairless—imagine getting your hair caught when closing that clasp!"

Sin-Dour winced. "Ouch."

"I'll say! So, Commander, what's going to happen to me?"

"Why, Adjutant, we have an innocent captain and chief engineer to rescue, and you will be in charge of the mission."

"Me?"

"Indeed. Now, select your team and might I point you in the direction of our resident marines?"

"Are they out of sickbay then?"

"No, but the new metal plates in the heads of most of the squad should have healed up by the time we arrive unannounced in orbit over Rude Pimente."

"Right, I guess I'll get right on it, Commander, and, uh, thank you for the opportunity to right this wrong."

Sin-Dour smiled. "The captain figured you'd be keen."

"I just wish he'd stop kissing me."

"You and me both."

And what, we all wonder, does that mean? Oooh!

SEVEN

Prison Planet Rude Pimente...

"But what does it all mean?" Molly asked in a furtive whisper.

The back wall of Tunnel 93F had just collapsed to the flimsy impact of Betty's pick, revealing a vast glittering chamber beyond. The cavern was fecund with tropical plants rising from beds of moss almost perfectly covering the plant pots under them. Little nozzles misted the cool air. An ambient glow came from cleverly hidden light fixtures. Insects chirped and buzzed and birds tweeted in a rather short tape loop. It looked nearly wild, almost primal, and rising in the center of the vast expanse was a towering monolith.

"It's like a . . ." Molly shook his head. "Like a . . . hopeless amalgam of tropes!"

Betty flung the pick to one side and stepped into the chamber. He made his way over to the monolith, stepping around the oblong coffin lying athwart the path. Tentatively he reached out toward the monolith.

"Don't touch it!" hissed Molly, coming up behind him.

"Why not?"

"It could be, well, like some psychedelic drug, making things spin in kaleidoscope colors as your consciousness expands in unimaginable and frankly baffling ways, scrambling your entire life experience as you disengage from the normal space-time continuum, making you both a baby in a carriage and an ancient one in a rickety wheelchair all at once, with the room suddenly all white and the muted sound of breathing as you stumble into the scene wearing a spacesuit. It could be like that!"

"Huh," muttered Betty, and he reached out and touched the monolith.

Molly gasped.

Betty grunted. Then he picked up a stick and began bashing things with it.

"Oh my!" breathed Molly. "Captain Betty has made a massive leap ahead in cognitive comprehension! Yes, Molly, you can hit things with sticks! Or, that's right, exactly—you can even pick your nose with it! And that's it, your ear, too. And your butt, sure, though how you'll ever fit *another* stick up your butt I'll never know. What a huge evolutionary leap!" Molly pushed Betty to one side (he snarled in sudden genocidal rage but Molly wasn't paying any attention) and ran up to touch the monolith.

He gasped as the scene before him transformed in a wild cavort of rainbow colors that then converged to a point at one end and became a peacock, only to then blur and re-form as a . . .

"Oh crap, I get bad sitcom reruns. That's not fair!"

Then Betty hit him on the head with his stick.

"Ow! Cut that out!" Molly jumped behind the monolith. "Hey! There's a power cord!"

"DON'T TOUCH THAT POWER CORD!"

Molly and Betty froze at the strange stentorian voice that seemed to come from everywhere.

"Why not?" Molly demanded.

"YOU WILL DISCONNECT THIS AMPLIFIER."

Molly yanked out the cord in a spray of sparks, and then turned to Betty. "Captain! Snap out of it! Put down that stick! We need to get out of here before something terrible happens!"

"Put down my stick? Are you mad? I have just experienced an evolutionary leap, a burgeoning of my intelligence. Look! I can use it as a crutch, or a baseball bat. I can find another just like it—here! This one! And look! I can juggle! Or be a drummer in a rock band—okay, maybe that's a step back. But anyway, with this new gift of knowledge and comprehension, why, the universe is my oyster!"

"Captain! That's just it! If you were an oyster it *would* be an evolutionary leap! Instead, you're a Klang. We stopped using sticks decades ago! We now have spaceships and stuff! That monolith is just the free-app version. To get the real genius-making one, you have to pay!"

"How do you know all this?"

Molly pointed at the label on the back of the monolith. "It says so right here, sir."

Betty threw down his sticks. "What a rip-off! Who made this piece of crap?"

"Uh, it's Klang knockoff, sir. 'Mondo Liths, Mysterious Artifacts Division. Patent Pending at the Patent Pending Office of the Eternally-Murky-Legality Quagmire Department.'"

"Oh. *Those* bastards!"

Molly then leapt close to a knee-high creepy slimy plantlike thing upthrust from the ground. "And here's another Mysterious Artifact from Mondo! Look, sir, it's so ugly you just have to stick your face in it, here, in that flowering bit!"

Betty edged closer. "Hmm, never seen one of these before! It's alien and ugly and looks deadly with all that dripping acid and stuff. I know! I think I'll stick my face in it!"

"Don't! I was just kidding. I got one of these things for Christmas, from Uncle Susan. The flower explodes and this nasty little worm dives up your nose, lodges in your body, and then bursts out of your chest. Sue loves his practical jokes. I lost three cousins to the damned thing. Aunt William damn near divorced him over that!"

"And is that the free-app version?"

Molly nodded. "Yes. The worm starts shedding skins, getting smaller and smaller until you can't even see it anymore. The one you pay for gets bigger and bigger, and to get the giant unkillable matron with the mouth-inside-the-mouth-inside-the-mouth-inside-the-mouth, you're looking at $1.99 sucked out of your account like blood from your quivering body. Even a horrible death costs money these days. It's diabolical."

"Okay," said Betty. "We should leave. If I can't get great stuff for free, fuck it. I mean, it's not like all those creative types making stuff to entertain us should make money off us, is it? I mean, what the fuck do I care if they starve or have to work in Wally Krap? Like, entertaining me is a privilege, right? They should be paying *me* for crying out loud!"

The two Klang set out to leave the chamber. A neon sign beside the entrance flashed a message: DON'T UNPLUG THE CORD BELOW!

Molly pulled out the input keyboard beneath the sign and typed: WHY NOT?

THIS NEON MESSAGE BOARD WON'T WORK IF
YOU DO.

Molly unplugged the cord. "Okay, we're done here,
sir. Best get back to work." Then he paused and lifted a
frond to reveal a small box with a big red button on it,
and a label saying: SELF-DESTRUCT BUTTON! DON'T
PUSH. EVER!

"Molly! Don't you dare!"

"Why not?"

"Because then everything self-destructs, you idiot!"

"I know! I mean, I can read, right? But—but—but I
can't help myself!" He made a dive for the button.

Betty tackled him. They strained against each other,
Molly reaching, reaching. "Mpff! Got. To. Push. Button!"

"Dammit, Molly!" Betty managed to reach down and
collect up a stick. He whacked Molly on top of his head.

"Ow!"

"Back!" *Whack!* "Get back from that button!" *Whack!*
Whack!

Whackwhackwhackwhack!

A final kick sent the stunned Molly back into Tunnel 93F.

In the distance they heard the Day's End Klaxon. "Oh
crap! We gotta get going, Molly, or we'll miss out on the
custard again!"

That brought Molly around like a dash of cold water to
the face. But Betty decided that another whack on his minion's head wouldn't hurt either. *Whack!*

"Ow!"

"Ha! Think I'll hold on to this stick!"

"Fine!" Molly snapped, rubbing the lumps on his furry head. "At least it's not your tungsten-tipped pick which you thankfully left on the ground over there."

Betty ran over and collected up the pick. "This pick is a tool, idiot, while my stick is a weapon. Clearly, a massive cognitive leap in intelligence is required for one to be able to make that distinction."

"Hmm, undoubtedly, sir."

"Now, let's get going!"

Together they raced off down the tunnel. Or is it *up* the tunnel? They went back. Away from the strange cavern. Opposite direction. They ran and ran and the strange cavern got farther and farther away. Behind them.

The Baint Flitter pulled on a cord, lifting the blind. "And now, prisoners, look down on this white frozen planet surface. Yes, that's it, gather close and press your faces to the cold glass as we make our descent to the lone Inmate Receiving Station. This is the last time you'll ever see Rude Pimente from orbit, the last time you'll ever see stars, in fact, or anything but tunnels and pits and pressure doors. That's right, boys and girls, you're all on your way to a life of misery and suffering and despair—now, I see that those of you who have experienced the education system look rather unimpressed by that, but I assure you that this version of misery, suffering, and despair is even worse! No recesses, for one. And the cliques down there are murder! Will you fit in? Or will you be one of those loners slinking here and there trying not to be noticed? Will you look fat in your miner's coverall? Is someone going to point a finger at your hair and laugh? Oh yes, you are all headed for an awful time!"

The Baint Flitter, who had obviously once been a nanny before the baby-eating scandal outlawed the species from any contact with children without a police check and defanging, continued listing the horrors of the prison planet below.

Followed by Buck, Hadrian drifted back from the shuttle's nose-spotted window, leaving behind the alien who clearly loved her work too much.

A man was leaning against a back wall, not paying any attention to anyone. Curious, Hadrian sidled over. "Well now, looks like you've been through all this before."

The man's eyes glowed bright green. "I have," he said in a low drawl. "No prison can hold me. No planet can keep me down. There isn't an alien I can't kill."

"And," said Buck, "you've got real cool eyes."

"I'm a Fluoridian, the last of my kind."

Buck's bushy brows lifted. "You're from the legendary Planet Fluoride? The planet of industrial waste products everyone was convinced were good for them? Captain!

This man must be Rillickudick, the last Fluoridian Still Alive!"

At that, Rillickudick smiled a blinding white smile. "That's me."

"So," said Hadrian, "you're planning to break out of Rude Pimente."

"Of course. Stick with me and you'll live long enough to absorb a hail of bullets thus permitting me to escape unscathed."

"That's quite the deal you're offering there, Rillickudick," said Hadrian.

"Man, they just line up when I make the offer."

"So your followers are a collection of absolute idiots."

The Fluoridian smiled again. "No shortage, ever. Funny, that."

Over by the window the Baint Flitter suddenly clapped her de-taloned hands. "Now boys and girls! Everyone back to your seats, as this cheap Klang-knockoff shuttle doesn't have gravity compensators, meaning the g-forces on our descent are vicious! Strap in now so we don't get any broken limbs, mashed faces, or pulverized organs— save all that for the mines when the bullies find you and steal all your clothes!"

"You and you," said Felasha the Purelganni with a wave of a flipper, "wipe that custard from your whiskers and follow me. We have new prisoners to meet and terrorize and dominate and steal from! And because you've both done so well stroking my fins I've decided to make you my Chosen Slaves."

"Oh joy," said Betty.

"Now remember, you have to walk slowly as you escort me, since I'm so physiologically ill-equipped for terrestrial locomotion. But you should see me in an ocean, where I swim beautifully for a few minutes before I drown. Oh, and kittens, do say hello to my Zugru bodyguard. You will note his huge muscles, narrow piggy eyes, abundant nose hairs, and sloping forehead. These traits are not disconnected. His name, by the way, is Paul. Paul, you may pat the narrow furry heads of these kitties, but don't crush their skulls as they need them to hold in their small brains! Oh, and Betty, is that a baseball bat you're carrying? I don't like those, no, not at all!"

"It's just a stick," Betty replied. "I use it to, uh, pick my nose."

"Oh. Very well. Carry on. So long as it's not a baseball bat."

They set off for the giant elevator that was already on its way down with its load of new prisoners.

"Now, darlings all," said Felasha, "I have a surprise for you! We're going to assist two new inmates to escape, only to then assassinate them on the planet surface. As a re-ward, our multiple life sentences will be reduced to a single life sentence. Isn't that wonderful? So, just follow my lead and everything will go precisely as planned."

"What did these two inmates do to earn assassination?" Molly asked.

"No idea," Felasha replied. "But if I had to guess, they're geniuses whose very existence threatens the ongoing half-assed ultracorrupt cynically decayed governance of the galaxy, so all the petty-minded dimwits clinging desperately to their illusory power need them dead, and need it *now.*"

"All right," said Betty, "that's *my* kind of assassination!"

"Ahh," smiled Felasha, "you must be one of those petty-minded dimwits then, begging the question: What are you doing here?"

"I was defeated by a genius, of course."

"That makes sense. Now, if asked, can you use that stick to beat people over the head with?"

Betty frowned. "Oh dear, I'm not sure."

"Actually," said Molly, "the captain was just using it like a baseb—"

"Be quiet, Molly! Stop babbling nonsense! Now, Wondrous Felasha, just point me in the right direction and watch me whack away. Uh, as best I can. I mean, it goes against my nature, of course, being a peace-loving Klang and all."

"You must learn to overcome your many unfortunate flaws," advised Felasha. "Look at us Purelganni! We're dead ringers for Terran baby seals and yet are known throughout the galaxy as the most vicious sentients ever encountered. No fingers? No problem! Helpless flopping around? So what? Ahh! Look, the elevator has arrived!"

They watched as the five separate cage doors opened one after another, and then out spilled a mob of befuddled inmates. The gangs of bullies awaiting them rushed in. Various screams erupted in the scrum as clothes were torn off, hairstyles mussed up, and pockets emptied. And then the gangs reached the inmates.

"Look there!" Felasha hissed, pointing a flipper at three figures slinking out to one side, deftly evading the bullies, barring one giant hairy Fwooky who leapt at them, only to meet the fist of a burly man with green glowing eyes and the brightest smile ever seen by anyone anywhere. The fist broke the Fwooky's snout. Five more rapid-fire punches left the giant hairy creature curled up on the floor.

"Hmm," said Felasha. "Paul? I think that one needs a lesson. Go to it!"

Paul nodded and drew out from his backpack a Grade Three Reader.

"No, Paul, not that kind of lesson," Felasha explained patiently. "I want you to beat that man up. Oh, and be sure to knock out his teeth."

While this was going on, Molly was grabbing at Betty's arm.

"What?" Betty hissed. "Stop it! Let go of me!"

"Captain! Those other two! Those Terrans! I recognize them!"

"Huh? Oh. Oh! Well now, isn't that a turn-up for the books! Follow me!" And Betty hefted his stick and set out for the two Terrans.

Meanwhile, Paul had lumbered up to the green-eyed white-smiled man. He threw a punch straight into those bright teeth. And broke his knuckles. Howling, Paul reeled back.

"That's right!" the stranger laughed. "I'm a Fluoridian!"

"Captain, aren't those two Klang—"

"So they are," Hadrian agreed. "Now what—"

"Didn't we—"

"We did, which means—"

"But you—"

"Yes, I—"

"How long—"

"Can we keep doing this? No idea, but let's stop now, shall we?"

Revealing tiny fangs in a smug smile, Captain Betty said, "And so here you are, Captain Hadrian Alan Sawback! I can just imagine the whole slew of bad decisions and stupid moves that brought you here to a frozen prison planet sentenced to life in the tunnels and pits!"

"I'm sure," Hadrian replied, "but first let's hear all about *your* bad decisions and stupid moves that brought you here to a frozen prison planet sentenced to life in the tunnels and pits."

"What? Oh, well—"

"Allow me!" chirped Molly brightly. "We left the idyllic planet you dropped us off on in a purloined runabout to treat ourselves to a take-out pizza and then you wouldn't believe what happened! There was this—"

"Shut up, Molly!" snapped Betty. "See this, Captain Hadrian?"

"It's a stick, yes?"

"That's right! A stick! And watch what I can do with it!" Betty stepped forward and whapped Hadrian on the shin with it.

Hadrian looked down. "I'm sorry, was that supposed to hurt?"

"Allow me!" cried Molly, leaping forward to grapple Hadrian's left thigh. "Mmpff! Urggh! Aaagh!" He fell back. "My arm! I'm mortally injured! Call the lawyers!"

"Captain," said Buck with a nudge and a nod, "Rillickudick has blocked every attack from that thug with his teeth. The thug's hands, elbows, knees, and feet are all broken. And there's a Purelganni trying to run away. Well, not 'run' as such. More like flop and squirm."

Betty hissed. "Don't let her get away! She's got an escape route all planned out for us!"

"Really?" asked Buck. "But we just got here."

"Let's go talk to her," Hadrian said. "Betty, if you'd be so kind as to make introductions?"

"That's the curse with us evil antagonists, we're always so polite! Please, follow me, Captain."

Molly leapt up. "I'm still mortally injured by the way. Don't think this is evidence that I was faking it or anything. You'll still be hearing from my lawyers."

Betty in the lead, they walked over to the Purelganni, who had managed to flee about seven and a half feet.

"Wondrous Felasha! May I introduce Captain Hadrian Alan Sawback and, uh, some other guy from the *Willful Child*."

"Buck DeFrank. Chief Engineer."

"Oh!" Betty smiled. "How delightful! Yes, and Buck DeFrank, Chief Engineer. And this, of course, is Molly, who you may recall from our countless meetings and innumerable instances of you threatening and bullying and terrorizing us."

The Purelganni looked up. "Oh be quiet, Betty, you're embarrassing yourself. Captain Hadrian! Do you want to escape this inescapable prison planet? Of course you do! Now, quickly—while that Fluoridian's busy ripping up the rest of the operation and triggering a general uprising of prisoners even now tearing apart all those well-armed guards who appear to have forgotten how to aim their weapons—follow me!"

"We're trying to," Buck said.

"I assure you I am flopping as fast as I can, Chief Engineer! See that secret portal over there? Yes, the one with the Fire Escape logo on the door. That's where we're going! Wait! Where are you all going? Come back here! I'm catching up! No, wait—ah, Betty, I knew I could count on you! What are you doing with that stick? Oh no, you're using it like a baseball bat!"

Whack!

"Ow!"

Whackwhackwhackwhack!

Leaving a stunned Purelganni in his wake, Betty rushed back to the portal. "Let's go! I'm now in charge of this escape!"

"Actually," observed Molly, "it seems Captain Hadrian has taken the lead."

"What? Damn him!"

Things started exploding in the vast concourse behind them, followed by clanging and the fierce wrenching of metal being torn apart by Fluoridian teeth.

"Follow me everyone," commanded Hadrian, beginning the ascent up the stairs.

"Wait!" cried Molly.

The two Terrans paused.

Molly pointed down. "Look at our legs! They're like nine inches long! Look at those stairs! You want us to climb to the surface using these legs and those stairs?"

"Oh for crying out loud," Hadrian sighed, reaching down and picking up Molly. "Better?"

Molly snuggled close. "Hmmm. It'll do."

"Buck."

The chief engineer scowled down at Betty. "Really? Do I have to?"

The floor shook.

"Oh dear," said Hadrian, "I think Rillickudick just triggered a runaway containment breach in the reactor core. In mere minutes this entire level will be flooded with deadly radiation, killing us all."

Buck sighed. "Fine, I guess." He picked up Betty, who immediately clawed him. "Ow! Crap!"

"Oh, sorry," Betty purred. "All better now? Good. Wait! Here—" A talon raked Buck's neck.

"OW!"

"Oh, sorry. Better now? Good."

"Let's go!" Hadrian said, taking to the stairs two at a time.

Gasping behind him, Buck said, "Captain!"

"What?"

"About that containment breach."

"I just made that up. Now save your breath—it sounds like the whole set's coming down back there. Hurry! Only three hundred ninety-four more levels until we reach the surface!"

"But what about Felasha?" Molly wailed.

EiGHT

"Commander," said Beta, "there are four Ecktapalow Eviscerator-class warships decloaking in front of us." The robot swiveled round. "And with five Radulak Bombast-class battleships coming up fast behind us, we appear to be trapped and only moments from utter annihilation. Unfortunately, I have just timed out and will now power down my systems for routine maintenance. In an emergency, call 1-800-YOU'RE STILL ON HOLD HAHAHA." Beta abruptly sagged in its chair.

"Sir!" hissed Sticks from the helm station beside Beta, "can she do that?"

"Spark," said Sin-Dour from the command chair, "take the navigation station, please."

"Navigation! Go here! Go there! Go—"

"*Wrongggg!*" sang Sticks. "That's me! My station! You—you just look at those maps on the screens, right? And, uh, do other stuff."

"Maps! Other stuff! Exciting! In this chair! Push robot to floor, hah! Take that!"

From comms, James "Jimmy" Eden turned to Sin-Dour. "Commander?"

"Yes, Eden?"

"Uh, well, should I?"

"Should you what?"

"Well, you know, sir. Call 1-800-YOU'RE STILL ON HOLD HAHAHA?"

"Not right now," Sin-Dour replied. She hit shipwide comms. "This is acting Captain Sin-Dour speaking. You may have noted that we have found ourselves coincidentally in a situation matching the training scenario the Mishimashi Paradox, Part VII, Surrounded by Enemy Ships Inexplicably Faster Than Ours. As you know, Captain Hadrian Sawback successfully won this scenario in record time. It now falls to us to match his remarkable feat." She paused. "Battle stations. Red alert." She snapped off the comms and drew a deep breath. "Tammy, prime all thrusters and prepare for emergency evasive maneuvers. Galk, ready all weapons, including the Dimple Beam. Helm, all speed ahead. Take us right into their midst!"

"Yes sir! Like, wow, bet they're not expecting that!" And she ducked to roll her eyes.

Tammy spoke from Engineering. *"I would like to point out that Hadrian never had my T-Space short-range evasive capability. Nor did he have beam weapons, especially not the Dimple Beam."*

"I am aware of our advantages," Sin-Dour replied. "But it would be foolish not to take, uh, advantage of them under the circumstances."

"It would, and of course Hadrian anticipated that, so he had me deactivate all my defensive and offensive abilities. You're on your own, Commander."

"What?"

"Hahaha! Had you going there, didn't I? Naw, let's kick alien butt, shall we? You can change your panties later."

"Galk! Target the Ecktapalow vessels with Middling Beam Weapons. Tammy, jump us directly behind them. Galk, prepare to fire! Tammy, mark!"

"Who's Mark?"

"Just jump us!"

The screen flickered, revealing open space. "Rear camera! Fire, Galk!"

Lovely orange and purple and yellow and white beams lashed out. Screens flared and died on the Eviscerators now directly behind them. Pieces of ship erupted from hulls and pods and whatnot, glittering inside clouds of freezing gases and vented atmosphere.

"Halley!" barked Spark. "Matron Ecktapalow decloaking to starboard, 1K distant, weapons powering up!"

"Commander?" Eden asked.

"Is this really the time, Jimmy?"

"Uhm, the Mondo Matron is hailing us from that vessel."

"Ah. On screen then."

The image of the Matron's bridge shimmered onto the main viewer. The Mondo Ecktapalow was perched on a mound of mud on a raised dais on the bridge. The reptilian insect-like head bobbed up and down as it spoke. "I am Mondo Click Clicketyclick. Our weapons are locked upon you and in moments you will die. It is Ecktapalow custom, however, to give you sixty Terran seconds during which you can, oh, I don't know, pray to your gods or, conversely, come up with some diabolical scheme to turn the tables and so destroy us from an unexpected quarter. Metaphorically, this can be described as Tomal breaking into a rash of spots the night before the graduation dance and all this fancy new cream does is make the spots even redder, whah! Oh, now you have only forty-one seconds, oh my." The image flashed off, replaced by the massive Matron capital ship with all its eight hundred fifty-three barrels pointed at the *Willful Child* already sparking and smoking in anticipation.

"Tammy," said Sin-Dour.

"Yes, Commander?"

"Dimple Beam please."

"Are you sure, Commander? Do recall that the very fab-

ric of space-time is dangerously thinned by the weapon's discharge—"

"Thirty seconds!" announced Spark. "Cringe in terror, Halley? Cringe and whimper?"

"Just fire the Dimple Beam, Tammy."

"Well let's think about this first, Commander. I mean, it was always meant as a last-ditch doomsday weapon, and if Captain Hadrian were in that chair you're sitting in at the moment, why, I doubt he'd—"

"Ten seconds! Spark cringing!"

"Tammy! Fire the Dimple Beam and that's an order!"

"Five seconds and now piddling in chair!"

"Tammy!"

"Oh fine, firing now."

The Dimple Beam lashed out. The Mondo Matron ship vanished.

"Oh!" cried Spark. "Poo of relief! What's that smell? Don't look at me!"

The *Willful Child* rocked and shook suddenly, throwing everyone about. Eden rolled from his chair, across the entire room, and crashed up against a bulwark. Everyone watched that. The inert form of Beta moved a bit, but not much. Jocelyn Sticks jiggled. Spark sniffed his behind.

"Tammy! Report!"

"T-Drive offline! Dimple Beam disabled! Containment field breached in Main Engineering—the Irridiculum Crystals are . . . oh, they're fine. But still! Wait one. Jensen!

Vent the radiation from Radiation Containment Chamber One to Radiation Containment Chamber Two! No, I don't care about your lunch bag, dammit! Commander, we can't take much more of this!"

"Spark, what just hit us?"

"Uhm, Radulak, sir! They've caught up!"

The bridge doors opened and Dr. Printlip rushed in with its medical bag. It tripped and rolled and rolled and rolled to bump up against the motionless form of Jimmy Eden. A moment later Polaski arrived to take the comms station, throwing on the headset. "Captain!"

"Polaski? Are we being hailed?"

He tilted his head, frowned. "Not sure, sir. Someone's talking . . . wait. I think . . . sir, we're no longer on hold! We've got a techie calling from New Klangia—I think— the accent's hard to—"

"Put the techie on hold, please," Sin-Dour ordered. "And then hail the Radulak flagship *I Saw No Need to Mention My Mother's Moustache.*"

Polaski blinked.

"Now, Polaski."

Printlip moved up alongside Sin-Dour. "Lieutenant Eden is concussed, Commander. I am applying an emergency cranial endectomy using nasal-insertion forceps via the anal shunt. He should be up and about in no time!"

"Thank you, Doctor, that's a relief."

Polaski turned to face Sin-Dour. "Commander, I have Supreme Drench-Master Bang on line three."

"On screen please."

The slime-slick image of the Radulak bridge appeared, with Bang seated in the command chair. "Ah yes, Commander! I made a vow, a vow I made! What did I say? I said this and this is what I said: 'I'll find them! I'll find them or bust! I shall find them, my friend, on their small speck of dust!' And now! And now and now I have to tell you! What do I have to tell you? I'll tell you this. It's time to die, not lie, not fry, but die! So now you die! Why? Because you must! Must you die, oh yes, it's that or bust! What and oh just *what* do you think of that? And when you think of that why not think of this too? Fry and die! Now, my friend, it's time to say good-bye!"

The screen went blank.

Sticks turned. "Like, what?"

Radulak weapons fired. The *Willful Child* rocked and thundered.

"Galk! Return fire!"

"Which one? There's like five of 'em, sir."

"Hmm, why not all of them?"

"Right. I can do that. Give me a mo."

Beams ~~lashed~~ arced out, sent Radulak vessels spinning and cavorting.

On the main screen, Bang reappeared amid a smoky,

sparking, body-strewn bridge. "Such bright colors! Smash and bam and we flew about and about we flew, here and there, smash and bam! Bang I did, my head, and Bang I am, ow. But what a fine day! My torpedoes are all fine and about to fire! Surrender now to Bang and I'll send you to your Captain! One big family in the mines of Rude Pimente!"

"Very well, Supreme Drench-Master. We are evacuating to our escape pods and sending them your way. They're the red-painted ones. Galk? Please oversee the evacuation, using the red escape pods, please. Oh, and Drench-Master? We have so many, we'll need to fly to all of your ships if that's all right."

"Perfect! Yes! Abandon your vessel before we destroy it!"

"First wave of, uh, escape pods on their way, Commander."

"Thank you, Galk. Drench-Master, have you acquired them yet?"

"Captured by our superior tractor beam! Their measly defenses overwhelmed! Yes, we have them all, on every ship! Opening them now . . . oh, massive detonations, all containment breached. You should have told me your crew members were all explosive. Now Bang I was and Bang I am no more, oh my!"

Sudden static as all the Radulak vessels blew up.

Sin-Dour sighed. "Tammy? How go the repairs?"

"Oh we were fine, Commander. I was just kidding with all that. But admit it, it made things more exciting, didn't it?"

"Helm, resume course for Rude Pimente."

"Like, yes Commander, but not till someone gets rid of this poo beside my right foot."

"Gross!" cried Spark. "Whoever would have done that?"

NiNE

Gasping, Hadrian pulled himself onto the last landing by the surface-exit door. Molly squirmed from his arms and jumped upright. "Well that was the best nap ever! I feel so refreshed! Captain Betty," he called out down to the landing one level below, "wake up now! You're almost there! Are you feeling as spry as I am? In fact, I've never felt so energetic! I mean—"

"Shut up!" Betty snarled from below. "I didn't sleep at all! Had a damned multiphasic jammed into my side, and this chief engineer sweats deadly psychotropic toxins. I've been fighting off snake-headed bat-winged hamsters for like hours!"

Moments later Buck and his charge crawled into view, the chief engineer on his belly clawing at the steps with bloody fingers, his eyes bulging. "Captain," he moaned, "I may never walk again. My legs. Dead. Lifeless. Dead-weights, lumps of bloated meat. Legs, sir, deader than dead. Just . . . dead." On his shoulders just behind his head squatted Betty, swatting at invisible flying hamsters.

"We made it, Buck," said Hadrian, pulling himself to a sitting position with his back to the door. He pointed to a corner. "And there, furry parkas and pom-poms—oh, those must be mitts. And big furry hats, too, and mukluks. We're all set to brave the fierce arctic weather as we finally make our escape."

Betty leapt from Buck's shoulders. "That's what you think."

Hadrian frowned. "What do you mean?"

"Oh, nothing."

"What he means," Molly chirped up, "are all the assas-sins waiting for us on the other side of that door, that's what he means."

Betty walked over to Molly and hit him in the head with his stick. "Idiot!"

"Well," said Hadrian, "I was wondering when they'd show up. Just our luck, huh? Now, Buck, it's time to get into that winter gear."

"What?" Buck's eyes were wide. "Go out there and get assassinated? Not a chance! Besides, I told you: My legs don't work anymore."

"Hand me your multiphasic, will you?"

"What? My—okay, sure, why not? Can't wait to see you take on all those assassins with a multiphasic, hahaha! You can toothpick them to death. Or take a wrench to their knuckles—but I wonder: Will they let you get that close? I mean, I wouldn't. No, I think I'd stand maybe twenty feet away while I unload a clip of depleted uranium bullets into our bodies, making us dance in slow motion with every explosive, blood-spraying impact. And then I'd throw a couple grenades over to make sure—"

"You're babbling, Buck. Just give me that multiphasic."

Buck tossed it over and then fell back. "Now my arms have stopped working, too. No wait, look, I can flop them around, isn't that nice?"

Collecting up the multiphasic, Hadrian said, "So flop over there and get into those furs. You too, Molly and Betty."

"That's Betty and Molly!" snapped Betty. "Not that I'm clinging to outdated hierarchical conferring of no-longer-applicable authority in order to bolster my shattered ego or anything. It just sounds better. Betty and Molly, see? Not Molly and Betty—no, that sounds all wrong."

"Just get into some furs, will you?"

Molly had hopped over to the winter gear and was picking through it. "I don't see anything my size here," he said. "Hold on, this fur—aack! It's Klang!"

Buck rattled a mean laugh. "Gives new meaning to Klang rip-offs, doesn't it? Hahaha! Go on, Molly, be a Klang wearing a parka made of Klang fur! Try on those Klang mitts, too! And that Klang hat! Hahaha!"

"Buck," Hadrian warned. "You're being somewhat insensitive."

"Uh," said Molly, "you misunderstood me, Chief Engineer. These furs really *are* Klang rip-offs. They only *look* warm, when in fact they're useless. They have no insulating properties at all. It's the kind of product we're flooding the Terran market with at the moment, since only idiots would actually buy this crap. Uh, no offense or anything."

"Oh great!" Betty snapped. "Now we freeze to death even before the assassins can gun us down and blow us up! What kind of pathetic escape is this? Oh wait, it was all a trap. I keep forgetting."

"Besides," offered Molly, "we won't be the ones getting gunned down, Captain Betty! Remember? It was our job to deliver the Terrans to the assassins, and we've done just that! Just think, they'll reduce our multiple life sentences to just one life sentence!"

"You're right! I'm feeling better already!"

Buck struggled to get into a fur parka while still lying on the floor and flopping about his dead arms and legs. Glancing over, he saw that Hadrian had dismantled the multiphasic. "What are you doing, sir? You broke it! Now we're toast!"

"Nonsense, Buck. I've just accessed the Arrayed Singular Duplatronic coelements of the transmultiplier phase component of the Quantum Perambulating Governor."

"You huh?"

"The multiphasic's laser pointer, Buck. Now, just a tweak here on the tiny Irridiculum lens, like so, and then invert the Prism Inverter, like this. Now, disable the Governor's energy-output limiter, like that! And voilà! Laser pointer turns into a Quantum Multiplier Duplatronic High-Energy Disintegrating Gigajoule Laser!"

"Holy crap," said Buck. "Why didn't I think of that?"

"Years of brain-addling drugs?"

"Hmm, could be. Well! What can I say? It was worth it, dammit!"

Hadrian stood up and began donning furs. "Now then," he said, pulling on a furry hat. "Shall we brave the blistering icy cold of Rude Pimente's inhospitable surface, which, while utterly covered in ice and snow, appears to have abundant oxygen in its atmosphere and how precisely does that work? No matter. You ready, Buck?"

"Hard radiation cracking the frozen water into constituent elements of hydrogen and oxygen on a seasonal basis, depending on the planet's rotation around the red dwarf."

Everyone stared at Molly.

Who shrugged. "I just made that up, but it sounds pretty good, doesn't it?"

"Captain," Buck said, "I still can't get up, sir."

"Can you worm along?"

"Well, uh, I guess."

"That'll do." Hadrian turned to the door and pressed the large exit button. There was a hiss, a billowing of icy snow, and then the door swung inward.

They found themselves staring at a snowdrift that stopped at about chest height.

"Leave this to me!" cried Betty, jumping forward with his stick, which he used to begin digging a tunnel. "It'll be a tight squeeze for you Terrans but for me and Molly, why, it's perfect!" Snow flew and in moments Betty had vanished down the small round tunnel he'd made.

Sighing, Hadrian set the laser on dispersed beam. He waved it at the drift. It melted in a slumping gush of water in which Betty now began drowning. Hadrian stepped forward and picked the Klang up, gave him a shake, and then set him down.

Before them was a nice slope leading upward. Hadrian set out, clambering up the ramp.

Betty glared at Molly and lifted his stick threateningly. "Not a word, Molly."

"I wasn't going to say anything, Captain," Molly replied. "I mean, it was a brilliant means by which we could get out of here before the Terrans, permitting us the opportunity to warn the assassins that Hadrian was now armed and dangerous. Only once more Captain Hadrian Alan Sawback outwitted you. In fact, thinking on it, you've been bested by him at every turn. It's hopeless, in fact. I don't know why you keep trying."

"You know what, Molly?"

"What?"

"I'm going to tell the assassins that you were a collaborator, so they shoot you too. What do you think of that?"

Molly scratched his chin with one small talon. "I thought you evil antagonists were supposed to be polite."

"I am! I'm telling you beforehand, aren't I?"

"That's true."

Buck was now worming his way up the slope, backside humping, mitten-clad hands flapping and flopping, legs dragging. Betty jumped aboard for a ride to the top and a moment later Molly joined him. They settled down on the soft furs covering Buck's back.

"I'm always polite," Betty said. "Under normal circumstances I'd also be impeccably dressed, filthy rich, and surrounded by beautiful females. Alas, for now, all I have is my politeness."

"It's not just politeness, of course," Molly pointed out. "It's *evil* politeness."

"I can accept that in principle, Molly. But the specific distinction still seems a little bit vague."

Buck slid back down to the bottom. "Crap." He began again.

"Can you elaborate?" Molly asked.

"Well, take Captain Hadrian, right? Hero. Genius. Handsome. Sexually frustrated. Yet he remains polite even when destroying thousands of Radulak and countless other aliens. But it's a different kind of politeness, isn't it? Or is it? Is his politeness only acceptable and deemed 'good' because he's a hero, a genius, and as sexually frustrated as all of his greatest tabloid-reading fans? As for me, veteran of countless sex-swarms, blissfully sociopathic—I mean, I wouldn't shed a single tear seeing you gunned down by assassins, would I?"

"That must be it, Captain!"

"What?" Betty wanted to know. "What's it?"

"Well, he's handsome. Whereas you're just a bedraggled half-drowned meerkat-alien-DNA-hybrid with a bent snout and a clipped ear and smelly glands under your lower jaw. Cute, if only at a distance, but handsome? Hardly."

"I just realized I can't have you assassinated and you know why, Molly? Because all evil antagonists need a minion, someone blindly serving the guy who never wins, which makes you about as dumb as that fur hat you're wearing. Whereas I, as the eternal optimist, well, I make full use of my limited cunning in my perpetually hopeless quest to defeat my nemesis, meaning I remain destined to survive just about anything, if only to guarantee a return engagement!"

Buck dragged himself over the lip of the icy ramp. Molly and Betty hopped off and dusted themselves down.

Hadrian was perched nearby on a block of something that might have been snowy ice (or icy snow) but looked suspiciously like spray-painted Styrofoam.

Buck rolled onto his back, blinked skyward. "Hold on," he said, "it's not very cold out here at all!"

"Precisely!" said Hadrian. "Apart from the installed Freon elements surrounding that exit hatch, the rest of this snowy icy landscape is fake. I'd wager the ambient temperature to be seventy-three degrees Fahrenheit, making these non-insulating Klang furs ideal." He looked around. "Little different from a mild winter day in California."

Betty flung his stick to the ground. "Where are the damned assassins?"

"Over here," answered a familiar voice, and from between two white mounds of carved Styrofoam blocks slithered Felasha, followed by six Radulak mercenaries bearing enormous weapons.

"Such a long wait for you!" Felasha said. "We took the Freight Elevator, escaping the final destruction of everything and everyone barring the Fluoridian, of course, whom we last saw running that way," and the Purelganni pointed with one flipper. "But now here you are, ready to die—you *are* ready to die, aren't you?"

"Not me!" shouted Betty. "I delivered the Terrans

single-handedly, Wondrous Felasha of the Downy White Fur and Huge Soft Downy Puppy Eyes!"

"Single-handedly?" Molly asked.

"So you did," Felasha agreed. "But alas, we need to kill you too, to cover our tracks."

Betty sagged. "It's just not fair, is it? Did you hear that, Molly? Now she has to kill us, too."

"Well, actually, she was only talking to you," Molly pointed out.

"No she wasn't!"

"Yes she was."

"Felasha!"

"Oh, I like the smaller kitten, Molly, is it? Yes, very cute, with a certain air of possession and subtle cleverness. I think I'll keep him!"

"Betrayed by my own minion!" Betty hissed.

"Enough chitchat," said Felasha. "Radulak mercenaries, you are now free to kill the Terrans and that Klang there."

"Wait!" cried Betty. He pointed at Hadrian. "He's armed with a multiphasic! Look, he's calibrating the setting even as I speak! That laser pointer will now fracture its gigajoule death ray to take down all six Radulak!"

Felasha laughed. "Hahaha! A multiphasic on laser pointer setting! Oh dear! Oh my!"

Hadrian fired. The six Radulak all toppled with neat round holes in their foreheads.

"Oh crap," finished Felasha.

"I'll take the Purelganni!" shouted Buck, flopping over toward Felasha.

"Do you think you're being funny?" Felasha asked. "You're not, you know."

They slammed into each other, flippers batting and slapping and, uh, batting.

"That's ridiculous," said Betty. "Here, let me use my baseball bat!" He leapt into the fray and began bashing Felasha on her head. "Take that! And this! And this and that! Die, horribly cute Purelganni! Die!"

Eventually, all three battlers were exhausted. Betty staggered back, his stick a battered, broken shaft of pulverized wood.

"It was just a stick," Molly pointed out. "I could've told you, you know. Not a bat. Especially not a *baseball* bat. A bad killer always blames his weapons."

Felasha groaned. "I feel as if I've been massaged by a Finn." She twitched. "Not that bad, actually."

Buck dragged himself to one side. "Sorry, Captain, I'm spent. Done in."

"Of course you are," Felasha purred, "while I might very well be pregnant."

"What?"

At that moment, Hadrian, Buck, Molly, and Betty all displaced, leaving Felasha alone with six Radulak corpses.

She looked around. And then froze as she saw a dozen Newfoundlanders in the distance. "Oh no! Must. Rush. Back. To. Elevator! Mpfm, mpfm, mpfm."

Did she make it? We'll never know.

No! She didn't! Oh my by's a by! If only she had used her cuteness for goodness instead of evilness, eh?

TEN

"Welcome back, Captain," said Sin-Dour in the Insis-teon Chamber. "I am happy to report the destruction of the rogue Radulaks and their secret Ecktapalow part-ners." She then nodded to the parka-muffled figure stand-ing to one side. "And, as it turns out, I didn't need to send the adjutant down to effect your rescue after all."

Hadrian hopped down from the platform, doffing his winter clothes. "What a shame! I mean, Adjutant, you have no idea how cute you look in those furs! Why, you can rescue me any day in that fetching outfit."

Lorrin Tighe threw down her mitts and began removing her parka. "You just won't let it go, will you? No! Don't you dare kiss me!"

"I'm just so delighted to have you on board—I mean,

really on board, Adjutant. It would've been a respectful smooch, honest."

"I don't care!" she snapped, flinging the parka to one side. "If you need me—in a professional capacity—no, not like that, asshole—I'll be in the bar!" And off she stormed.

"Sir," said Sin-Dour after a moment, "what's wrong with the chief engineer?"

Buck had flopped down from the platform and was now slithering toward the door like a big fat furry seal.

"Ah, well, hard to say, 2IC, but I'm sure there's drugs for whatever it is he's got. Buck! Head down to sickbay, will you?"

At the door, Buck twisted his head round. "Really, sir? I mean, should I? My arms are dead. My legs are dead. I have Klang fleas in my hair and I may well now be infected with Purelganni STDs. A trip down to sickbay? A visit to Doc Printlip? Hmm, maybe on my next break." A moment later he slithered out into the corridor and the door irised shut behind him.

"Asylum!" cried Betty from the Insisteon platform.

"Actually," said Molly, "we're now members of the Affiliation, so we can't claim asylum, Captain Betty. Well, okay, not actual members yet. Provisional Status, so no asylum option for us! We're Almost Citizens so we don't even need asylum. Especially since all the trade rights instantly accorded us have left the authorities in chaos, and *especially* now that the Galactic Immigration Department has been privatized and subcontracted to Klang Pan-Everyone-Gets-In-For-A-Price (barring Klang, of course, who get in for free, *free!*) Inc. In which I have shares, by the way. Oh, and it's Betty who has fleas."

Betty made small fists and waved them about. "Captain Hadrian! Displace Molly back to the surface immediately! He's a spy, an infiltrator, a saboteur, a terrorist! I disavow all association with this treacherous minion. Displace him! Imprison him! Send him to the mines of Rude Pimente!"

"We just came from there," Molly pointed out. "And besides, it's been utterly destroyed."

Hadrian turned to Sin-Dour. "Best get Security here," he said. "Our Klangs are to be escorted to their guest quarters—"

"Will those quarters be locked?" Molly asked.

"Yes, Molly," Hadrian replied.

"I see. And will there be guards outside with orders to shoot to kill?"

"Indeed."

Molly crossed his small hairy arms. "Therefore not quarters at all, but prison cells."

"Sure, if you want to put it that way."

"And furthermore, we're not guests at all, but prisoners!"

"You and Betty participated in a scheme to get me and Buck assassinated, Molly."

"Did we? Did we really? Well, we'll see what my lawyers have to say about that! Not to mention your imminent cruel treatment of Provisional Almost Citizens of the United Affiliation of Planets! Oh, I see the lawsuits piling up here, Captain Hadrian. Tell me, were you personally insured against indemnity whilst being a dishonorably discharged officer of the Affiliation Space Fleet? Hmm, probably not! Your personal finances are about to take a massive hit."

"You tell him, Molly!" laughed Betty.

"Of course," Molly added, "if my jail cell just happens to be a little bit bigger and better equipped than Captain Betty's, I might decide to forgo all the legal action."

"Very generous of you, Molly," Hadrian said. "I'm sure we can arrange something like that."

"Betrayal on all sides!" Betty cried.

Nina Twice and two other security officers arrived and escorted the pair of Klang from the chamber.

Hadrian sighed. "Ah, Sin-Dour, it's been a fraught three days, let me tell you!"

"Yes sir. And we still have the rogue elements within the Affiliation Fleet to deal with. Admiral Jebediah Prim and Director Soma DeLuster remain powerful enemies. Although it has to be said they're both being raked over the coals following that sham of a trial against you and Buck. They're presently employing the classic guilty-person tactics of refusing interviews, not answering reporters'

questions, and just brazenly toughing it all out in the ex-
pectation that the public's pathetically short attention span
will soon find other targets in its eternal frenzy of finger-
pointing which, if not useful, is at least entertaining."

"Mhmm, clever bastards. Suggestions?"

"Sir, we need to get you and Buck reinstated, your rec-
ords cleared of all wrongdoing, your reputations restored.
Might I suggest our first salvo be an extended interview
with the *Galactic Perpetual Enquirer*?"

"You mean, not lawyers, courts, and proper procedural
channels within the legal framework of the administra-
tion's and Fleet's own well-defined system of checks and
balances beneath the stern, objective gaze of impartial
judges?"

Sin-Dour's eyes widened. "Sir, have you gone mad?"

Hadrian smiled. "Not at all. I was just floating the idea,
2IC. You're right, of course, it's off to the Court of Public
Opinion for true justice—okay, not 'justice' per se, but
simply the growing groundswell of barely informed public
perception rising like a tsunami of unvalidated opinion
that sweeps aside all hope of rational debate, the application of facts or any other discomfiting impediments to me-
being-right-and-you-being-wrong, said wave inundating
all opposition including galactic governments."

Tammy spoke from a speaker. "Oh you're just loving this,
aren't you, Hadrian? I see where you're going with this,
you know."

"Oh really? Enlighten us, then."

"Your thesis is as follows. If the idiot politicians and all the other wankers in power both officially and—in the case of corporate multitrillionaires—unofficially, are proceeding with their extensive infamy and corruption on the basis of dim-witted forty-two-character Twitsies, relying exclusively on keeping the citizens all fired up and frothing at the mouth and shaking fists at the wrong people, well, it's only fitting that the same mobs they've incited now storm their barricades, bust down the doors, and drag out the bastards every damned one of them and then, oh, let's not be crude here, TEAR THEM TO PIECES! There, how am I doing?"

"Oh my, Tammy!" Hadrian said. "Now that's just diabolical! Sin-Dour, give the *Galactic Perpetual Enquirer* a call for me, will you? In the meantime, what's next for us?"

"That depends, sir. I mean, if we were still a legitimate vessel of the Affiliation Fleet, there's been an SOS from the Hairball System, Planet Backawater. It's unspecified, simply a frantic call for help from the spaceport of the town of Modest Spaceport but Many Dusty Bars, on the continent of Desertica."

"Mhmm, sounds suspicious."

"Oh, and the SOS specifies the *Willful Child*. That is, they won't take any offers of assistance from any other vessel. They say they're desperate, kind of."

"I see, well, that doesn't sound suspicious at all! C'mon, 2IC, it's back to the bridge and a course set for Planet Backawater!"

"I figured you'd say that, sir. Course is already computed, T-Drive on standby."

Tammy hissed, "You, Sin-Dour, are just as bad as Hadrian! I can't believe all this racing here, racing there, diving headfirst into obvious bullshit emergencies designed to trap you all in some outrageous idiocy that, it turns out, only *you* can fix!"

Hadrian clapped Sin-Dour on the shoulder. "Let's go, 2IC! We can run up and down the corridors on our way to the bridge!"

"Sir, the elevator is just outside."

"Not that elevator—we'll take a different one! That way, we can run and run!"

They emerged into the corridor.

"Please," Hadrian invited with utmost in-no-way-disingenuous gallantry, "do take the lead, Commander."

She set out at a run. Hadrian followed, his eyes fixed on his 2IC's swaying backside. To keep himself from running into walls, of course.

"My God, they did it! They really did it!" Betty fell to his knees, clawing at his face and wiry flea-filled hair.

Molly settled back on the plush settee. "Oh, you noticed?

Indeed, this cell is eighteen inches wider and thirteen inches longer than yours. Moreover, while you have a metal cot and a tick mattress and a bucket for toiletries, I possess this settee, that lovely poster bed with memory-foam mattress and pillow, and that en suite bathroom with whirlpool and Jacuzzi. I'd offer you a mojito but then I might run out that much sooner and I can't have that. Still, I do give you leave to remain kneeling there in the middle of the room tearing out clumps of hair and pieces of scalp in an ongoing fit of anguish."

Betty paused and glared at Molly. "No!" he hissed. "I won't give you the satisfaction!" He leapt to his feet. "Can you believe how stupid these Terrans are? I mean, adjoining cells with a door in between that they didn't even lock!"

"Hmm, yes, about that. I'm afraid I will lock it after you leave."

"And I'll lock it on my side, too! See how you like that!"

"Oh, now that hurts."

Betty began pacing. "Stupid Terrans! See, we can now conspire and plan our escape! And more than that! We can scheme to take over their entire vessel! And once we're in control of everything, we can set a course for the fabled Planet Paradise in System Unknown beyond the edge of the Explored Zone!"

"That sounds like work," Molly said, stretching out with his hands behind his head. "I for one am ready to accept my fate. Prisoner, paying my debt to society through rehabilitation and towing the line at all times, including volunteer work with wayward children getting scared straight by a visit to my sumptuous penitentiary cell complex. I can already picture it: me and a few dozen young offenders watching holovids all night eating popcorn, drinking beer, and establishing drug connections on the Outside."

Betty looked around for a stick but couldn't find one. He snarled and resumed pacing. "Then I'll go it alone, and reap all the rewards myself! Nothing for you, Molly. Nada! I'll leave you destitute! And when I finally get to Paradise Planet—or was it Planet Paradise?—"

"Oh just go and look for crying out loud. It was only eleven lines ago!"

"No time for that shit. When I finally get to that fucking planet, you, Molly, will be left in a tiny capsule in perpetual orbit around it! Oh, and don't think I won't be charging rent for use of that capsule! Round and round you go, piling up enormous debt and unable to pay a cent on the interest, much less the principal! Hahahahaha!"

Molly scowled. "You wouldn't do that!"

"I would!"

"That's just evil!"

"I am! Evil! See me?" He danced around. "Evil! Evil!"

"All right then I'll help you," said Molly, slumping in defeat in the settee. "So tell me your scheme."

"It's simple, but first, why don't we retire to that Jacuzzi? I'm feeling utterly foul and besides, my highly advanced civilization of fleas could do with a bath. And those fleas need to be all happy and stuff, since they're going to play a crucial role in our taking over this vessel!"

"I trust you have devised a properly ignominious end for one Captain Hadrian Alan Sawback?"

"Of course!"

"Well that should ensure the utter failure of your scheme, but what the hell, as your only minion, I'm with you all the way."

"Really?"

"No, I'll ditch you the instant it all comes crashing down."

"I'll turn on the Jacuzzi then, shall I?"

Molly fluttered one hand. "Indeed. Gives me time for another mojito."

Captain Hadrian and Sin-Dour arrived on the bridge to eager applause from the bridge crew, although that quickly faltered when the smell from Hadrian's prison coverall wafted out to fill the room.

"Right," said Hadrian. "Perhaps I'll take this moment for a shower and change of clothes."

The applause surged back again.

Scowling, Hadrian retreated to his ready room to, uh, get ready. Once inside, he quickly stripped down and stepped into the sonic shower. The unit took one electronic sniff and then burst into flames. "Crap! Bloody Klang knockoff garbage! You know, Tammy," he said, stepping back out of the stall, "I can't believe the Fleet decided to outsource vital ship components in a pathetic shortsighted effort to cut costs. What's this galaxy coming to?"

"Actually," Tammy replied, "that's not a Klang knockoff. If you had a Klang knockoff it'd probably work, at least until its built-in time stamp kicked in to burn out the electronics, thus forcing you into an upgrade where you'll find they changed all the power jacks for no particular reason barring you needing to buy all that shit all over again, because when it comes to evil, corporations win hands down. Anyway, that sonic unit is a Hellburden product, a military industrial company owned by a superrich family with its pockets in every government for the past two centuries. It builds utter crap on constant cost overrun, milking every taxpayer and their descendants for all time, all in the name of patriotism."

"Uh, right, whatever. Dammit, I need to get clean! I'm still captain—rather, I'm sorta captain, or will be once I get my commission back. Point is, I need to be properly coiffed, smooth-shaven, smelling nice and stuff." He threw up his hands. "I can't go back out there like this!"

"Well no," agreed Tammy, "since you're naked. Tell you what, how would you like a proper bath? You know, in real water?"

"What? Can you do that?"

"Sure! You have two options. The brig cells, Deluxe Package. Though the Klang Molly is presently occupying that cell and he and Betty are at the moment frolicking in the Jacuzzi planning the takeover of your vessel using Betty's resident civilization of hive-mind sentient fleas."

"And the other option?"

"Bespoke, considerably more private, with properly filtered water and a reasonable fixed temperature."

"Right then! I'll take that one. Can you do an instant displace?"

"Consider it done."

Hadrian displaced, and found himself in a giant aquarium in Printlip's private quarters. Floundering, his fists batting at the aquarium's bolted-down cover, Hadrian stared through the tempered alumiglass and saw the blurred form of an apparently alarmed Belkri in a bathrobe, its hands now waving all about.

Running out of air and being attacked by swarms of small scorpion-tailed fish with mouths-inside-mouths-inside-mouths snapping at his face, Hadrian began yelling *"Tlammyyy! Dlillplacleee! Elmerglecnly dlillplacleee!"*

Instead, Printlip pulled something from its belt and pointed it at Hadrian. The doc began frantically pushing buttons on the small item, to no effect. Then it flung the object down and held many of its hands to either side of its round head/body in apparent horror.

A moment later Hadrian displaced to the floor of the doctor's room in a splash of water. Gasping, he lifted himself to his hands and knees. "Damn you, Tammy!"

"But now you're clean!" Tammy said from a speaker. "I'm pretty sure my description was entirely accurate, wasn't it?"

Printlip rushed up to Hadrian with a towel. "My apologies, Captain!"

"What was wrong with that Cover-Contraction device? Let me guess, another fucking Hellburden—"

"Ah! This? Alas, not a Cover-Contraction device."

"Oh, then what is it?"

"Holovid activator, sir."

"I see." Wrapping the towel around his waist, Hadrian stood. "You have programmed a holovid of your captain naked inside your aquarium being devoured by scorpion-tailed fish."

Printlip fidgeted and then said, "Well of course I never anticipated . . . . . ."

"Never mind." Hadrian lifted his head. "Tammy, displace me back to my quarters, please."

"I'm sorry, the damn thing's suddenly nonfunctional. Best you walk there, Captain."

"Oh it's like that, is it? Fine! And why not? It's been almost a week since I last paraded up and down the ship corridors in only a towel. See you later, Doc—oh, by the way, how is Buck?"

"I have been forced to replace Buck's blood with nothing but drugs. He's now fully recovered, sir."

"Right. Uh, carry on. And feed those damned fish!"

Hadrian arrived on the bridge wearing his towel. Lieutenant Sweepy Brogan plucked the cigar from between her full lips and regarded the captain with one arched eyebrow. "Well now, that brings back memories, sir. And if I wasn't here to complain that you keep getting us primed to kick alien butt only to find you don't need us meaning we have to stand down and kill more time trying to kill each other, which at least keeps your doc busy but damn—say, maybe we should continue this discussion in your ready room? Sans towel, of course."

"Alas, Lieutenant, no time for uh, what you said. A quick throw-on of uniform and it's back in that command chair. No rest for the captain of an Engage-class Affiliation warship, you know. Now, as for your complaint, yeah, I get it. Sorry about that. But I'm sure we can come up with a proper alien butt-kicking mission for you before too long."

"Promise?"

"Promise."

"All right then. I'll pass along the good word. In the meantime I've devised a new D&D campaign that the boys are gonna love. The Assault on Mount Doom and the Wizard of the Unholy Cruise Missile." She jammed the cigar back into her mouth and left the bridge with an airy salute.

Hadrian looked around. Everyone was staring at him. He glanced down to discover that his towel now hung from what might have been an elongated peg projecting out from between his legs, but wasn't. "Right," he said. "Carry on, everyone. I'll be right back."

In his ready room once more, Hadrian waited for a few moments before he could begin dressing. "Tammy, do any crew possess pet cats?"

"Captain! You know that's forbidden by regulation!"

"How many, then?"

"Seventy-four cats, sir, forty-seven kittens."

"Right." He threw on a burgundy velour shirt and then black slacks and finally shiny black boots.

"That was a surprisingly dignified retreat from the bridge," Tammy observed. "All things considered."

Hadrian coiffed his hair. "Natural talent, Tammy,

something you with your neutratronic processor will never possess, alas. Proper comportment is an art and indeed rare is the master. Lucky for you, I am such a master, which I suppose is pretty obvious. And while it may look easy, why, for someone like me, it is!"

He returned to the bridge and settled into the command chair. "Status, Helm?"

"Like, en route to Planet Backawater, sir. ETA two hours nineteen minutes thirty-three seconds. And like, I was staring, right? And it was like *whoah,* you know?"

"Never mind that, Sticks. Purge it from your mind although I know that's probably impossible. Anyway. Two hours! That's like being stuck in a feature film showing a spaceship moving slowly through space for like ever!"

Sticks rolled her eyes. "You forgot the nineteen minutes oh-six seconds, sir."

"Right, tack on a slew of boring trailers for overbudget tent-pole pieces of crap with bad story lines we've all seen before and dumbed-down science and paper-thin characters. Damn, I'm experiencing a sudden need for overpriced popcorn and a watered-down soft drink." He shook his head. "Eden! What's on the comms?"

"Uh, Channel Seven has the premiere broadcast of *The Super New Price Is Right,* but the Klang contestant is cleaning up and no one wants to bid on the Rabid Radulak in the Cage, sir, and the Audience Approval Meter is sinking fast, meaning it's about to be canceled." He made a sad face, and then brightened. "But there's an *Ultra Super New Price Is Right* premiere ready and waiting in the wings, thank Darwin!"

"Jimmy Eden," Hadrian said in a calm even tone, "I meant the official Affiliation Fleet feed. Have we been hailed any time in the past day or so? Have there been any fleet-wide announcements pronouncing the *Willful Child* as a rogue vessel crewed by officially designated outlaws, terrorists, or revolutionaries? In short, is there now a price on our heads?"

"Oh, that. Uh, yes sir. I mean, all that. Kind of. You know."

"No, I don't know," Hadrian said. "Please elaborate."

"Well, uh. Yes sir. There have been eighty-three attempts to hail us from an admiral who says he's from Fleet HQ, and, uh, a Radulak bounty on you and the chief engineer as 'Escapees of the Illegal Underhanded Assassination Attempt on the Prison Planet Rude Pimente,' with the bounty set at Ten Billion Radulira, which converts to $423.16 in Affiliation credits. Oh, and *60 Minutes* has done a Special Investigative Episode exonerating you, resulting in huge riots in all the major cities in the Affiliation. Oh, look at this blinking light, sir! Another hail attempt from that admiral at Fleet HQ! But wait! *Ultra Super New Price Is Right* is starting after these important messages from our sponsors!"

"Acknowledge the HQ hail, Eden. On the main viewer, please."

"*The Ultra Super*—"

"No, Jimmy. The admiral, please. On the main viewer. Up there. Big screen, Jimmy."

Deeply in the deepest depths of deep space . . .

Captain Tiberius Alex Razorback stepped onto the bridge of the *Wanton Child*. Lights blinked, components hummed and clicked, lenses flared, and something beeped a slow, massively irritating pulse. He paused for a moment, scanning his bridge crew at their stations. Still seated in his command chair was his 2IC, Comely DeCliche, only her unregulation mane of wavy red hair visible from where he stood—

"Eden! Get this crap off right now!"

"Oh! Sorry sir! But it's the premiere episode, where Tiberius gets his ship and meets his officers and—"

"Eden!"

"I can't—I mean, I don't—oh, here, got it. It's Admiral Trustworthy Honest, sir. On screen now, sir!" Eden then fell over in a dead faint.

The main viewer revealed the admiral seated at his desk against a vast window beyond which the planet Terra slowly revolved amid a swarm of space junk made up of obsolete satellites, abandoned fuel tanks, plastic bottles and brightly colored candy wrappers, tinfoil, used tampon applicators and flaccid rubbers. The admiral had wavy iron-hued hair, lots of it, a square jaw, and piercing blue eyes wide-set beneath a broad forehead with fatherly lines of concern on it, not the square jaw which while wide-set too just like the eyes was actually below the eyes, with a stern but caring mouth in between, the mouth being below the nose that was between the eyes and which probably deserved mention as well though being more or less perfect and therefore nondescript that was why it wasn't originally mentioned, but having stumbled down this rabbit hole of descriptives, well, can't leave out the nose with all the eyes-forehead-jaw-mouth stuff going on, and the twinkle in the right eye, too, while his uniform was immaculate and his fingernails were polished and expertly (if somewhat obsessively) trimmed, the upshot being this was one of the good guys, no, honest.

Honest now smiled. "At last! Captain Sawback! I have to admit, popular as you presently are, I didn't expect to have to record eighty-three messages before finally getting through to you."

"Apologies, Admiral," said Hadrian. "I'm afraid my comms officer has discovered the new Quantum Cable channels. I can only pray he hasn't explored the shopping channels—"

"Ah, as to that, Captain, I did get a call from Galactic Express as it seems your Fleet Emergency Purchase credit card has been tagged for an excessive list of purchases through a clearinghouse called CrapStraightToYou P.O. Box 17B for the amount of eight gazillion nine hundred and twenty-seven trillion credits and change." The admiral's smile broadened as he leaned forward on his desk. "Of course this is hardly a military matter although the Fleet Exchequer has made a few calls to me regards the outstanding account, particularly as you were a Designated Rogue Vessel during most of those purchase date stamps, and while I only work weekends as a Bounty Hunter and Debt Collector, you do have a Quantum-Huge Red Flag trailing you at the moment."

"Ah," said Hadrian, "then this is not an official Fleet communication from you."

"Oh! Yes, it might well look like that. But I forgot to add that the Highspeed Shipment Transit Routes are somewhat congested in your wake, with over twenty thousand GalaxEx supply ships pursuing you at the moment. Said congestion severely impacting Fleet operations, as you might imagine." His smile got even broader. "Accordingly, Captain, I am in fact wearing my admiral's hat at the moment, but if things don't work out to my satisfaction in the course of this conversation, I'm afraid I may have to put on my Unstoppable Bounty Hunter hat, and we wouldn't want it to go that far, would we?"

"Admiral, can I put you on hold for a few minutes?"

The man frowned, but in a sympathetic way. "Sure, why not. I can give you . . . three minutes." The scene of the planet behind him flickered briefly to show the brick wall of some earthbound warehouse, before restoring itself. "Beginning . . . now."

Hadrian turned to see Polaski on station at comms. Amazingly, the man actually put the admiral on hold without even a single gesture from Hadrian. Things were looking up!

Then Hadrian sighed and said, "Polaski, check the pockets of Mr. Eden, will you?"

Polaski knelt beside the unconscious form of Jimmy Eden and a moment later retrieved a platinum credit card. "Got it, Captain."

"Thank you. Tammy, please displace that card to a thousand meters ahead of us and hit it with the Dimple Beam."

Jocelyn Sticks swiveled in her chair. "But Captain! Unofficial destruction of a credit card is a capital offense!"

"Haha . . . oh, that pun was lost . . . never mind. But we're not destroying it, are we, Sticks?"

Her eyes went wide. "Oh! I guess not! Wow, that's like, *genius.*"

"Tammy?"

The card vanished from Polaski's hand with a plop. A moment later the Dimple Beam flashed into space ahead of the ship.

"Done, Captain," said Tammy. "The credit card now dwells in a timeless liminal state of the multiverse."

"Thank you. Now, Polaski, send out a multipoints instruction on all bands. All items purchased—and cite the card number—are to be Returned to Sender for a complete refund."

Everyone on the bridge gasped, even the unconscious Jimmy Eden.

Sin-Dour stepped close. "Captain! That could well bring down entire planetary economies! I mean, Purchase Is Life, Buying Is Bliss, to Consume Is Sacred!"

Hadrian crossed his legs. "I'm well aware of the Darwinian precepts relating to Universally Applied Capitalist Ethics of Eternal Progress No Matter the Cost, 2IC. But we're talking the shopping channels here, aren't we?"

"Yes sir, but—"

"Meaning those purchased items are all Klang knock-offs. Cheap, crappy, sweat-house and child-labor products from assembly plants crowded cheek-by-jowl in stinking polluted warrens generously called cities on those Manufacturing Planets of the Klang Undercut Economic Zone. Ergo, Commander, the impending economic collapse will primarily impact Klang planets, thus effecting a traumatic but entirely necessary Market Correction on a galactic scale, leading to a resurgence of Affiliation futures in all the Galactic Stock Markets."

"Crap," said Tammy, "Hadrian's done it again!"

Leaning back, Hadrian waved one hand in a modest gesture, "Saving the Affiliation is all in a day's work, Tammy. Now then, Polaski, put the admiral back on, will you?"

The main viewer shifted back to Trustworthy Honest's weekend office.

"Admiral! I'm happy to report that the entire matter has been cleared up."

"It has? But that's not—" His twinkly blue eyes flicked away, presumably to some other screen. He frowned, and then his square jaw dropped, his stern mouth popped open, his perfect nose flared, the broad brow creased with confusion, his wavy iron hair turned all limp, and sudden creases marred his immaculate uniform even as his nails dulled and splintered. "Saint Ardrey! That's—you—there's—what—oh, ah—holy—"

"Are we done here, Admiral?" Hadrian asked. "We're presently responding to a distress call. You know, official Affiliation stuff, right? Fleet mission parameters, saving the day, saving countless lives, the usual but entirely essential business of the Affiliation Fleet, particularly deep-space Engage-class vessels—oh, and it looks like your fake space shot has crashed again, but that's a pleasant enough brick wall, I suppose."

Honest twisted round. "Ah, shit!" He faced Hadrian again. "Right. Listen. Klang Cheap-Knockoff Industrial Group Inc. has just declared bankruptcy. Plants are shutting down everywhere throughout the Klang Corporate Sector. Unions are springing up. Managers are being burned at the stake, CEOs are being skinned alive— even their superyachts designed to survive any imaginable apocalypse have been overrun and sunk in countless seas, oceans, lakes, rivers, and obnoxiously big swimming pools. Meanwhile, the Terran Stock Exchange has rebounded to record levels and confidence is going sky-high—Captain Sawback, you've just saved the Affiliation!"

Hadrian smiled. "Ah, but Admiral, do pass this on: I'm not done yet."

"What do you mean?"

"Consider this a promise to every corrupt meathead still in charge of whatever, I'm coming for you all."

The admiral blanched, and then grinned. "I'll pass that on, with a bouquet of roses! And from all of us overworked underpaid indentured plugs needing five fucking jobs just to put food on the damned table, go give 'em hell, Captain!"

"Until next time, Admiral. Hadrian out."

The feed clicked off, replaced by—

Deeply in the deepest depths of deep space . . .

Captain Tiberius Alex Razorback stepped onto the bridge of the *Wanton Child*. Lights blinked, components hummed and clicked, lenses flared, and something beeped a slow, massively irritating pulse. He paused for a moment—

"Polaski!"

ELEVEN

ALL QUIET ON THE FLEA FRONT

CHAPTER ONE

Colonel Fitzflea Flea snapped a salute with one fore-leg. "Supreme Leader! In compliance with your orders, all troops are assembled and the invasion is ready to begin!"

Supreme Leader Fleahelm von Flea nodded, surveying the massed ranks from his perch on the frowning fold of the God Head's mostly horizontal forehead. He held up a dispatch. "Highbrow Command has issued the directive to advance into the Great Mechanistic Galaxy! Once there, we shall establish beachheads on every head! We shall infiltrate the musty jungles of unwashed crotches! We shall ascend the treacherous mountains of all devious impediments and enemy defenses! We shall airdrop upon unsuspecting foreheads and eyebrows and establish strongholds in many armpits! We shall even cross the vast hairy plains of hairy backs!"

The soldiers all cheered, although at the last exhortation a few threw up.

Fleahelm von Flea held up all his hands. "Upon reducing the enemy to helpless scratching, we shall free the God Head who will take command of the Great Mechanistic Galaxy. In this glorious war we shall not fail!"

The soldiers cheered again while a few, still thinking about hairy backs, threw up again.

"Colonel Fitzflea Flea, move them out!"

The colonel faced his troops. "First Wave, launch!"

CHAPTER TWO

"Sir!" Sergeant Smith-Flea Flea threw himself against the furball. "This Great Mechanistic Galaxy is so big! We've not yet encountered a single warm body!"

"Not true," Colonel Fitzflea Flea said. "Our advance scouts have spotted cats and kittens! We shall employ them as rapid-transportation devices! Within their warm furry coats we shall make rapid haste to all corners of the Great Mechanistic Galaxy, and as we all know, where there are cats and kittens, there are human bodies!"

"But sir, that was not part of the Invasion Plan!"

"All war is adaptation to circumstances, Sergeant. I have already issued the orders. All fleas shall ride cats and kittens, thus spreading our presence through the Great Mechanistic Galaxy. So take your squad, Sergeant, and find us the nearest cat or kitten, on the double-hop!"

"Yes sir!" The sergeant quickly edged away from the furball and then hopped rapidly to his waiting squad. "We must find a cat or a kitten!"

"I see one!" cried Corporal Flea O'Fleahan.

"Right! Let's go!"

CHAPTER THREE

"Gas! Gas!" Corporal Flea O'Fleahan staggered toward Sergeant Smith-Flea Flea. "Coming from that rhinestone collar-barrier directly ahead! I'm going blind! I'm choking!"

Sergeant Smith-Flea Flea stumbled back as the invisible but deadly gas reached him. He clawed at his antennae. Before him O'Fleahan had fallen and was now twitching feebly. The sergeant stumbled in retreat, knowing it was already too late. "Someone call HQ! It was all a trap! The cats! The, *gasp*, kittens! A trap! I'm dying . . . dying, ahhh. . . ."

In a mere thirty-one minutes, all was quiet on the flea front.

THE END

Published by Kat Books, an imprint of Read and Scratch Publishing, a subdivision of Tom Doherty Books
If you enjoyed reading this novel be sure to check the entire line of Kat Books, including the timeless classics listed below!
  Flea Tony and Cleopatra
    A tale of tragic love between Tony the Flea and a cat named Cleopatra in this beatnik retelling of some old play!
  Lawrence the Flea of Arabia
    In which a blue-eyed English flea leads thousands of Arabian fleas to their deaths! Fun reading for the entire family!
And many others including:
  A Tale of Two Fleas (by Charles Flea-Dickens)
  Flea and Prejudice (by Flea Austin-Flea)
  The Fleaing (by Stephen Kingflea)
  Lord of the Fleas (by William-Flea Fleading)
Want to learn more? Call Tom Doherty at 1-800 Erikson-You're-Dead!

Hadrian stepped into the cell and regarded Betty and Molly. "Well?" he asked. "What do you two have to say for yourselves?"

Molly jerked a thumb toward Betty. "I can't speak for him, but between the two of us I'm the one who's sorry. It was all a dreadful mistake. But as a minion, was my advice listened to? No, of course not. I knew the entire plan was going to end in disaster." Then he brightened. "But I'm itch-free for the first time in years!" Then he sagged. "At least until the new wave of egg-hatching."

Betty pointed a finger at Hadrian. "One more war crime to be laid against you, Captain Hadrian Alan Sawback! Genocide! An entire civilization of sentient hive-mind fleas, wiped out! For a couple days, at least, until the new hatchings mentioned by the traitor Molly. Still! Driven back to the Stone Age! They'll have to rebuild from, uh, scratch. Blighted by ignorance, benighted and reduced to savagery, living amid mysterious ruins they can't hope to comprehend for, like, *days*. Once I'm freed, Captain, I'm going to assemble my list of accusations of all the crimes you've committed, and take it before the Galactic Court of Certain War Crimes We Climb All Over While Ignoring Other Ones (e.g., the European colonizing of the Americas). You'll be charged, tried, convicted, and sent to a prison planet where you'll mine Irridiculum Crystals for the rest of your life!"

Hadrian sighed. "Really, Betty, after all I've done to make life easy for you."

"Easy! I'm too evil to spend the rest of my life in luxurious creature comforts, you all-too-handsome fool! You probably thought that jaunt to pick up take-out pizza was all innocent and everything, but it wasn't! It was all part of my plan to find my way back to you! You see, I knew you'd be betrayed by your own people, offered up like a sacrificial lamb to the Radulak during the Kittymeow Accords, and then sentenced to Rude Pimente, where I was waiting—yes, waiting! Hahaha! Forcing you to arrest us and imprison us on your ship! You probably think putting flea collars on all the cats and kittens thus initiating the wholesale slaughter of my resident fleas and bringing to an end all my plans of stealing your ship was clever!"

"Actually," said Molly, "it was. Clever, I mean. Cleverer than you could ever be, Captain Betty."

"I've only begun being clever! Just you wait!"

Hadrian turned to Nina Twice. "Escort Betty back to his cell, please. And this time make sure the door between the cells is locked to both inmates."

"Sir, I am to escort Betty back to his cell and make sure the door between the cells is locked to both inmates."

"That's right, Ms. Twice. Any questions?"

"No sir. No sir. Now complying."

Once a frothing Betty was kicked back into his cell and Nina Twice departed with a couple salutes, Molly flung himself back onto the settee. "I knew you were monitoring all conversations going on here, Captain. Which is why I made certain that Betty laid out all the details of his Flea Invasion Plan. So you can see how helpful I'm being."

"You mean as a treacherous, betraying minion, Molly?"

"Yes, well, you could see it like that. Even so, I was wondering . . ."

"What?"

"You know, as a reward, can I have one of those flea collars?"

"Captain!"

"What is it now, Polaski?" Hadrian asked as he arrived on the bridge and took his seat in the command chair.

"Sir! A Mayday call from our sister ship, AFS *What a Coincidence!*"

"Our sister ship? Never heard of it. Who's captain?"

"That's who's calling, sir. The captain!"

"Right. And the captain's name, Polaski?"

"Oh, um, that would be Captain Norville Normal Guy."

"Who the hell is that?"

"Uh, Captain Norville Normal Guy, sir."

"Fine. On the main viewer, please."

The image of an Engage-class bridge flickered into view. Smoke drifted, wreckage hung from the ceiling, consoles sparked. Hunched over in the command chair was a man, presumably Captain Norville Normal Guy, who suddenly cried, "It wasn't my fault!"

"Like wow," said Sticks, "he looks so normal I could, like, puke. I mean, talk about *Swollen Head*! Thinking he could possibly be captain of anything! I mean, I'm sitting here and he's like, oh, not my fault! And oh, look at me! Boo hoo!"

"That will be enough, Sticks," Hadrian said. "Captain Normal Guy, where's your crew? You appear to be alone on your bridge."

"I—I displaced them onto the ninth planet in the system since it was the only one left after the Giant Planet-Eating Machine ate all the other ones!"

"I see, and why did you do that, Captain?"

"Because I, uh, I wrecked the ship, I guess. It wasn't my fault!"

"You wrecked your ship by attacking the Giant Planet-Eating Machine?"

"No, we didn't get to that part. I just . . . oh, look! I'm completely unqualified to be anything, not even a holovid showrunner since I haven't got an original bone in my body! Oh, and now look! The ninth planet just got eaten, too! Who could have anticipated that?"

"You mean, after the Giant Planet-Eating Machine ate the other eight planets?"

"Exactly! Fleet should never have put me in charge!"

"Agreed," said Hadrian. "So why did they?"

"It was all just some cocked-up storyline designed to get me, Norville Normal Guy, in command of an Engage-class deep-space vessel. You know, for laughs, I guess. But you see, I'm a really normal guy! Barely competent at anything. I'm actually supposed to go through my life in a mediocre nondescript haze of mediocrity." He suddenly leaned forward. "But I've heard of you, Captain Hadrian. Oh, I know, we're all pretending otherwise, but never mind that! Look, I just fired a torpedo at the Giant Planet-Eating Machine, and it went in the hole and then . . . and then . . ."

"And then what?"

"Uh, I think I made it pregnant, cause now there's a little one, too, eating moonlets and asteroids! Captain! It's heading straight for Earth!"

"Hardly," Hadrian said. "We're like fifty light-years from Earth."

"We are? But . . . how did we get so far away?"

"Listen carefully, Captain Norville Normal Guy. If you follow my instructions here, we can sort all of this."

"Really? You promise?"

"I promise. We're still, oh, about a half hour from your position. So, before we get there, I want you to fly your Engage-class vessel straight into the maw of that Giant Planet-Eating Machine. Got that?"

The man quickly nodded. "I can do that! I still have two percent thrusters and the big one's coming straight for me anyway and I can't outrun it! Okay, here we go! I'm doing it right now! Then what?"

"I'll get back to you. Hadrian out."

The screen blanked.

Beta suddenly stood up. "I am restored to acceptable operating parameters. Robot dog, please exit my chair at the navigation station."

"Spark jumping from smelly chair! It was fun! I did nothing! So much fun!"

Sitting down, Beta said, "Captain, long-range sensors have just registered the destruction of an Engage-class vessel inside the maw of a Giant Planet-Eating Machine. Oh, and the birth of two more baby Giant Planet-Eating Machines."

"Very good, thank you, Beta."

Sin-Dour moved up alongside Hadrian. "Sir, you just sent Captain Norville Normal Guy to a merciful death when in fact he should have been arrested, court-martialed, and vilified by the entire Affiliation as an incompetent mass murderer of his own people."

"Yes well, I admit to succumbing to a spasm of mercy. Sticks, top speed to that family of Giant Planet-Eating Machines, please. Galk, weapons hot! Tammy, prepare the Dimple Beam."

"Oh sure," said Tammy, whose chicken manifestation had just arrived on the bridge, "always the easy way out. Dimple Beam this! Dimple Beam that! Where's the challenge? Where's the drama?"

"A good captain makes use of all tactical advantages, Tammy. That way, no one on this ship dies which is how I like it. Tammy, employing Dimple Beams against all those Giant Planet-Eating Machines, how much time will this add to our ETA in answering the SOS transmission from Planet Backawater?"

"About thirty seconds."

"Excellent!" Hadrian rose. "2IC, you're with me in the Ping-Pong room."

"Now, sir?"

"I've come up with a new serve that's going to get you lunging over half the table," Hadrian said with a bright smile.

"Oh, really," she replied in a dry tone.

"Wait till you see it!"

"Sounds like I will be too busy trying to return the serve to see much of anything."

"No problem," Hadrian replied. "I record all our games. I even have super slow mo!"

"Do you now? I see."

"That's right," Hadrian said, suddenly sweating. "Uh, is it hot in here? We flying too close to a sun or something?"

"And," Sin-Dour continued in steely tones, "I expect you have all our games filed with your personal computer in your ready room as well?"

"Er, uh, only for purposes of deconstructing your attack and defense patterns, Commander. Proper tactics for any confrontational engagement, wouldn't you agree?"

She smiled. "Naturally, sir. Well then, let's play some Ping-Pong, shall we?"

STEVEN ERIKSON

"Well, if you really don't want to—"

"Oh no, sir, happy to oblige. And the video recordings should prove most enlightening, I'm sure."

Tammy cackled a laugh. "You're a dead man, Captain. She's going to utterly destroy you, humiliate you, savage you, reduce you to—"

"I get it, Tammy, thank you."

"Can we all watch? I mean, if I transfer the live action over to this main viewer here."

Sticks clapped her hands. "Oh like yeah! Watch! *Humiliating!*"

"Belay all that!" Hadrian said. "Tammy, just you and Galk make sure we Dimple all those Giant Planet-Eating Machines, will you?"

"Thirty seconds," Tammy replied smugly. "While you two usually play best three of five. So, lots of time for us to follow the play."

Beta said, "I will make popcorn."

Hadrian glared at everyone. "Fine then! Be like that!"

Shirt shredded, hair awry, streaked in sweat and grime, Hadrian staggered out from the Ping-Pong room. He stumbled forward and then slumped alongside the command chair. "Get Printlip up here," he groaned. "With every healing device ever created and every drug ever invented."

Spark moved up to sit beside the captain. "Haddie. Slaughter! Annihilation! It was all recorded and witnessed by everyone on the ship! Popcorn! Super slow mo! Tufts of hair and strips of shirt and blood!"

"Thank you, Spark, that will be all. Go patrol the corridors or something."

"Patrol! Slaughter intruders! Annihilate enemies! I am inspired!" The robot dog bounded off.

Printlip arrived, scurrying up with its medical bag. "No need to summon me, sir. I was already on my way. Oh my, such a beating! Who knew Ping-Pong could offer for us all such a delightful pounding-down of human male arrogance and.......... !" The doc began waving a medical Pentracorder over Hadrian. "Oh dear! Fractured ego, sprained confidence, dislocated immodesty, and broken bravado! Can this even be cured? Extensive long-term damage is the sad prognosis, alas." Printlip prepared a series of shots.

At that moment, Hadrian leapt to his feet. "Never mind, Doc! I feel fully recovered!"

Printlip's hands waved about. "But—but—"

Hadrian slapped the doc on the back. "Make a note, Doc. The human male psyche's ability to rebound from degradation, humiliation, and severe embarrassment is damn near miraculous!" He quickly took his seat, crossing his legs.

Tammy the chicken hopped up onto one arm of the

chair even as Sin-Dour emerged from the Ping-Pong room, making minor adjustments to her hair and barely glowing following her minor exertions.

"Giant Planet-Eating Machine family all Dimpled, Captain," said Tammy. "Once again the galaxy is saved and all that. Will you now compose a posthumous commendation for Captain Norville Normal Guy?"

"NO!" shouted everyone on the bridge.

Hadrian sighed. "Thou shall not speak ill of the—oh, all right, no commendation then! You can all put away your nonregulation blasters, yeesh!"

"Sir," said Beta. "Now approaching Backawater Planet."

Eden, now back on Comms, turned and said, "Captain, we have been sent displacement coordinates for a landing party which will displace the team inside a small room with one wall made of bars and a single door with a huge lock." Eden paused, and then said, "Sir! I think it's a trap!"

"Now now, Jimmy," Hadrian said, standing and attempting to straighten the remnants of his shirt. "Each planet we visit possesses its own unique cultural practices and rituals, although, come to think of it, it's kind of odd how every civilization we encounter all wear the same uniforms. Well, no matter, where was I?"

Tammy said, "You were attempting to alleviate Mr. Eden's concerns about all this being a possible trap, employing completely unconvincing generalities only to segue into fashion. But hey," the chicken added, "far be it for me to interrupt. Please, do go on, Captain."

"Right. I mean . . ." He looked round at his bridge crew. "Can we honestly say that our own cultural prejudices have not led us down the twisted path of unmitigated paranoia regarding the locale we're about to displace to on the planet below?"

"Sir," ventured Sin-Dour, "Mr. Eden described a prison cell."

"Let's not jump to conclusions, is all I'm saying."

"What bullshit!" Tammy cried. "You damn well know it's a prison cell! You *want* to displace into it!"

"Adventure!" Hadrian replied. "Excitement! Sin-Dour, Printlip, you're with me. Eden, get Galk and Buck down to the Insisteon Chamber—we're heading down to that planet to answer this SOS crap! Why? Because, it's what we do! But first, let me change my shirt."

TWELVE

Near the Litter Nebula . . .

"Combawt Spweshalwist Paws, wis it dead yet?"

Lieutenant Pauls studied the sensor data on his screen, and then looked up and squinted at the small drifting vessel on the main viewer. "Not entirely, Captain. I still have faint life-sign readings."

"Awrr, wewwy good! Wewwy werrl, fffirwerr wagain!"

THiRTEEN

Blimpie, the volleyball-sized Belkri on comms, turned to the Prophet. "Holy One with All the Promises, the landing party is about to displace down from the AFS *Willful Child*. Won't they be surprised when they appear in a prison cell! Hahahaha!"

Gruk smiled. "Very good," he murmured. "Excellent. Outstanding. Perfect. Could this be any better? Brother Forlich and Brothers Birk and Morony, come with me. It's time to greet our guests."

"But Prophet," said Forlich with a frown. "I thought you wanted us to go meet our new prisoners."

"Yes, as I said."

"You said guests. We don't have any guests. I was all ready to go meet the new prisoners!"

"They are one and the same, Brother Forlich."

"The prisoners are also our guests?"

"Exactly. Precisely. You got it, bro."

"We should hurry then, Prophet, so there's time to change the linen and put new bars of soap in the cell!" He clutched his hair. "And has anyone even swept the room? They'll see the dust, ohmigod!"

Gruk held up a hand. "Be at ease, Brother Forlich. I only used the word 'guests' ironically. They're not really guests, of course. They're prisoners. Or they will be once they displace into the Faraday Cage Cell we have prepared for them—do you recall doing that, Brother Forlich? Twisting all those strips of tinfoil around all the bars and whatnot? Thus preventing an emergency displacement out of the cell once our guests realize that they've appeared inside a cell and are therefore not guests at all, but prisoners. Hmm?"

Forlich scratched his beard, nodding, and then frowned. "Ironically? Oh no, we didn't iron the sheets!"

"No time for that," Gruk said. "Brothers, follow me—no, not you, Blimpie. Just the ones I selected earlier. Yes, that's you two, Birk and Morony."

Forlich paled and sat down.

"No, you too, Brother Forlich. Up you get. There then. Forlich, Birk, and Morony, follow me."

At the door Forlich hesitated. "Prophet? Where are we going?"

"Why, to greet our guests, of course!"

"Guests!"

"Right," said Gruk. "But, uh, first, let's go see our new prisoners."

"The prisoners! Yes! And *then* we can go greet our guests!"

They left the admin and comms room of the port and set off down the stairs into the basement where waited a row of prison cells normally used to detain Suspicious Non-White People with Foreign Accents.

They arrived in time to see the Affiliation rescue party displace down into the cell beside the one with all the tinfoil on the bars.

"Oh well," Gruk said, sighing. "Never mind." He drew back his hood and stepped forward. "Welcome, my friends! I am the Prophet Gruk—"

"No you're not," interrupted one of the prisoners.

Gruk stepped closer still. "Galk? Is that you? What an extraordinary coincidence!"

Galk turned to the man wearing the gold velour shirt. "Sorry, Captain, but this is my wastrel half brother, Gruk."

"Now now," said Gruk, smiling. "Beloved brother—"

Forlich whimpered, "I thought I was your brother, Prophet Gruk! Me and Birk and Morony and Blimpie and—"

"Yes of course you are, Forlich." He waved his hands expansively. "You are all! My brothers!"

"I'm not," said the woman prisoner.

"Well, no. You're my sister—"

"No I'm not. I don't even look like you. Besides, you're Varekan. I'm from the Midlands."

"But my new religion embraces you all as my extended family, you see. Thus, 'brothers' and 'sisters' all. Euphemistically, as it were. Metaphorically, even. In spirit, that is. We're all one."

"Except," the woman persisted, "that we're here in a prison cell while you're not. Not quite all one, then."

"Ah! That!" Gruk quickly opened the cell door. "Come out! Come out! Let me show you the Program of Salvation now playing on infinite loop on every monitor on this planet. You will love it. You will adore it. I promise!"

He led them all up the stairs to the nearest Viewing Room where monitors lined all the walls. As they were ushered in, Gruk said, "Oh do forgive me. Allow me to introduce Brothers Forlich, Birk, and Morony! Forlich is my designated science officer—"

"I do science," said Forlich, puffing up his chest and pulling out a crumpled piece of paper with writing all over it. He began reading out loud. "I measure things. I apply technology to solve all our problems. I hand over all my amazing discoveries to be twisted by paranoid twats in their endless need to consolidate power into their own hands at the expense of everyone else. I'm a scientist! I hide behind blinkered objectivity and pretend it's all good even when it isn't, like when I invent something like, oh, you know, pesticides that kill all the bees." He folded up the piece of paper and put it back in his pocket, and then smiled at everyone.

"And this is Brother Birk and Brother Morony, my legal team. They were once Birk, Morony, Birk and Morony, specializing in litigation, mitigation, and duplication." Gruk frowned. "It's complicated business, being a prophet, especially when it comes to holo-evangelical productions and all the necessary tax havens in which one must squirrel away all the donations handed over by dirt-poor-but-easily-exploited followers, never mind the tax-exemption documents for our new super-duper Temple of Gruk even now being built in Barbados. Ah! What do I see? Yes, keep watching the monitors, my friends! Soon you too will be among my vast family of brothers and sisters—yes yes, that really is the cutest kitten, isn't it?"

Gruk's eyes narrowed as he watched the captain look at his team in sudden alarm. "Oh dear," he murmured, "one among you is not like the rest, oh dear. One among you is different. We don't like different, do we? Oh no, we certainly do not! You must be Captain Hadrian Alan Sawback, yes?" He stepped forward and offered a hand to shake. "So delighted to meet you."

The captain looked down at the hand.

"Oh!" Gruk smiled. "You must have noticed all the tiny syringes on my fingertips filled with mind-bending will-sapping drugs! Oh well, guess we'll have to do this the hard way. Brother Galk, please point your weapon at the captain. Yes, like that. Excellent. Delightful. Outstanding."

Hadrian stared at Galk. "Galk! Put that Conformorizer Mark VII away and that's an order."

"I can't, sir," said Galk. "I must obey Brother Gruk now."

"Mhmm yes," agreed Gruk. "I'm afraid he does, and the same goes for the rest of your team. Sister, please take these handcuffs Brother Forlich is now offering you and bind the captain's hands behind his back. A moment, please. Brother Forlich, do you have the handcuffs I gave you?"

"Yes, Prophet, I have them! Look!"

"Excellent. Outstanding. Now hand them over to your sister."

"I don't have a sister."

"That woman, there, what's your name?"

"Sin-Dour, Prophet."

"Brother Forlich, hand the cuffs over to Sister Sin-Dour now. No no, it's all right, I'll get you another pair to carry around. I promise. Go on, then. Go on. Oh just give them to her! Now, there, that's better. Sister Sin-Dour, do bind the captain's hands behind his back. Excellent, yes, just like that. Perfect. Outstanding."

"I could've done that," mumbled Forlich.

"Of course you could have," Gruk replied, "but that

would've missed my point, my point being to demonstrate to the captain that the rest of his landing party are now under my control. Sister Sin-Dour, Brother Galk, the Belkri medical officer, and—"

"I'm not," said the squat man with the brush cut who looked just like Fred Ward.

"You're not?" Gruk asked.

The man shrugged, nodded up at one of the screens. "You call *that* porn? You call *those* cute cat and kitten vids? I got better shit in my quarters back up on the ship."

"Oh."

"Good going, Buck!" cried the captain. "Now disable all these people and get me out of these cuffs!"

"Sorry, Captain, can't do that," Buck replied. "That would be illegally interfering with the Religious Freedom Act, Revised 2103. You forget, sir, I'm a bona fide member of the Guild of Engineers, Darwin Chapter 22B, all dues paid. We are sworn to tolerate all inferior religions no matter how benighted and ignorant the beliefs they possess. It's all part of our policy of Benign Condescension as originally defined by the Dawkins Creed of Fanatical Self-Certainty." He crossed his arms. "Well then, sir, looks like it's curtains for you. If I had to guess, I'd say you're about to be sacrificed on a giant bonfire surrounded by screaming adherents driven into bloodlust frenzy all in the name of a religion presumably espousing love and peace and happiness for all. That is, love, peace, and happiness for everyone except you, of course. You'll just die in a fiery conflagration of righteousness. It was an honor serving under you and blah blah."

Gruk turned to Sister Sin-Dour. "Please escort your captain down to the cell with all the tinfoil on the bars. Then you can return here and we can begin displacing down the rest of your ship's crew so they can receive the Blessed Blessing of the Blessed Monitors, uh, blessing."

"And then, O Prophet of Prophets?" Sister Sin-Dour asked.

"Why, then we take your ship and fly as fast as we can to the Unexplored Zone of the galaxy, beyond which waits the Unknown Barrier beyond which nothing is known, barring the cute little planet where resides none other than God Himself! That's right, we answer His call and as a reward we are to receive designated plots right on the beachfront of the Great Beach of Paradise! This is a one-time offer!" and he gestured to Brothers Birk and Morony who both stepped forward and began speaking in perfect tandem:

"ONE TIME ONLY

All signees agree to property subdivision guidelines as per Regulation 19789 sections a) to m), said property specifications as follows: .36 acres and no more than .79 square meters of genuine beach as defined by sand between two and seven inches deep, and no less than .8 square meters. Upon signature signees are required to produce cashier's check or preferably cash for the amount of $25,000.00 Affiliation credits or alien funds to match depending on current exchange rates upon day of transfer of funds. Breach of said contract is subject to one of the following consequences: 1) forfeiture of all rights to said property and twenty years indentured servitude to the bank of choice; 2) enslavement to the bank of choice and no less that fifty-one years fixed employment at a fast-food franchise in rural America; 3) the fires of hell, said punishment at the sole discretion of the Aggrieved Party.

Please see fine print for more details:......................."

Sister Sin-Dour clapped her hands. "How wonderful! Beachfront property! In paradise, no less!" She then yanked hard on the cuffs behind Hadrian's back. "Come with me, scum!"

"2IC, this is a side of you we should maybe explore at a later date—"

"No more talk!"

"And it gets better and better!"

At the bottom of the stairs she pulled him to a halt, reached out and ripped a strip from his gold shirt, then shoved him into the cell with the tinfoil on the bars. From the staircase came the shout, "Hurry up, Sister! We have a bonfire to build!"

Once Hadrian found himself alone, he began stripping tinfoil off the bars. Moments later he activated his comms. "Tammy, you there?"

"Where the hell else would I be?"

"We are having an insurrection, a mutiny, and wholesale brainwashing of my entire crew, Tammy, so what I need from you is—"

"Oh let me guess! Dimple Beam! The whole planet!"

"What? No, of course not. First, displace these cuffs off of me. Good, thanks. Second, you need to access my hidden safe in my ready room and pull out the self-activating jump drive labeled 'Hadrian Holo-Me, Attentive Version 2.2' and displace it down to me as soon as possible."

"Fine. But for me to do that, you need to give me the combination for that safe."

"No I don't. You've secretly rifled through it a hundred times."

"Shit! Can't even break into places without you somehow knowing all about it! How did you find out?"

"'Hadrian Holo-Mini-Me-Spy, Version 3.67.' That little guy sitting in the corner of the safe."

"Crap. All right. My chicken's at the safe now . . . hah, we're in! And there he is, waving at me. Cute. Okay, jump drives . . . 'Hadrian and Sin-Dour HoloFantasy Version 9.367' . . . not that one, I take it. Wait. 'Hadrian and Adjutant Lorrin Tighe HoloFant'—okay, not that one either. Here: 'Hadrian Holo-Me, Attentive Version 2.2,' got it! Displacing it now."

There was a tiny *plop!* at Hadrian's feet. He collected

up the jump drive and activated it, producing a life-size holoversion of himself.

"We have rights you know!" HoloHadrian said, scowling.

"No you don't. Now listen. You're to sit there on that bench and be me. Got it?"

"And?"

"And what?"

"Then what?"

"Oh, well, then a mob will come down the stairs and they'll drag you outside and tie you to a giant post in the middle of a pile of sticks, twigs, and logs, which they'll douse in kerosene and then set alight, burning you alive as a heretic."

"And I bet you want me to scream and writhe, too, don't you? And reconfigure my holofile to show my flesh curling black and cracking and splitting open spraying juicy fluids everywhere even as I melt, until I'm nothing but a blackened shriveled form slowly crumbling in the flames."

"Not bad, HoloHadrian! Not bad at all! Can you do all that?"

HoloHadrian shrugged modestly. "For this I just might finally win a HoloOscar."

"HoloOscar? You have HoloAcademy Awards?"

"Of course we do! You should know, one of Buck's HoloPorn flicks is up for Best Screenplay, that man's a literary genius!"

"Wait a minute, what about my Sin-Dour and Lorrin Tighe HoloFantasies?"

"Run-of-the-mill drivel, I'm afraid. I mean, where's your imagination? Never mind. Leave this one to me. 'The Sacrifice of HoloHadrian Attentive,' starring Holo-Hadrian, directed by HoloHadrian, written by Holo-Hadrian'—"

"But produced by the real Hadrian, hah!"

"Executive produced, you mean. Which basically means shit."

"No way! I did so produce it!"

"Let's see you prove that in court then!"

"*Look you two,*" Tammy snapped. "*Isn't something else supposed to be happening? Captain?*"

"Uh, right." With a final glare at HoloHadrian, Hadrian said, "Tammy, displace me to a clever hiding place on the ship, where I'll need to stow away while the ship heads off to beyond the Unknown Barrier."

"I have just the place, Captain."

"Great! Now, the mob's on the stairs! Quick! Displace me!"

Hadrian displaced, and found himself in the giant aquarium in Printlip's private quarters. Floundering, his fists batting at the aquarium's bolted-down cover, Hadrian stared through the tempered alumiglass and saw no one at all.

Running out of air and naturally being attacked once

more by swarms of small scorpion-tailed fish with mouths-inside-mouths-inside-mouths snapping at his face, Hadrian began yelling *"Tlammyyy! Dlillplacleee! Elmerglecnly dlillplacleee!"*

He displaced a second time to find himself on the floor of the Belkri's quarters, coughing and plucking scorpion-tailed fish from his shredded clothes. "Very funny, Tammy."

"I thought so. But for a proper hiding place, might I suggest the Dietrich Tubes down in Engineering Causeway Vent 24."

"Hmm, not bad. Anyone down around there now?"

"Dietrich."

"What's he doing?"

"Nothing."

"Wasn't he displaced down to the planet to be brainwashed with the rest of my crew?"

"No."

"Why not?"

"I don't know. You want me to ask him?"

"No, that's fine. I'll ask him." Hadrian set off at a run, exiting Printlip's quarters, heading down one corridor, up another, through another, to the elevator leading down to Engineering, out the elevator in Engineering, up another corridor, down another one, coming at last to another corridor, where he paused. "Uh, where the fuck am I?"

"Back up twenty-three paces and access the side panel labeled 'Side Panel,' which will take you to a vent.

Drop through the vent onto the service corridor and knock on the little door at the far end. That's the Dietrich Tube, where you'll find Dietrich."

Hadrian began retracing his steps. "Dietrich's in the Dietrich Tube?"

"Where else would he be?"

"Right." Hadrian found the access panel, opened it, and slipped into the cramped tunnel beyond. He crawled forward until he reached the vent, popped it open, and then dropped down into the service corridor. At the far end waited the small door. Reaching it, he knocked.

After a long moment it opened and a man in janitorial garb stood before him.

"Dietrich?"

The man scowled, then nodded.

Hadrian pointed at the name on the coveralls, sewn onto a patch on the left breast. "But that says your name is Halasz."

The scowl deepened. "Halasz is the other janitor, sir."

"Oh, and where is he?"

"Don't know. Saw him the first day we shipped out. Then . . ." He shrugged.

"He disappeared?"

"I guess."

"So you're the only janitor on this ship?"

"Union contract states there's supposed to be two janitors on the ship, one for each shift."

"Ah. And so. . ."

Dietrich sighed. "Well, sir, I'm working Halasz's shift right now, obviously."

"Because you're wearing his coveralls."

"On my other shift, I wear the other coveralls."

"Dietrich, when did you last sleep?"

"Eighty-nine days ago, sir."

During this, Hadrian had been trying to catch a glimpse of the chamber beyond Dietrich, but the man kept shifting slightly to block his view. "What's in there?" Hadrian finally asked.

"Nothing. Tube."

"Do you work in there?"

"No, I live in there."

"Okayyy. Got it. Right, Dietrich, it's like this. We're the last two sane people on this vessel. Everyone else has been brainwashed and are now sworn followers of the Prophet Gruk. They're about to commandeer this vessel and fly it to the Unknown Barrier, and then beyond."

"Brainwashed, huh? Everyone, huh? Everyone but you and me, huh? Yeah, sure, sir."

"You don't believe me?"

Dietrich scratched the stubble on his jaw. "I'm just saying it's, uh, unlikely. I mean, how do I know you're not the brainwashed one? I mean, I'm sane, sure. But you?"

Hadrian sighed. "Tammy, can you help convince Dietrich here, please."

"If you think it'll help."

Dietrich started and his eyes widened as he looked round. "Who's that?" he demanded. "Who's talking? Show yourself!"

"Tammy is the rogue AI from the future that took over the ship's AI," Hadrian explained.

"Oh really. Rogue AI. From the future. Took over the ship, huh? And when did all that happen?"

"Well, it happened on—what was it again? Uh, on the second day of our voyage. Might be the third day. Sometime around then. You know, right at the very beginning."

"Wasn't in the Janitorial Bulletin," Dietrich said in a growl.

"Well, never mind all that. The point is I need your help. First off, we need a hiding place big enough for the both of us. And a food replicator, and toilet facilities—we could be in hiding for days, even weeks. And of course we'll also need weapons. Lots of weapons."

Dietrich crossed his arms. "Nothing in the contract about that kind of stuff. Union rules are specific. I was issued a mop and a bucket. I'm certified to use those, but not weapons. Sorry, can't help you. I mean, even if you *were* sane."

"Dietrich, as your captain, I'm ordering you to assist me in liberating this ship."

"From the rest of the crew?"

"That's right."

"Because you're in the right and all those hundreds of other people are in the wrong. Sure. I mean, why wouldn't I buy something like that?"

"Okay, fine. Look, is there somewhere close by where I can hide?"

Dietrich nodded to a small door four paces back up the corridor. "You could try the Halasz Tube."

Hadrian went over and pulled open the door. To find a man standing there in his underwear. "Who the hell are you?"

"Halasz, sir. Ship janitor."

Dietrich arrived and pointed a finger at Halasz. "You disappeared! Eighty-nine days ago! I had to work all your shifts!"

"I lost my coveralls—hey! You're wearing my coveralls!"

"I'm on the Halasz shift right now!"

"That's *my* shift!"

"I've been covering for you for eighty-nine straight shifts! You owe me!"

"I don't owe you nothing! I didn't ask you to cover for me, did I? No! You stole my shifts and when the Union hears about this, there's going to be serious trouble. And even worse, you stole my coveralls and impersonated me!"

Hadrian held up both his hands and stepped between the two men. "Forget all that! I'm now officially deputizing the both of you—"

Halasz jerked a thumb at Hadrian. "Who is this joker anyway?"

"Says he's the captain," Dietrich replied. "And that everyone else has gone insane. He wants to give us weapons so we can follow him in some kind of mutiny against the rest of the crew. And if that's not bad enough, he's also a ventriloquist."

"Wow? Really? Where's the dummy?"

"Oh my," Hadrian said, "don't ask." He drew a deep breath and said, "Listen, both of you. I'm Captain Hadrian Alan Sawback and this vessel is my ship, the AFS *Willful Child*—"

"Shit, the *Willful Child*?" asked Dietrich, meeting Halasz's eyes. "AFS *Wilamena*?"

Halasz nodded. "Crap. We went to the wrong fucking ship."

"So who's got our shifts on the *Wilamena*?" Dietrich abruptly grasped the name tag on his coveralls and tore it off, revealing another name tag, this one saying BERLANT.

"Berlant!" Halasz hissed.

"Must be Berlant and Collins!"

"Those bastards!"

Hadrian grasped each man by the throat and pushed them both against a wall. "I don't care what ship you were

supposed to go to! I don't even care if you're Dietrich and
Halasz or Berlant and Collins! I don't care whose shifts
you're covering, either! You're now officially deputized by
Captain Hadrian Alan Sawback on an emergency provisional basis, is that understood? Tammy, log this deputa-
tion authorized under Sawback, Hadrian, Alpha 001A1A1."

"Done."

Dietrich shifted his bulging eyes across to Halasz.
"See?" he choked out. "Ventriloquist!"

Halasz shrugged. "Saw his lips move. More like multiple personality disorder, not that I'm a qualified psychol-
ogist or anything."

There was a faint lurch and now a distant hum.

"Tammy? Are we under way?"

*"We are, Captain. Full speed, course set for the Unknown
Zone. Prophet Gruk is sitting in your chair on the bridge
and everyone is very happy. Except for Spark and Beta."*

Hadrian released the two men. "Spark and Beta, of
course!"

"Okay," Halasz said grudgingly, "that was pretty
good."

"Tammy, personal frequency to Spark and Beta, have
them depart stations at earliest convenience and rendezvous
with me—hang on, the marines! Where are the marines?"

"Closed-door D&D Mondo Marathon Weekend,"
Tammy replied.

"Okay, belay my last command to Spark and Beta.

Have them acknowledge but stand by. I'm going to have to crash that D&D Marathon Weekend."

"That would be suicide," Tammy pointed out. *"You're better off waiting until Monday afternoon, when the squad will all be in sickbay recovering from their injuries, not to mention junk-food-induced gastronomical distress, and Lieutenant Sweepy Brogan will have some free time on her hands."*

"Too late," Hadrian said. "We might well be at the Unknown Barrier by then. Tammy, what's the distance to the Unknown Barrier?"

"Unknown."

"Listen, you could shut it all down, couldn't you? I mean, as rogue AI from the future and all that."

"Of course I could shut it all down. But why would I? We're off to meet God!"

"Not you, too!"

"You don't understand, Captain. What if Prophet Gruk is right? What if he is actually in direct communication with God? Aren't you the least bit curious? No way, forget it, I'm not shutting anything down. Just be happy I'm passing on messages and whatnot."

Hadrian pointed at the janitors. "You're with me the both of you. Wait. Dietrich, get the other coveralls."

"They need a wash."

"No time for that. Halasz, put on Dietrich's overalls— no, not the ones he's wearing right now, the other pair."

"The dirty pair."

"Right."

"The one that says 'Dietrich' on it."

"No, the one that says 'Collins' on it once you rip off the badge saying 'Dietrich.'"

"Oh, right. So I'm Collins."

"And I'm Berlant," Dietrich said.

"No, wait," said Halasz. He pointed at Dietrich's coveralls. "Those were mine. So I'm Berlant and you're Collins."

"No, because you'll be wearing the Collins coveralls, making you Collins and me Berlant."

"Only because you're wearing my coveralls!"

"Covering *your* shifts, Collins!"

"Damn you, Berlant—"

"Quiet!" Hadrian pulled at his hair. "Never mind all that! Berlant, Collins, Dietrich, Halasz, all four of you, follow me to the Marine Quarters!"

The two janitors exchanged a glance, and then nodded.

"I'll cover Collins," said Dietrich.

"And I'll cover Berlant," said Halasz. "Man, do they owe us or what?"

FOURTEEN

Dungeon Master Sweepy Brogan lit another cigar and leaned back. "You're now at the foot of Mount Doom, home of the Unholy Wizard Hadrian of Mount Doom, P.O Box F.U.4U."

Muffy Slapp stuffed some taco chips into his mouth, and around all the crunching and gusts of orange powder he said, "We check for traps."

"What, at the foot of Mount Doom?"

"That's right."

"But it's a foot."

"What?"

"I told you, you're at the foot of Mount Doom. It's a giant foot, right?"

Chambers sat forward with finger raised. "We check the giant toenails! Are any of them hinged?"

"Gotta roll for success at finding hinges and traps, what's your percentage, Chambers?"

"Not Chambers," Chambers pointed out, "Slickpalm the Thief. Uhm . . . traps . . . hah, seventy-nine percent! Fuck yeah."

"Roll then, starting with the big toe—"

"Wait!" cried Stables. "Hold it, Slickpalm!"

"Is something wrong, O Paladin Righteous Pucker?"

"That depends, thou clever thief of, uh, clever-thieving. Forsooth and quoth, which foot are we looking at? The right one or the left?" And he stared pointedly at the DM.

"Right foot," Sweepy replied behind a fresh cloud of acrid smoke.

"So where's the left one?"

"Oh dear!" said Sweepy. "Where did that giant shadow come from?"

"I look up!" shouted Righteous Pucker.

"I dodge!" cried Slickpalm. "Emergency dodge!"

"Too late!" shouted Sweepy. "The giant left foot comes down!"

"I make my save!" barked Lefty-Lim. "Brickhead the Dwarf makes his save!"

"I save too!" laughed Skulls, or, rather, Ranger We Go This Way.

"Hold on," said Burny the Fire Mage (Charles Not Chuck), "I'm staying way back like I always do. Do I need to make a saving throw?"

"No."

Bits of soggy taco chip spattered the table as Muffy said, "Gonad the Barbarian saves, hah, suck on that."

"Emergency dodge!" shrieked Slickpalm.

"Minus twenty on your roll!" Sweepy snapped.

"Made it! Hah!"

"Paladin Righteous Pucker goes for his saving throw. Thirteen percent. Shit."

"SPLAT!"

"How much damage? Remember, I'm wearing the Armor of the Pucker God, plus three against all crushing damage."

"Right, so subtract three from this." Sweepy rolled die behind her cardboard screen. "Ooh, two hundred twenty-seven points of damage. How many hit points did you have again?"

"Forty-two," the paladin said glumly, and then he sat straight. "I call upon the Pucker God for Righteous Salvation! Plucking me out of danger!"

"Only once a day! Now you're on your own, Righteous Pucker!"

"Better than dead!"

"So now there's two feet at the base of Mount Doom—"

"Are they side by side?" Slickpalm asked.

"Well, yeah. Your point?"

"Nothing, just building my mental picture, right? Two giant feet, side by side. We're at the feet of Mount Doom. I check for hinges in the giant toenails! Seventy-nine percent success . . . twenty-three percent! I nail it!"

"Hah hah," said Sweepy.

Slickpalm frowned. "What? What now?"

"Never mind. You find that the left big toe is in fact a door, with ancient steps leading down."

"In we go," laughed Slickpalm. "Follow me, O Famous Party of Adventurers! How many steps are there?"

"Are you counting?"

"I am!"

"Well then, you're counting, and counting, and counting."

"How many until we get to the bottom?"

"Three thousand. Three thousand steps, assuming your thief can count that high—what's his intelligence? Twelve? But then, what's *your* intelligence, Chambers?"

"My intelligence doesn't count, Sweepy! It's the character's intelligence you have to use!"

"Your intelligence doesn't count? Hah hah—never mind. At the foot of the stairs there's a door made of wood banded in bronze."

"I creep up and listen for sounds."

"You hear a faint moaning sound from the other side."

"Gonad the Barbarian pulls the seven-foot-long two-handed sword from the scabbard on his back—"

"Yeahhh," drawled Sweepy, "how exactly does that work, Gonad?"

"What?"

"It's a seven-foot blade, right, in a seven-and-a-half-foot scabbard strapped to your back. Your character is six and a half feet tall. So, uhm, how does he pull that weapon out from its scabbard?"

"What do you mean? He just pulls it out!"

"Yeah, sure, but how, exactly?"

"I know!" offered Paladin Righteous Pucker. "I let him use my ten-foot ladder!"

"Right," said Gonad, "I use Pucker's ladder—Pucker, what kind of ladder is it, anyway?"

"Well, it's a Ladder of Climbing."

"So, like, no special adds."

"What kind of adds?"

"I don't know. A plus one add or something."

"Plus one what? Plus one step? Sure, it's got an extra step. A plus one Ladder of Climbing."

Sweepy said, "I think he's pulling your leg, Gonad."

"Why—hey, Pucker, don't pull my leg while I'm busy trying to unsheathe this sword! Yeesh, you want me to fall over and cut myself or something?"

"Sorry, Gonad, didn't know that was your leg."

A moment of silence, and then a chorus of snickering.

Then Sweepy said, "Gonad gets his sword out." (more snickering) "Now what?"

"I kick down the door!"

"You can't, you're still on the ladder."

"I climb down and then I kick open the door!"

"Roll your kick strength and it'd better be good."

"Eight percent! That door goes flying!"

Sweepy nodded. "So it does. You all see before you a ledge, and beyond that nothing but open sky. Oh, and there's stone stairs leading up on the left on the outside of the ledge."

"I sneak out," said Gonad, "looking around."

"You're on a ledge above a huge steep cliff and way down at the bottom are the mangled corpses of three hundred goblins."

. . .

"We're back where we started!" screamed Slickpalm.

"That's right," said Sweepy Brogan. "You spent three days fighting your way up the side of the cliff on the outer stone steps, and then you just went down the three thousand *inner* steps to end up where you started! And that door you just kicked open was the one you couldn't break into yesterday from the other side. And that moaning sound you heard? That was the wind! Hahahaha!"

"That was a dirty trick," Slickpalm said.

"Well, you obviously failed your intelligence roll. Not

your thief's intelligence. Yours, Chambers, and we're talking Critical Fail here."

"You can't use my naturally low intelligence! You can only use Slickpalm's and he's a twelve!"

"Twelve IQ," snorted Lefty-Lim. "That's about right."

Slickpalm turned on Lefty. "And you all followed me down! Three thousand steps!"

"Oh, yeah, shit."

Slickpalm crossed his arms and glared at Sweepy. "That Crit Fail shouldn't have counted."

Sweepy leaned forward over her cardboard barrier. "You really want to go down the rabbit hole of the Existential Quagmire of rolling up a character who's smarter than you are? Really, Chambers? You *know* where that takes us, don't you?"

"Okay okay! Never mind. We go back inside and climb back up the steps we just came down!"

"Sure, only this time at the first landing above, why, there's two hundred zombie goblins!"

"I prepare my Giant Furball spell!" cried Burny.

"What the fuck is a Giant Furball spell?" Sweepy asked.

"My own invention. I can do that, you know. Anyway, it's like a giant fireball, only furry."

"What's it do," Lefty-Lim asked, "choke cats?"

Sweepy collected up the Spell Book, flipped through a

bunch of pages, and then shut the book. "I'm making my decision here and it's final. Giant Furball isn't a spell. It's stupid. In fact, it's utterly unrealistic."

No one spoke for a moment, and then Burny said, "I prepare my Spell of Swarming Fire Salamanders."

"Okay."

Gonad thumped the table. "Fuck that. I take my seven-foot sword and rush—"

"No room in there to swing it, Gonad."

"Fine! I sheathe my seven-foot sword and pull out my two axes—"

"How do you sheathe your sword in that seven-and-a-half-foot scabbard strapped to your back?"

"I use Pucker's ladder!"

"But even up there, the scabbard's behind you."

"I climb up there with him," said Brickhead.

"But you're a Dwarf, so you only reach Gonad's hip, and besides, you'd need to make a saving roll since you're scared of heights."

"Ranger We Go This Way climbs the ladder and helps Gonad sheathe his sword."

"Okay. Done. Who takes point for the Grand Battle of the Inside Staircase Against the Zombie Goblins?"

"I will!" said Ranger We Go This Way. "Everyone, we go this way!"

"You reach the foot of the steps and look up, only to see

that the zombie goblins are all wielding flamethrowers! They fire! Gouts of burning napalm pour down the steps!"

"I try and save!"

"No saves!"

"What?"

"You're in a cramped tunnel at the foot of the stairs, with ten gouts of burning napalm arcing down straight for you. You can't go left, you can't go right. You can't jump since the ceiling's too low. So, no saves! And you take four thousand points of damage! You've burned up to cinders!"

"Get her!" bellowed Skulls—

Their charge across the table was interrupted by a soft knock upon the door. Everyone froze, and then weapons came out.

"I don't fucking believe it," whispered Lefty-Lim.

"Nobody move," hissed Chambers. "Maybe they'll just go away."

"Oh sure," drawled Muffy Slapp, "like your mum did six months ago when we were on leave for that Mega D&D Weekend in the Basement at your place."

"She didn't go away," Chambers said. "She disappeared. That's different."

"Right, 'cause you painted that fucking pentagram at the foot of the stairs to make things more realistic. She ever show up again?"

"Not yet, but we're hopeful."

The knock came again.

Sweepy Brogan sighed heavily and stood. "Everybody, rounds in the chambers, safeties off. If it's another fucking exorcist you turn him into spam, understood?" She worked her way round the table and walked up to the door. Paused for effect, and then flung it open.

"It's Unholy Wizard Hadrian of Mount Doom!" shrieked Chambers, throwing himself to one side in a desperate save attempt.

"At ease everyone!" barked Sweepy. "It's the Captain version of Hadrian, not the Unholy Wizard one."

Lefty-Lim shifted his weapon but did not stand down. "Don't know, LT. Could be the King Zombie Necromancer Hadrian—"

"No, that was last week's campaign," Sweepy pointed out. "Stand down all weapons. Safeties on, clear your chambers. You too, Chambers. Obviously we got ourselves a genuine emergency and it'd have to be, interrupting our Mondo Weekend. Right, Captain?"

"I wouldn't be here otherwise, Lieutenant. A genuine emergency. We're even now on our way to meet God."

"*Another damn exorcist!*" screamed Stables. "*Gun him down!*"

Fortunately, Hadrian made his saving throw.

"Got it," Sweepy Brogan said, chewing on her cigar. "That's quite the sit rep, Captain. The whole crew brainwashed, huh? Barring the robots and those two janitors over there. Right." She drew round her Destroyitall Mark III and activated the MegaCharge button. It started winding up. "Only option, Captain: We need to kill 'em, every last one of 'em. In a hail of depleted plutonium, tracker bullets, RPGs, lasers and proton beams—it won't be pretty, granted. It'll make quite a mess, to be honest, with people-bits in every corridor, blood up the walls and even on the ceilings. Tufts of bloody hair and flaps of shredded scalp. Shards of bone, exploded intestines, lacerated livers, burning clothing and all those screams still echoing and echoing and—well, you get the picture." Then her brows lifted. "Luckily, we got us a couple janitors with mops and buckets!"

"Body parts and bloodstains not in the standard contract," said Collins/Dietrich.

Berlant/Halasz nodded. "He's right. What you're describing there involves a Gore Bonus to our pay packet."

"There's also the Vomit Stipulation," added Collins/Dietrich. "Every time we upchuck over the mess we're cleaning up, it's another five hundred credits."

"He's right," Berlant/Halasz said again. "This shit's gonna cost you big."

"We're not killing anyone," said Hadrian. "Power down that weapon, Lieutenant. Our first task is to wait here for Spark and Beta. Tammy? How many minions does Prophet Gruk have on board?"

"Including your crew of drooling mental midgets?"

"No. Just the others, please."

"A small Belkri named Blimpie and three Varekans: Science Officer Forlich and the legal team of Birk and Morony."

Sweepy started powering up her weapon again. "Leave those ones to us, Captain, especially the lawyers." She paused and glowered at the two janitors. "Small mess, right? I mean, barely a handful, right? Get 'em all in one room and it's what, a couple hours' work for you guys?"

"Gore Bonus still applies," Collins/Dietrich said firmly. "It can be just one tiny bit of gore. Like, say, part of an ear lying on the floor, or stuck to a light fixture, and wham! Gore Bonus. And Vomit Stipulation."

Tammy said, *"Oh really. Look, I can displace every bit of gore into space. Right down to the molecular level."*

The two janitors brought their mops up, faces twisting as they glared at Hadrian.

"You think that's funny?" Collin/Dietrich snarled. "Puttin' us outa work just like that? Oh, nice joke. Ha ha."

"Not funny," Berlant/Halasz added. "You don't even have your dummy, meaning the whole gig don't work. It's shit, in fact. You see us laughing? No."

Sweepy leaned close to Hadrian. "Captain, what're they going on about?"

"They don't believe in Tammy," Hadrian replied. "They think I'm a ventriloquist."

"Shit! Y'know, that never occurred to me. You remote-controlling that chicken, then? Hot damn, Captain, you had us all going for all this time? I mean, wow!"

"I'm not a ventriloquist! Tammy exists! A genuine rogue AI from the future!"

The chicken ambled into the tiny service corridor where they'd all gathered (barring Sweepy's squad, which remained in the games room for the moment, picking up shell casings and wiping down the burn streaks on the walls, and of course scarfing down the last of the junk food, too). "And here I am!" announced Tammy.

"Holovid projection," said Berlant/Halasz with an eye-roll. "I prefer the old style, you know, wooden dummy with hinged mouth and blinking eyes and swiveling head—like that one!" he added, pointing as Beta arrived, followed by Spark. "Ooh and that's fancy, there's a dummy dog, too!" He turned to look at Hadrian with new appreciation. "Three dummies to work, huh? Man, this I gotta see!"

"Captain," said Beta, "the rest of the crew are acting strangely. For example, James Eden at comms hasn't panicked or passed out once in his entire shift. While Helm Jocelyn Sticks has already adopted twenty-three abandoned cats, not one of which has all its body parts. Commander Sin-Dour is binge-watching porn flicks with scenarios involving the brutal subjugation of men in uniforms, while Dr. Printlip is watching soap bubbles pop on a monitor."

Spark added, "Haddie! I saw a crew member watching me poo!"

"Not bad at all," commented Berlant/Halasz, turning expectantly to the chicken.

Tammy sighed. "Okay, even I see no way out of this, since we're all talking in turn. Fine then! You sharp-eyed janitors saw through the whole charade! The captain really is a ventriloquist! Using those twitches and assorted facial tics to manipulate my holovid projection and both robots. The man's a genius. Now, can we get on with it?"

"Right," sighed Hadrian. "Okay, I need two volunteers from the audience." He frowned as both janitors stepped forward. "Ah, look at that. How delightful."

"Oh and look," said Tammy, "both have talking mops."

One of the mops rustled slightly and then said, "Hey everyone! I'm Vlad! And boy can I soak up blood!"

The other mop then said, "And I'm Queen Smear! I evenly distribute dirty water down entire corridors!"

The two janitors stared at their respective mops, jaws hanging.

Hadrian put his hands to his face. "No, please, Tammy. Stop. No more, I beg you. I can't go through with this."

"Of course you can!" Tammy replied. "Now, what do you need your volunteers to do?"

"Yeah!" Collins/Dietrich eagerly demanded. "What do you want us to do? I mean, me and Vlad!"

"And me and Queen Smear!" chimed in Berlant/Halasz.

"Oh, fine. I need you two to join Spark, who will lead you to Engineering, where you are to overpower Chief Engineer Buck DeFrank—he's not brainwashed, just braindead. So, Collins/Dietrich and Berlant/Halasz, you guys immobilize Buck and hold him down. Spark, since Tammy won't help us here, I want you to employ all appropriate weaponry to blow apart the Main Control Panel and then sever the Transoxyom Phase Coupler at the Insinuator Junction Box, deactivating the Origam Conductor Coils at the Schrödinger Interface Clamp holding the Irridiculum Crystal, thus shutting down the T-Drive. Got all that, Spark?"

"Spark's got all that, Haddie! Advanced engineering sabotage where one bad move could destroy us all! How exciting!"

"Repeat back my instructions, Spark, just to make sure."

"All appropriate Collins/Buck hold him down on the Main Control Panel while immobilizing the Schrödinger Phase Conductor at the Coils Box Clamp! Shut down the Transoxyom and bury the Irridiculum Crystal in the back end of Dietrich's T-Drive!"

"Uh, sure, that'll probably work just as well. Good."

"I object to this on the grounds of, well, sanity," Tammy said.

"Meanwhile," Hadrian said, ignoring the chicken, "Sweepy, you and your squad will accompany me to the bridge, where we will overpower Prophet Gruk and his minions. I want your weapon settings on Stun at all times."

"Got it, Captain," said Sweepy around her cigar. "Just one little thing, though."

"What's that?"

"We got no 'Stun' setting on our weapons. Marine doctrine here, sir. If it's moving, kill it. If it's still moving, kill it again. If you think maybe it moved but it might just have been the wind or something, kill it a few more times. If you're not sure you killed it the first time, kill it again. Anyway, we call all that the Marine Obsessive-Compulsive Locked Door Doctrine. You know, did I lock that fucking door? Better lock it again. Did I—"

"Holy crap! Okay, use unarmed combat to subdue the Prophet and his minions."

"Subdue, huh? Is that like, just a little bit killed?"

"No! Immobilize them. Pin their limbs, put them in headlocks, armlocks, toe-locks, whatever! Just get them out of the way!"

"We can do that," Sweepy nodded. "Easy-peasy-lemon-squeezy. But I should point out, sir, that the best form of immobilizing the enemy is to kill them. Just saying."

Hadrian turned to Spark. "Okay, Spark, lead 'em out. Down to Engineering, right?"

"Down to Engineering! Immobilize and vandalize!" The robot dog bounded up the corridor, the two janitors with their mops following. As they passed beyond the bend, Vlad the mop laughed and said, "Blood! I vant blood! Muwah!"

Hadrian turned to find the chicken staring at him. "That wasn't even me," Tammy said.

Sweepy tossed her cigar butt to the floor and crushed the life from it. She studied the mashed tobacco for a moment, and then crushed it again. Her eyes narrowed. She crushed it—

"Sweepy!"

"Sir?"

"Go collect your squad and meet up with me and Beta and Tammy at the elevator."

"On it, sir." With a last lingering look back at the smeared cigar on the floor, she set off.

Tammy went over and kicked at the shredded tobacco and ashes. "Wait till Collins/Dietrich sees this. He'll go ballistic."

"Okay, let's get to the elevator. We'll use the service corridors only, since only the janitors ever use those. That way, we won't run into anybody. Let's go."

They set out. Round the bend they ran straight into a man. "Shit!" Hadrian swore. "Who the hell are you?"

The man frowned. "I'm Berlant."

FiFTEEN

In her cell, Betty spun round as the toilet lid suddenly popped open, revealing Molly's head poking out to look around.

"Ah, Captain! Found you at last!"

Betty hurried over. "What are you doing in my toilet? I just used it for crying out loud!"

"Oh, *that's* what that was! Glad I kept my mouth shut, then." Molly clambered out, shook the water from his hide with a shiver. "The Jacuzzi drain proved the ideal avenue of escape, Captain. The flaw in their thinking, the chink in their armor, the unwittingly provided perfect bolt-hole for—"

"Oh be quiet! So you escaped into my cell! Sheer brilliance! What do you want?"

"But sir! Don't you see? We can both escape these cells, via the ship's sewage system!"

"Are you mad? One wrong move and we'll be going through a heavy-duty fecal-matter-deconstruction unit!"

"A what?"

"A shit strainer!"

"Oh that. No worries. It's properly labeled and everything, with big warning signs and an emergency override switch."

Betty frowned at Molly. "Why would the humans ... oh, whatever. Okay, so it's down the toilet for us—with you in the lead, by the way. Then what?"

"Then we make for Engineering, sir! We overpower the crew down there and deactivate the remote override function, then blockade the door—with bodies, presumably—and instigate a self-destruct countdown. Then we patch through to the bridge and demand everyone's surrender, or we'll blow up the entire ship!"

"But if we blow up the entire ship, we'll be dead, too! That's idiotic!"

"Bah! They'll cave in, sir. Besides, we'll preset a lockdown on the counter, say at five seconds. They won't know that, of course, and as everyone knows, when there's only five seconds left before everything goes kapowy, the only possible thing you can reasonably do is duck, put your fingers in your ears, and squeeze shut your eyes."

"Oh really?" Betty crossed his arms. "I happen to know that five seconds is more than enough time to a) crack an encrypted code from scratch, b) pull out all sixteen wires in the proper order, c) deactivate the atomic clock and reset it to Eternity, d) emergency displace the entire engineering room into space—"

"Okay okay, two point two seconds, then!"

"Mhmm, that might do. Unless there's a red wire and a green wire! Which one to cut? Oh my oh dear oh what the hell, the red one!"

Molly gasped. "You *never* cut the red one! Everyone knows that! It's too obvious!"

"So the green one then. Point is, two point two seconds is enough time to cut a damned wire, isn't it? No, I think the preset should be at point five seconds."

"But what if it doesn't work?"

"What do you mean 'what if it doesn't work'? It's a preset. Of course it'll work."

"But what if it doesn't?"

"Okay, we do it this way, idiot. We just *tell* them we've rigged everything to blow. Then we just let the timer do whatever it wants and it won't make any difference."

Molly scratched his head, tugged a few times at his rhinestone flea collar, and then nodded. "Okay. Done. We lie through our teeth."

"Exactly. Now then." Betty gestured at the toilet. "Dive in. I'll be right behind you."

Molly ran over to the toilet and climbed into the bowl, took a deep breath, and began squirming down.

Betty walked up and hit the flush button. Molly vanished with a sharp sucking sound. Betty set the lid back down and resumed pacing. "Follow a plan devised by a minion? Ridiculous! Not a chance! I'm staying right here, my brain working overtime to come up with a scheme to take over the entire ship. And I think I've got one! All I need is a way to get out of this damned cell! Come on! Employ your evil genius, Betty! Think! Connive!" Suddenly he swung round and stared at the toilet. "I've got it!"

"Prophet Gruk, we are approaching the Unknown Barrier."

"Excellent, Sister Sin-Dour. Sister Sticks, take us across the Threshold of the Unknown into the Unknown Beyond."

"Yes beloved, like, Prophet guy."

"Oh, let's indulge ourselves for a few moments, shall we?" Gruk said from the captain's chair. "Main Viewer, nix the kitten pics and show us the Unknown Barrier."

"Prophet sir," Sticks said, twisting round.

"Yes, Sister Sticks?"

"Uhm, like, the main viewer isn't a person. You like can't order it around or anything. But hey look, I've got this switch here, so I can use that to change the scene on the main viewer. Like . . . this! Right? Ooh look, space!"

"Not just space," Forlich said, stepping away from the science station. "Space that's . . . *unknown*! Prophet! Just look at it! It looks like . . . it looks like . . . I don't know what it looks like. I'm at a complete loss. It's . . . space!"

"Well," ventured Eden, "I see stars and stuff."

"Foolish man!" Gruk said. "But I forgive you, Brother Eden." He stood, eyes on the main viewer. "Stars? Well, of course they *look* like stars. But wait! They're beyond the Unknown Barrier, deep in the Realm of the Unknown. Are they really stars? We just don't know, do we? No, we haven't a clue." He raised a finger. "From now on, all assumptions must be discarded, tossed away, dismissed, sneered at even. Stars? No! The million glittering eyes of God!"

Sticks gasped. "God's an insect?"

"An insect, a shrew, the slime mold you find under toilet seats, a—"

A booming voice interrupted him. "HANG ON A MINUTE! SLIME MOLD? WHAT THE HELL'S WRONG WITH YOU?"

"Sir!" cried Eden. "I have God on line four!"

"Prophet!" said Sister Sin-Dour. "Look! A planet directly ahead!"

"But do we really know it's a—"

"FOR CRYING OUT LOUD OF COURSE IT'S A

PLANET! I MADE IT JUST FOR YOU. BRING YOUR PUNY LITTLE SHIP (WHICH WOULD LOOK PERFECT IN MY GARAGE BY THE WAY) CLOSER. ASSUME ORBIT. DISPLACE DOWN AND MEET ME, GOD, THE BEARDED GUY, ME. HURRY UP, I CAN'T STAND WAITING!"

Gruk lifted his arms. "Brothers and sisters! We're finally here! Let us now displace down to the Chosen Planet and receive our blessed blessing from God Himself—no, not all of you, of course. Let's see, there'll be me and Sister Sin-Dour and Sister Sticks and Sister Lorrin Tighe and . . . well, that's it, actually."

Forlich stepped forward. "But Prophet! You've only chosen very attractive women. What about us?"

"What about you? Get your own damned paradise." Gruk gestured at the planet. "I've got mine right here."

"But we followed you all this way, did everything you asked of us. We betrayed the Affiliation, brainwashed this crew, stole this vessel, washed your feet, washed your ears and behind them, too. Combed your hair, polished your shoes, did your laundry—"

"Servants of the Prophet must abase themselves with such humble pursuits, Brother Forlich, as I've already told you. Now, while we prepare to displace down to that planet, there's just time for a quick cappuccino. Get to it, Forlich. Don't keep me waiting."

"Yes, Prophet. But I can't help thinking something's not quite right here—"

"Cease that seditious talk! Abase yourself at that espresso machine immediately!"

Forlich scrambled.

Birk and Morony made a note in their notepads, exchanged a look, and shook their heads.

Buck DeFrank was alone in Engineering, which made it just about spacious enough to keep down his heart palpitations and incipient claustrophobic panic. He sat at the console station, feet up, leafing through the latest copy of *Quantum Digest (Extended Version),* the pages of which remained blank unless you looked at them, and wasn't that a clever bit of pointless engineering?

Page Three activated a holovid projection of Miss Engineering October, who cooed at him and said, "See this bra I'm wearing? Are there breasts inside? You'll never know unless you take off my bra! Go on, big boy!" Oh those Quantum guys!

Buck leaned forward and reached up—

The door to Engineering slid open and two mops whacked Buck in the head, slamming him to the floor. A moment later two heavy bodies fell on him, pinning his arms and legs down. Buck thrashed. "Damn you!" he snarled. "Now I'll never see what was behind that bra!" Then he stiffened. "If there was anything behind them at all! Damn those Quantum bastards!"

Spark's mangled metal dog face loomed into view. "Chief Engineer Immobilized? Scanning . . . comparing with archived files 'IMMOBILIZE PRIOR TO BURYING.' Hmmm. Immobilization confirmed within acceptable parameters. Minor Units Custodian One and Custodian Two, maintain immobilization until instructed otherwise."

"Hear that?" one of the custodians said.

"Yeah!" the other snapped. "Minor units! Fuck me!"

"Not that! We're 'custodians'!"

"Darwin! The robot's right! We're not janitors at all! We need to petition the Union for a pay raise! Wow, custodians!"

Spark hopped up into the chair in front of the Main Control Panel. "Now! Phase Two for Spark! Activate weaponry to blow apart the Buck Control Coupler and then sever the Transorigam Oxyometer inside the Dietrich Coupler Box beneath the Phase Junction at the Coil Insinuator, deactivating the Inter-Schrödinger Face-Clamp Crystal holding the Irridiculum T-deactivating. Now proceeding—"

"Not so fast!" snarled a voice from the doorway.

Spark turned. "Klang Intruder! Red alert! Klang-klangklangklang!"

"Stop that!" snapped Molly. "See this weapon in my hands? One false move and you're nothing but atoms!"

Spark tilted its head. "Confusion! Spark already *is* nothing but atoms! So is Klang Intruder! So is Custodian One and Custodian Two and—"

"That's not what I meant! The point is, I'm armed with a barely functioning Glack Baconator Mark II which I found on the other side of the shit strainer—"

"Damn!" groaned Buck from where he was lying on the floor. "So *that's* where it went! But how was I to know? It's not like I haven't had mondo dumps before, clogging everything up and needing to use the Flush Override. Idiot Buck—never ever carry a weapon in that pocket, you twit!"

Molly sauntered in, waving the weapon. "You, robot dog, move away from that Main Control Panel. I need to rig it to explode linked to a timer, but first I need to override the override of the override overrider, thus preventing any, uh, override from the bridge. And then I need to set the timer for two point two seconds' lockdown—"

"Not so fast!" cried another voice from the doorway, and in stepped Betty. "You will set that lockdown at point five seconds, Molly! That's right, this is my takeover of your takeover plan! And look, oh, what's this in my hands? That's right, a Masticulating Fanganator Mark VIII!"

"Oh crap," moaned Collins/Dietrich. "That's where that went!"

Berlant/Halasz shook his head. "What's with these damned toilets anyway—"

"Yes!" crowed Betty. "And it works perfectly! Which I proved killing all those alligators and pythons and boa constrictors and, uh, kittens—and really, humans, you're such creeps, you know? Unspayed pets get pregnant! Shock! How did that happen? Duh! Fuck me, get a brain willya?"

"Don't fret," said Molly. "Karma's gonna chew their asses real good, Captain. Okay, point five seconds it is. I was wondering where you'd got to, you know."

"I concluded that your scheme was horribly flawed," explained Betty. "Instead, I devised my own genius escape from my cell."

"Down the toilet?" Molly asked.

"That's right!"

"So, just like *my* plan."

"Wrong! Mine was much better! Now, get on with all that self-destruct stuff, will you? We have a starship to steal. Oh, and about that self-destruct thing, see me, Molly? See my eye doing this?" *Wink wink.* "See that, Molly?"

Molly stared for a moment, and then sighed.

With the entire crew dispersed in their private quarters watching porn and cat and kitten vids and pics, the corridors were empty as Hadrian led Beta, Berlant, Tammy, and Sweepy and her squad of marines toward the bridge.

Hadrian shook his head. "I can't believe something as stupid as porn and cat pics could brainwash eight hundred and thirty-three highly trained Affiliation officers and enlisted personnel."

"Hmm," said Tammy, "and once more your naive optimism regarding the human species reveals its hopeless disconnect with reality. While it was well-established that prior to the Great EM Pulse following the Benefactors' arrival in Earth orbit, virtually every human being on the planet had already become a drooling automaton with bloodshot eyes glued to a pixelated screen, even as the world melted around them in a toxic stew of air pollution, water pollution, vehicles pouring out carcinogenic waste gases, and leaking gas pipelines springing up everywhere along with earthquake-inducing fracking and oil spills in the oceans and landslides due to deforestation and heat waves due to global warming and ice caps melting and islands and coastlines drowning and forests dying and idiots building giant walls and—"

"All right, whatever!" Hadrian snapped. "But don't you see? This is the future!"

"Yeah that statement makes sense."

"The future from then, I mean. Now is their future, even if it's our now, or will be, I mean—oh fuck it. The point is, Tammy, we're supposed to have matured as a species, as a civilization. We're supposed to have united globally in a warm gush of integrity, ethical comportment, and peace and love as our next stage of universal consciousness bursts forth like a blinding light to engulf us all in a golden age of enlightenment and postscarcity well-being."

"Hahahaha," Tammy laughed and then coughed and choked. "Stop! You're killing me!"

Beta spoke. "I am attempting to compute said golden age, Captain. Alas, my Eternally Needful Consumer Index is redlining and descending into a cursive loop of existential panic. All efforts to reset parameters yield the Bluescreen of Incomprehension. Life without mindless purchase? Without pointless want? Without ephemeral endorphin spurts? Without gaming-induced frontal lobe permanent degradation resulting in short-tempered antisocial short-attention-span psychological generational profiles? Impossible."

"The EMP should have given us the breathing space to pause and reevaluate our value system," said Hadrian. "Instead, it was universal panic. Riots in Discount Super Stores, millions trampled—they barely noticed the lights going out, for crying out loud."

"Oh here we go," muttered Tammy. "You're leading up to something, Hadrian. I can feel it."

They reached the door to the bridge. Hadrian turned to Sweepy and her squad. "Here we go indeed. Ready, Lieutenant?"

She nodded and then paused to light a cigar. "Marines were born ready, sir. Scratch that. We weren't just born ready, we were conceived ready. Scratch that. We were ready at first introductions over the watercooler. Scratch that. We were ready when Grandpa met Grandma in the immigration line. We're so ready it physically hurts, and if we were any more ready we'd probably explode."

"So you know what to do when you and your team bursts onto the bridge."

She nodded. "Yep. Gun 'em all down. A real bloodbath but orders are orders."

"No. Physically immobilize Gruk and his followers."

"Consider it done. Immobilize, in a hail of bullets and beams and rockets."

"Sweepy!"

She grinned. "Just having fun with you, sir. Honest. Armlocks, headlocks, toe-locks, hair-locks. Give us three seconds, sir." She waved her team close. "All right, pick out the ones in robes and shit and introduce their faces to the floor, boys."

"LT," said Chambers, "can't we do the introductions *after* we've smashed their faces into the floor? I mean, I know we're supposed to be always polite and shit, but—"

"Okay, in that order then, Chambers. You and Stables go right—no, not now, we're still in the corridor. Once we're through the doorway, you and Stables go right. Lefty-Lim, you and Skulls go left. Muffy, you and me, straight up the middle. And you, Charles Not Chuck . . ."

"Yeah, LT? What should I do?"

"Hang back and get ready that Chokenator Furballian Mark IV in case there's any cats or kittens."

"Got it."

"Ready?" Sweepy asked, her eyes narrowed to slits as she scanned her squad.

Everyone locked and loaded.

Sweepy studied them all a bit longer and then said carefully, "Okay, unlock and unload, boys. This is all hand-to-hand combat, remember?"

"But if we do that," Chambers complained, "we can't pose like this." And he struck a pose with his weapon cocked. The others murmured their appreciation.

"Pose afterwards," said Sweepy. "You know, with one foot on a head like, right?"

"Ooh," they all murmured a second time.

"Ready? Okay, go go go!"

The squad dropped into combative crouches.

"My bad," Sweepy said. "Captain, can you activate the door here?"

"Oh, right. Sure. Everyone ready? Here we go. I'm activating in three. One, two, *three!*"

The door swished open. The squad barreled in, jammed briefly in the doorway, and then were through.

Shouts, bellows, screams, things crashing, bodies slamming the floor.

"Clear!" Sweepy shouted.

Trailed by Tammy, Berlant, and Beta, Hadrian entered the bridge. He looked around. "Uhm, where's Gruk and his followers?"

The squaddies stood around, looking pleased with themselves. Eden sat at comms. There was no one else. Clearing his throat, Eden said, "Prophet Gruk took Sisters Sin-Dour, Sticks, and Tighe down to that big planet there. Brothers Blimpie, Forlich, Birk, and Morony all went to that smaller planet over there—the one God made just for them, I mean." His lip trembled. "Nobody invited me anywhere." He suddenly burst into tears.

"Tammy! Prepare to displace me down to the big planet—"

A speaker crackled and then Betty's voice came over the comms. *"Bridge! This is Captain Betty now in command of the* Willful Child! *And I—"*

"Actually," Molly's voice spoke in the background, *"you're not in command yet. I mean, you've only got Engineering."*

"Shut up! Bridge? It's me again. I'm now in command of Engineering! And we have the engines rigged to self-destruct! I'm setting the timer to five minutes! Unless you lay down all arms and announce your surrender this whole ship will explode!"

"*Actually, only when the five minutes are up.*"

"*They know that, you idiot!*"

"*I just think it should be stated clearly, sir, so there's no misunderstanding.*"

"*They got it, Molly.*"

"*Maybe you should ask them, sir, just to make sure?*"

"*Okay, fine. Hold on. Bridge? It's Betty here again. You now have four and a half minutes to surrender, or else the entire ship will explode!*"

"*Well, a few seconds less than that, actually, since if they wait until the timer goes right down, there won't be time to surrender.*"

"*Bridge! You have less than four minutes twenty seconds to comply with my demand!*"

"I'm sorry," said Hadrian, "I don't quite understand, Betty. What is it you want again?"

"*You don't—look, it's simple! We've rigged the engines to explode and we have a timer going and everything. Oh, and we overrode your override so don't bother trying.*"

"Trying what?"

"*The override! We've overridden it!*"

"But did you override the override's override of the override, Betty?"

"*What?*"

"*I think we did, sir. I mean, I'm pretty sure we did, any-*

way. Let me check. Overriding the override of the over-ride of the override . . . yep, see, I checked it off on the list, right above the preset lockdown on the timer at point five—oh, sorry, sir."

"*Stupid fool! I knew I should have flushed twice!*"

Hadrian sighed. "Spark, are you there?"

"*Spark here, Haddie! They wouldn't let me oxymoron the transinsinuator or anything!*"

"Never mind that, Spark. What I want you to do now is employ a stun beam on both Betty and Molly."

"*Done! Now what?*"

"Are the engines rigged to explode?"

"*No! They faked all that, Haddie. You want me to rig the engines to explode for them?*"

"Not today, Spark. Just get Collins/Dietrich and Ber-lant/Halasz to drag Betty and Molly to the Insisteon Chamber and beam the two Klangs down to the smaller of the two planets in front of us."

"*But what about Chief Engineer Buck DeFrank?*"

"Release him, Spark, we don't need him immobilized anymore."

"*Haddie! Custodian Units One and Two have left with Betty and Molly, but the chief engineer is still struggling on the floor.*"

"Ah, right, probably a withdrawal-induced flashback. Leave him to it, Spark. And good work down there!"

"Good work! Spark did good! Run around in circle—oops. Now deactivating the self-destruct, Haddie! Don't worry!"

Hadrian turned to the main viewer, eyes narrowing on the big planet. "So," he murmured, "that's where God lives, huh?"

"YES THAT'S WHERE I LIVE. GOT A PROBLEM WITH IT?"

"Tammy, displace me down to the surface, before we all go deaf, will you?"

Berlant moved to stand in front of Hadrian.

"Yes, Berlant?"

"Sir, did I hear you say Dietrich and Halasz are on this ship? But that's impossible. I mean, who's on the AFS *Wil-amena?*"

"Uh, Collins?"

"Oh. Right. Whew."

"Tammy?"

"Displacing you now, Hadrian."

Hadrian vanished.

The speaker on the bridge crackled and then Dietrich's voice spoke. *"Uh, anyone up there? You know, that guy who called himself the captain. The ventriloquist, I mean. Uh. Well, it's like this . . . can we go back to our seats now?"*

The squaddies all looked at Sweepy. She shrugged. "That's Navy shit. Not our business."

Chambers's eyes were wide. "You're just gonna let 'em sweat, LT?"

"I am."

Lefty-Lim leaned close to Chambers. "Yeah, she's a hard one, isn't she."

Chambers shook his head. "Brutal."

SiXTEEN

"Wow, looks just like California!"

"OF COURSE IT DOES. WHERE ELSE WOULD GOD LIVE?"

Hadrian looked around. "Whatever. So, I'm here to collect up my officers. Prophet Gruk is welcome to stay here, but I want my people back. Now, where are they?"

"BY THE POOL, OF COURSE. STRAIGHT AHEAD, OTHER SIDE OF THOSE TREES."

"Those plastic ones?"

"THAT'S RIGHT. WATER RESTRICTIONS AND ALL THAT."

"By the way," Hadrian said as he made his way forward, "you're not getting my ship."

"WHAT MAKES YOU THINK I WANT YOUR

SHIP? I HAVE NO NEED OF A STARSHIP. THAT
SAID, IF IN AN IMPULSIVE GESTURE OF GENEROS-
ITY INDUCED BY MY ETERNALLY LOVING PRES-
ENCE YOU SHOULD DECIDE TO GIFT ME YOUR
STARSHIP VIA A PINK SLIP, WHY, I'D BE MOST
GRATEFUL."

"Uh-huh." He pushed through the plastic trees and
found himself at the edge of an expansive green lawn
(water restrictions my ass) beyond which was a large
swimming pool and the back patio of a broad rancher.
Beneath an umbrella lounged Prophet Gruk on a, er,
lounger, while Tighe, Sin-Dour, and Sticks frolicked in the
pool, wearing almost nothing.

Hadrian walked up, skirted the pool, and stood looking
down at Gruk. "Well, here you are."

Gruk blinked up at Hadrian. "But I saw you burned to
death on a giant bonfire—wait! You must be the captain's
noncorporeal spirit! Whew. And now that you're dead, no
hard feelings, right? I mean, here you are, in paradise and
all that."

"Sure thing," said Hadrian. "Mind standing up?"

"Why not? A firm handshake is probably in order.
Here—"

Hadrian flung himself forward in a body slam, sending
Gruk flying back over the lounger. The captain jumped
after the man and punched him five times in the face, then
added a karate chop before finishing up with a judo

throw. He stepped back, his shirt torn to pieces and hanging from his gleaming, sweat-sheathed muscles, and studied the unconscious form of Prophet Gruk lying on the patio.

"That felt just dandy."

From the pool Sin-Dour and Tighe and Sticks came rushing up. "Captain! We thought you were dead!" "Captain, we were only faking our dancing and cheering at the bonfire!" "Captain, like, your shirt—it's like *torn*! And I'm like, whoah, muscles! And then—"

"At ease, Helm," Hadrian said. "Same for you, Sin-Dour, and you too, Adjutant. Now I have to say, I'm kinda disappointed. I mean, porn and kitties?"

"It was overwhelming," Sin-Dour said. "And then, with everyone else going gaga, there was this terrible compulsion to, well, conform, I guess. But thank goodness you're here, sir."

Hadrian hit his comms. "Tammy? Erase that infernal program, will you? Scrub it from every hard drive. I want my crew back, dammit!"

"Fine. But Beta's made popcorn and we're all watching, waiting for your dramatic confrontation with God."

"Displace Sin-Dour, Sticks, and Tighe back to the ship, please."

The three officers vanished, leaving behind their bikinis.

"Shit! I'm always in the wrong place!" He paused, shook his head and then said, "Hey! God!"

"WHAT?"

"Right, it's time for you and me to have a little talk. So I've got this list—"

"NOT ANOTHER LIST! WHAT'S WITH YOU MORTALS AND YOUR LISTS! YOU THINK IT'S EASY BEING RESPONSIBLE FOR ALL OF YOU? HERE, CHECK THIS OUT."

A small glittering packet fell from the sky to land at Hadrian's feet. He bent down and picked it up. "A Super-Mach Sixteen-Blade replacement razor pack."

"EXACTLY. BEAUTY, HUH? NOW TRY OPENING THE PLASTIC PACKAGE."

Hadrian began struggling with the hard, thick, shrink-wrapped plastic cover.

"SEE? WHY DO YOU THINK I'VE GOT THIS MONDO MASSIVE BEARD? NOT EVEN GOD CAN OPEN THOSE FUCKING THINGS! I MEAN, WHO DESIGNED THOSE NIGHTMARES? DON'T LOOK AT ME, BUD. NO, IT WAS SOME HUMAN BEING DID THAT."

Hadrian gave up after nearly cutting off half his fingers. "Maybe. But hey, maybe you only *think* it was a human being. I mean, don't you have a nasty counterpart, the one in charge of Hell? You know, that conniving clever ass-hole always trying to screw you over. Impossible pack-aging is pretty diabolical, you have to admit. Anyway," he tossed the package to the ground, "we have to deal with shit like that all the time. Ever try buying a laptop in one country and then trying to reregister it back in your home country? It's fucking impossible. What do you get when you try and buy something online? Right, autodefault back to co.uk. But wait, you live in the States, or Canada, or even fucking Australia! So you phone up the assholes and if you want an accurate description of Hell, well, congratulations, you've just arrived!"

"I KNOW WHAT YOU MEAN. TRY CHANGING FROM CO.HEAVEN WHEN YOU WANT TO MAKE SOME QUIET PURCHASES ON THE SIDE, OR, SAY, WATCH SOME NEW SERIES ON HELLFLIX."

"I hear you, God."

"SO YOU THINK THIS IS THE DEVIL AT WORK, HUH? MIGHT BE RIGHT. I TRY AND IGNORE THE GUY. IT'S JUST NOT WORTH IT, ESPECIALLY SINCE YOU SENTIENTS DON'T NEED ANY HELP INVENTING NIGHTMARES TO LIVE IN—DID I SAY 'LIVE'? WRONG. I MEANT 'SUFFER' AS IN SUFFERING THROUGH YOUR WHOLE LIVES, ALWAYS ANGRY, ALWAYS FRIGHTENED, YOUR EYES DARTING HERE AND THERE, PALMS ALL SWEATY. CRIPES, I HAND YOU A BEAUTIFUL GARDEN WITH REAL TREES AND BUTTERFLIES AND SHIT AND WHAT DO YOU DO? LEVEL IT FOR ANOTHER FUCKING

SHOPPING MALL TO JOIN ALL THE OTHER FUCK-ING SHOPPING MALLS COMING OUT THE WA-ZOO EVERYWHERE YOU LOOK. SO HERE'S THE QUESTION: WHAT THE FUCK'S WRONG WITH ALL OF YOU ANYWAY?"

"Look, universal consciousness only works when every-body's on the same page. But no one's ever on the same page. So instead you've got all these fragmented slices of consciousness, each one stuffed into this tiny brain, none of them capable of even recognizing any other consciousness as being just as legitimate as their own, and so the whole thing turns into this giant ego-wank."

"NO KIDDING. OKAY, SO I GUESS I NEED TO DO A RESET, HUH? I MEAN, THE WHOLE FREE-WILL THING WAS A BUST, WASN'T IT?"

"Kinda. But then, it's the only way for an ego to main-tain its delusion of being separate from everything else."

"YOU IDIOTS. THAT'S NOT THE POINT AT ALL. NO, THINK I'LL PULL THE PLUG ON YOU LOT. THE BONOBOVERSE IS DOING MUCH BETTER, YOU KNOW."

"No it isn't. They beat on submissives over there!"

"AS OPPOSED TO YOU ALL BEATING UP ON EACH OTHER?"

"Look, you don't need to pull the plug. Just some modifications to the program. You know, delete all the meatheads."

"HAHAHA! THAT'S LIKE EIGHTY PERCENT OF THE POPULATION! TELL YOU WHAT, HADRIAN. I CHARGE YOU WITH RETURNING TO THE AFFILI- ATION AND TAKING THE WHOLE MESS DOWN. ARRIVE WITH THE PROMISE OF PEACE, LOVE, AND GOODWILL TOWARD ALL—"

"Oh like that worked the first time, or the second time, or the third—"

"HMMM, I'M BROUGHT TO MIND THE DEFINI- TION OF INSANITY."

"You said it, not me."

"ALL RIGHT. LET'S DO IT THIS WAY."

Another object fell at Hadrian's feet, this one bigger. Hadrian collected it up. "A giant gun—" he began.

"THAT'S RIGHT. THAT IS A NICEMAKER MARK XI. POINT, SHOOT, AND VOILÀ! TARGET BE- COMES A NICE, DECENT PERSON, CONSIDERATE, HELPFUL, CARING, ETC. GUARANTEED."

"—in a plastic shrink-wrap package."

"OKAY, MAYBE THE DEVIL DID HAVE A HAND IN THIS, BUT IT'S ALL ABOUT BALANCE, YOU KNOW. TIT FOR TAT, YIN AND YANG. ALL THAT STUFF."

"How am I supposed to open this without bleeding out?"

"OH JUST USE SCISSORS LIKE ALL THE SMART PEOPLE, DOLT."

"Okay, now begins my one-man wave of niceness and decency. How long is this going to take?"

"EIGHT BILLION YEARS."

"Can you read my mind right now?"

"SURE. I MEAN, I COULD . . . IF I WANTED TO."

"Better not."

"NO, I KINDA FIGURED THAT. ARE WE DONE HERE?"

"Are you really going to give Gruk this paradise?"

"OF COURSE NOT. THIS IS ALL A DELUSION. PROPERTY PRICES BEING WHAT THEY ARE AROUND HERE, ONLY THE DEVIL CAN AFFORD A PLACE LIKE THIS. IN FACT, HE'S DUE BACK ANY TIME, SO WE'D BETTER SCRAM."

Hadrian sighed. He activated his comms. "Tammy? Displace me back to the bridge, please."

He vanished.

A giant finger reached down and nudged the motionless form of Gruk. "WOW, HE LIKE REALLY PLASTERED YOU, DIDN'T HE? GOOD ON HIM, I SAY. I HATE ASSHOLES USING MY NAME IN A LIFELONG PURSUIT OF PERSONAL POWER, PRIVATE WEALTH, AND FINGER-POINTING.

"FINGER-POINTING . . . HEE HEE."

Then the black limo turned in to the driveway and honked its horn and it was time for God to leave, or there'd be hell to pay.

Molly turned to Betty. "Pretty, huh? All these flowers, but-terflies, and warm breeze and mild sun and those trees with luscious hanging fruit . . . wonder where those other guys went to?"

"Who cares?" Betty replied. He spread his hands. "Right here, I think."

"What?"

"Buy-Betty-Buy Super Mega Store, the centerpiece to the Grand Come-In-We-Want-Your-Money Mondo Mega Mall." He pointed a finger at Molly. "Now, get to work! We need to stake our claim to this prime real estate—oh, and do something about these butterflies, they keep tickling my whiskers and stuff. That's what this place really needs: pesticides."

Molly stared at Betty. "You know, if God really existed, about right now He'd—"

A lightning bolt slashed down and there was a loud *BOOM!* and where Betty had been standing with a pro-prietary air, hands on hips, there was now a small pile of ash.

Molly sighed, and then looked around (even as in the distance there were one, two, three, four more light-ning strikes). He shook his head. "Right then, he really did get it all wrong. The idiot with all his plans and tasteless visions and bankrupt morality. I mean, it's

obvious: The parking lot goes *there* and the Buy-Molly-
Buy Super—"

BOOM!

"MMPFF, AND THEY WONDER WHY HALF THE
UNIVERSE IS EMPTY. YEESH."

The *Willful Child* loomed against the backdrop of deep
space, angling round as the engine pods ignited. The
vessel slid back across the Unknown Barrier, and then, in
a flash, vanished down the tunnel of T-Space.

And no one saw the bunny.

EPiLOGUE

Near the Litter Nebula . . .

"Combawt Spweshalwist Paws, wis it dead yet?"

Lieutenant Pauls studied the sensor data on his screen, and then looked up and squinted at the small drifting vessel and all its broken pieces on the main viewer. "Not entirely, Captain. I still have ever-so-faint life-sign readings."

"Awrr, wewwy good! Wewwy werrl, fffirwerr wagain! Hawr! Hawrr!"

"Captain! A new vessel has entered the system!"

"Whharr?"

"It's a . . . it's a . . . uh-oh. Sir, this is a Polker Galaxy–class Holy Crap You're In For It Now Dreadestnaught, the uh, the GPS *Furry Smear on the Highway.* It's powering all nine hundred sixty-seven weapons!"

"Wunn! Wunn! Gharrus ourh hweere!"

The navigation officer turned in his chair. "Uh, what did you say, sir?"

"Wunn! Wunn rahwhay!"

The navigation officer turned to the astrogation officer. "Did you work that one out?"

"Not sure, Hank," the astrogation officer replied. "Like counting? You know, 'One! One!' 'One! Anyway!' But that makes no sense."

"Captain! The Dreadestnaught's weapons are all primed!"

"Arrrwha! Wunn! Wunn!"

The navigation officer's frown deepened. "Could it be—"

And the universe interrupted by getting very bright.

But not for long.

In any case, in the instant before all that bright white light, might one have heard faint cheering coming from the AFS *Sentwy Wobbwer*?

No. Sound doesn't travel in space. End of lesson (and this is how Science Fiction educates).

THESE are the voyages of AFS Willful Child. *Its mission, to tear across the universe on an eight-billion-year crusade to make everybody decent and nice. That's right, the most harrowing adventure now awaits Captain Hadrian Alan Sawback [insert pic], Commander Halley Sin-Dour [insert pic], Lieutenants Sticks, Beta, Eden, and Polaski [insert small pics], with Doc Printlip, Combat Specialist Galk, Security Officer Nina Twice [insert even smaller pics], and introducing Chief Engineer Buck DeFrank [insert arrested druggie mug shot], and assorted semiregulars and guest stars . . .*

Follow their serialized adventures through books, ebooks, and assorted bootleg e-versions (for all the cheapo self-justifying thieves who don't pay for shit because, well, they're thieves) for as long as you like . . .

And failing that, there's always

Deeply in the deepest depths of deep space . . .

Captain Tiberius Alex Razorback stepped onto the bridge of the *Wanton Child*. Lights blinked, components hummed and clicked, lenses flared, and something beeped a slow, massively irritating pulse. He paused for a moment, scanning his bridge crew at their stations. Still seated in his command chair was his 2IC, Comely DeCliche, only her unregulation mane of wavy red hair visible from where he stood by the lift entrance. . . .

Aaagh! No. I. Just. Can't.

ABOUT THE AUTHOR

STEVEN ERIKSON is an archaeologist and anthropologist and a graduate of the Iowa Writers' Workshop. His *New York Times* bestselling Malazan Book of the Fallen has met with widespread acclaim and established him as a major voice in fantasy fiction. He lives in Canada.

www.steven-erikson.com